I0638794

FRACTURED HALO

A BROKEN HALO NOVEL

JILLIAN NEAL

Photography by GOLDEN CZERMAK / FURIOUS FOTOG

Cover Model CALEB BLANCHARD

Edited by HAPPILY EDITING ANNS

REALM R PRESS

Written by Jillian Neal

Copyright © 2019 Jillian Neal

All rights reserved.

No part of this book may be reproduced in any form or by any electronic or mechanical means including information storage and retrieval systems, without permission in writing from the author. The only exception is by a reviewer, who may quote short excerpts in a review.

This book is a work of fiction. Names, characters, places, and incidents either are products of the author's imagination or are used fictitiously.

Any resemblance to actual persons, living or dead, events, or locales is entirely coincident

Published by Realm Press

ISBN: 978-1-940174-49-5

Library of Congress Control Number: 2019934540

First Edition

First Printing – March 2019

There isn't one single word I've written that I could've done without his love and support. But for this book in particular I needed my own personal computer guru's help, and just like always he was right there every step of the way. So, this book is dedicated to my husband. Thank you for being my forever and always.

1

S mith Hagen kept his focused gaze locked on the woman in the apartment across the street, via the high-end telephoto lens in his hands.

"We need food." Voodoo slammed the refrigerator door making several bottles jangle in the process.

"So, go get food." He'd been done with his partner's bitching about their latest mission a week ago. A relatively empty apartment in Kansas City was a hell of a lot better than the desert or some South American swampland, where they'd spent their years in Special Forces together. As recon missions went, this wasn't that bad. They had heat, carpet under their sleeping bags, and food. By army standards, they were staying at the Ritz.

Voodoo spun one of the two folding chairs they'd acquired and straddled the seat. He poured a sleeve of peanuts from the local service station into his mouth.

Click. Smith took yet another photo. Voodoo shook his head at him. "She's been reading for an hour. You don't have to keep snapping pics."

Irritation stiffened Smith's spine. If that had been the only thing rapidly stiffening in his body, he wouldn't have been concerned. The grin that had captured his attention through the lens was still painted on Mercy Valon's beautiful lips. Whatever she was reading made her happy, and he desperately wanted to know what it was. He wanted to know how he could make her grin like that. They'd been following her for weeks, and this was the first time he'd seen her smile.

Her delicate features were constantly plagued by apprehension. She seemed to fear her own shadow. Some ridiculous, primal instinct deep in his gut wanted to banish anything that frightened her. He longed to reassure her that he knew how fucked up her existence had become, and by the might of his own two arms, he would make everything better. She would likely insist that she didn't need his help, but she didn't know what was coming for her.

He gave one last appreciative glance at those full, pouty lips, curved in delight, before making up an excuse to explain away why he was so fascinated with their target. After all, she did have the kind of lips that made very intelligent men do very stupid things. "I have to know what she's doing, every second of every day. We don't know when she'll try to take the plans. I thought you were going for more food." If he could talk his partner into getting more snacks, he could try to get a grip on reality.

Mercy was a pawn in a very dangerous game she didn't even know she was playing. Their job was threefold. Keep her, a master hacker, from accessing the drone sequencing radar plans from the Department of Defense, keep her from being arrested by the feds, and keep her away from her brother, Julian, the heir apparent to the Castellas drug cartel. Julian Valon was happy to stay behind the curtain while dangling his sister out as bait. Fucker. He was the one thing out of Smith's control. They had no idea when he might contact his sister again or if he'd kidnap her and stash her behind the walls of the cartel making her inaccessible to anyone. If all of that couldn't help Smith get a grip on some of his better judgment, he could get a grip on his cock again, the way he'd been battling his rampant attraction to this woman for the past few days.

When she set her iPad on the coffee table and grabbed her laptop, Smith and Voodoo both sprang into action. Popping the tension out of his fingers, Smith traded the camera for his own computer. She had no business going after those files, and if anyone could keep the high queen of hackers from accessing them, it was him.

Voodoo kept the camera trained on their target, zooming in on her computer screen. "Finally. Something interesting."

Smith shook his head. "She's not going to do this from her apartment. She's smarter than that." IP addresses were far too traceable, but they had to be ready for anything.

"Let's not take anything for granted," Voodoo reminded. "Roman needs her to stay out of a federal pen if we're going to help the Drug Enforcement Agency access the cartel."

Smith didn't need the reminder. He knew Mercy wasn't going after the plans that night. He could feel it. Besides, she'd already changed into those worn flannel pajama pants—the ones with polar bears wearing nightcaps and that black ribbon he'd fantasized about slowly tugging loose more than once.

He was certain the plans were secure at least until morning. He did, however, need to know if her brother had sent her more emails. Naturally, he could've hacked his way into her laptop to read anything he wanted, but hacking a hacker was never a good idea. Until Julian actually made contact with instructions, it wasn't worth the risk. One thing he knew for certain about her, she was one of the best hackers in the game. He was better, but not by much.

Come on, sweetheart. Open your email for me. As if she could actually hear his mental prodding, she flipped to the screen with her open email. His cock throbbed out its intrigue. He had an endless list of far more interesting things he'd like her to do— things that had nothing to do with emails, secure servers, and VPNs. His cock had so many requests: *Spread your legs for me. Sit right here in my lap and let me touch you. Show me how wet you get for me.* Damn thing was going to be the death of him.

Ordering his mind back to the head above his belt, he scanned the emails. Nothing from any of her brother's email addresses. She went through the tedium of sending most of it to spam, and then she opened *RexArmis*, his current online game obsession. Voodoo started to drop the camera.

"Keep it on the screen. You have to see this," Smith ordered. After giving him an eye roll, Voodoo did as he was told. "She's a Rogue Half-Elf. I'm only a Second Rank Mage."

"I assume in nerd speak what you're trying to tell me is that you're jealous."

"I'm not jealous. I'm...impressed." Yeah, that was it.

"Bullshit. Maybe you could go over there and geek it up with her. You can tell her that her brother is a fucker who doesn't give a damn about her, even though he keeps telling her he does. Then you can explain that you've had a boner for her for weeks. You two can screw like digital second rank elf-rabbits or whatever the hell you just said, and I can go home because this blows. I'm a medic. I'd always thought boredom couldn't be a cause of death, but this seems to prove my theory wrong."

"Our job is to keep her safe. If you're so bored, try being more helpful. And I do not have a thing for her."

Voodoo laughed at him outright. He yanked the laptop from Smith's grasp and brought up the camera feed from the past week. "You took thirty-seven photos of her drinking coffee. Oh, and then another dozen of her making Chef Boyardee. You're on a direct flight into stalker territory, my friend."

Guilt throbbed in Smith's head. He'd been calling himself the same thing for a week. "I wasn't taking pictures of her cooking. I was trying to see her screen. See, her laptop is open on the counter." At least, that's what he'd told himself he was doing.

"Good point. In fact, I can even almost make it out around the shots of her ass in those blue jeans. Look, I get it. There probably aren't a lot of women out there who speak binary. Perfectly natural for you to be jonesing for some nerd love, but at some point her brother's gonna show up here, and we're going to have to snatch her up to keep her away from him. If you want, I could help you convince her to play with your joystick. Women happen to be my specialty. You're going to have to be careful with her, though. As you just pointed out, she's elf-sized. But, you never know, she might have a thing for giants."

Smith smacked the back of his friend's head with his massive hand. Voodoo jerked away. "Damn. That hurt."

"Good. You're not convincing her to do anything, and her being a half-elf has nothing to do with her height, dumbass. It's her class in... just never mind. Go get food."

"Fine. You want anything?" Voodoo pulled on his boots.

"Are we still rating all Kansas City barbecue joints by their brisket, or have you turned enough of your blood to sauce at this point?"

"It's the only thing I'm living for, man. Don't take it from me."

"Fine. A rack of ribs and a few pork sandwiches." He couldn't stomach any more brisket no matter how delicious it was.

"When I get back, can you be less pissed about her? You're doing that *thinking* thing you do again. She's pretty, and you two have a lot in common. You're a red-blooded dude with functioning testicles, and that stalker territory thing I said was out of line. I shoulda kept my mouth shut. God knows it's about time you had a thing for someone. I was starting to wonder if you really were a robot." His shoulders lifted in a shrug as if to say everything spewing from his mouth was painfully obvious. "Stop overthinking this. You're not an asshole." With that, he grabbed the keys to one of their many rental cars and headed out the door.

Smith brought the camera back up to his face, but ordered himself not to take any more pictures. Overthinking everything was his job. That's how he'd become one of the youngest comm sergeants in Special Forces. It was frequently how he saved the remaining members of their team in their new venture—owning the hotshot national security firm, Tier Seven. Telling a guy like him not to over-think something was like telling him not to breathe.

Mercy had replaced the laptop with her iPad again. Her teeth raked over her bottom lip, and he grunted his approval. His eyes zeroed in on the tight white shirt she'd pulled on with those pajama pants she somehow managed to make sexy. Her nipples were drawn to tightened beads at the crest of her lush breasts. His mouth watered. He could just make out the rosy imperfect circles as they strained against the cotton. God, he wanted to memorize their precise color and shape. He needed to discover just how dark they became when she was aroused. He longed to know the flavor of her breasts and how good their weight would feel in his hands.

She arranged a blanket over herself and returned to her reading. She must've been cold. He wanted to tuck her against his massive form and keep her warm. He wouldn't have minded if she wanted to keep reading, so long as he got to hold her against him until he knew she was safe and content, until he'd erased that worry from her brow.

A shiver quaked through her. He ached with the need to protect her. She stood to adjust the thermostat, and he burned with a fascination he had no idea how to control.

2

Something collided with Smith's foot tearing him from his restless slumber. The slick exterior of his sleeping bag slipped along the carpet as Voodoo nudged his foot, with the toe of his own boot, again. Smith lifted his head. Sleeping four hours a night was getting old. "What?" he sighed.

"She's on her laptop. Black screen. Color text. Looks like hacker shit to me."

That was enough to get Smith moving. He lumbered out of the bag, rubbed his hands over his beard, and settled at his laptop. Popping the kink out of his neck, he blinked in the feed from the camera and tried to determine just what his little hacker was up to at zero three hundred. Had she not been able to sleep? Had some kind of nightmare frightened her? Was she cold again, perhaps?

The idea of Mercy alone in a cold bed razored through his gut. The thought that she'd needed him and he hadn't been there mounted frustration in his chest. He was clearly losing his mind. The lack of sleep, or the workload, or something had gotten to him. Now, he was imagining that this woman needed him. She didn't even know him.

"What woke her?" he asked. Lightning fractured the sky, illuminating Mercy seated at her cheap desk with fingers flying over her keyboard. The ensuing rumble of thunder had her tucking herself away from the windows. "Never mind." The knowledge that she was frightened only further cemented his guilt over not being close enough to comfort her.

His little sister Hannah had been scared of storms when the two of them were kids. In the middle of the night, she'd tug on his blankets with that terrified look in her eyes and a wobbling lower lip. He'd cave every time. She'd outgrown it in elementary school, but before that, Smith had frequently woken up with her feet in his back, since she was incapable of staying on her side of any bed. He was practically an expert at warding off the wrath of Mother Nature.

If he'd been with Mercy, she could've laid her head down on his substantial shoulder. He could wrap her up in his arms until she knew there was nothing to fear. He'd cradle her to him, making certain she felt safe and warm. He'd stare down her demons and damn them back to hell. That was his mission, after all. Keep her safe from everything out to do her harm. He refocused.

Voodoo took another sip of coffee. "She got up as soon as it started raining and carried a can of tuna outside to that kitten that lives under the stoop, the one she's been trying to coax inside for a week. Took her a while, but she finally got it to come out. That's why her hair's soaked. Once she got the cat back in the apartment, she started doing whatever it is she's up to now."

"No contact from Julian?" Smith watched everything flashing across on her screen. She was running some kind of vulnerability scan on a server, but he hadn't yet determined which server she was checking. Definitely wasn't any of the DoD's systems. It was some cheap, off-the-shelf CMS.

"If her shit-wagon of a brother had emailed and she'd started typing, don't you think I would've told you that right off?"

"Sorry. I'm trying to figure out what she's after."

Voodoo stalked to the kitchen and poured another cup of coffee. He set it next to Smith. "Caffeinate. It'll help."

"Thanks." He downed a few sips and decided to hack into the

server ahead of her. He was running on CIA equipment, thanks to Tier Seven's latest contractor, Operative Roman Becker. Mercy didn't have that kind of power and access.

With a few lines of code and a password breach that was far too easy, he scanned the sites hosted on the server she was still trying to crack. Glancing back at the camera feed, he grinned. She was in. *All right, sweetheart. Where are we going?*

She went after the firewall on a site called Sub Q.

"Pull up subq.in for me. I need to keep my eyes on what she's doing. I'm gonna take this firewall down for her."

Voodoo pulled his phone from his back pocket, hit a few buttons, and scowled. "Jackasses that run sites like this make us all look bad," he huffed. "This is why the girls I get with are so hesitant to send me nudes."

Smith rolled his eyes. "What is it?"

"Revenge porn site. You upload the images to them, they spread them all over the internet. Bastards."

Smith's eyes narrowed. He should've known it was something like that. K155, Mercy's hacker name, only went after the barnacled, sludge-slicked underbelly of the internet, unless someone paid her to do otherwise.

Voodoo scrolled through the home page. "You want me to see if there are any pics of her on here? Maybe that's what pissed her off."

"No." He couldn't go there. Fury snarled low in his gut. If some asswipe had uploaded pictures of her like that, he wouldn't sleep until he'd hunted him down and expressed himself with his fists. Men should have more respect for women than to post private photos as a shitty way to deal with a breakup. His desire to rearrange the internal organs of men like that didn't concern him. But the fist of possessive ire that wrapped around his own throat, along with the hollow char in his lungs after his flash fire of rage, did. If he ever had the honor of having her exposed and vulnerable all for himself, he would worship every delicious curve of her body. The thought that someone else might've been bestowed a gift like Mercy made him want to drive his fists through several walls. Jealousy was never an attractive emotion. Jealousy over someone he'd never even met was borderline insane. And yet, it was right there, smoldering in his chest.

"So, now you're helping her hack this thing? Aren't we supposed to keep her from hacking?" Voodoo yawned.

"We're supposed to keep her from hacking the DoD. Everything else is fair game. Sites like this shouldn't exist in the first place. Besides that, their security is so lax, they deserve whatever she dishes up."

While she deleted the database of images and destroyed the backups, he took down the alerts system on the site, paving the way for her to exact revenge without sounding any alarms for some half-wit IT clown.

"Uh, is this bad?" Voodoo held up his phone a few minutes later. Sub Q's previous homepage had been replaced with Mercy's ASCII art signature—lips with a skull and crossbones. *Hacked by K155* was in its standard place under the artwork, only this time, she'd added *and friends.*

Smith fought not to bang his head on the table. Then again, maybe it would knock some sense into him. In his quest to help her, he hadn't been quite as covert as he should've been. She'd seen him. She was now aware of him, even if she had no idea where he was. He'd disobeyed direct orders from T-Byrd, the head of their team, to remain out of sight until the last possible moment. Disobeying orders went against everything he was. What was wrong with him? He no longer recognized himself.

His eyes sought the camera feed once more, but Voodoo no longer had it pointed at her screen. Now, it was on her face. Another one of those beautiful eye-crinkling grins lifted her cheeks just before she sank her teeth into her bottom lip in obvious delight. This smile was different than the one he'd seen earlier. Stupid, ridiculous, arrogant pride filled his chest. He had some small claim on this smile, and that pleased him far too much. Dammit. That grip on reality just wasn't coming. He cared far too much about her smiles, those he'd seen and all of the others that he hadn't, and not nearly enough that he'd just indirectly blown their cover.

3

"Make it stop," Mercy whimpered. There was a hammer driving some kind of railroad spike into the base of her skull, or maybe it was someone pounding on her front door. She couldn't be sure. The pain in her head chose to believe the more violent version of the story. By that afternoon, the incoming migraine would take her out at her knees. The pain in her neck never lied, and she did not have time for this.

The rhythmic thuds picked up pace. "Mercy, are you home?" Edgar's deep Colombian accent rapid-fired against her skull.

Forcing one foot to wiggle out from under the covers, she planted it hesitantly on the carpet. Progress. She popped open one eye when four tiny paws landed beside her head. "You aren't supposed to be here, and that's my landlord," she whispered to her newly acquired kitten as she ran her hand down the cat's downy-soft fur. "Keep quiet for me, and I'll get you another can of tuna." Scooping the cat up, she managed to make the steps necessary to carry it into the master bathroom. "Don't give me that look. If he catches you in here, we'll both be homeless." A heartbroken yowl escaped from the tiny animal. "I'll be right back. I promise." Poor thing. He'd finally let Mercy rescue him last night in the middle of the storm. Now, he probably thought he was being abandoned again. Mercy's heart weighted with guilt. "Just let me get rid of him," she vowed through the door.

Incoming pain marched steadily toward her eyes. Pausing to switch on her coffee maker, she tried to remember if she'd paid her rent that month. She was fairly certain she had, but that one check she'd been expecting from the vacation rental site had come in late. Maybe that's why he was there. A slight case of nerves gripped her chest.

Couldn't he have just texted her? Was coming over all the time really necessary? Her landlord checked in with her almost every day. For the most part, Mercy considered human interaction to be completely unneeded. There was Netflix, Amazon Prime, *RexArmis*, and sexy e-books, so really, what more did she need? Of course, she was also the woman out in the middle of a storm rescuing a kitten, just so she'd have someone to talk to. As she headed to the front door, she made a vow to get out more. Soon. Someday. Maybe even a someday relatively soon. Her brother thought she ought to try online dating sites. It was just that people like her couldn't help but see the puppeteer behind the marionette.

She knew how to figure out which men on the dating sites were actually sleazy creeps. Every stolen photo, every posted tweet, that dick pic they'd sent three years ago trying stupidly to get someone's attention, she knew the code behind them all. She could incinerate every string they'd ever pulled and expose the cretins, but there were just so many of them. Taking down sites like Sub Q reassured her that at least she was doing something to fight back, some small thing to reclaim civility.

She'd given up looking for chivalry. There were no heroes left anymore. Guys with any semblance of manners no longer existed. The Smithsonian should be adorned with framed photographs of men in suits from days of yore opening doors for their girlfriends, buying dinner, and refraining from whipping out their dicks until the appropriate time. Not that she necessarily knew when the appropriate time was. Not getting out much hadn't helped with her still-a-virgin status.

She tried not to let the whole of humanity get to her. She opened the door and forced a smile she was certain never climbed all the way up to her eyes. Edgar towered over her five-foot frame and his mustache always seemed to be eating his own lips, preventing a smile from emerging. His eyes were murky pools of black concern. They always were. What was he so worried about all the time?

"Hi, Edgar. Everything okay?" Her voice faltered. She tried to shake off her nerves. When a distinctive meow accompanied a pawing on the bathroom door, she coughed as loud as she could, which did nothing to help her incoming headache. Her eyes throbbed, and defeat taunted her.

Edgar's eyes narrowed. "You sick?"

"Um... maybe." She wasn't certain what the correct answer might be.

He thrust a laptop toward her. "They broke it again, but if you're sick..."

"Oh." Relief eased a little of the tension in her head. She took the laptop. "It's fine. I can fix it. I'll bring it up as soon as I'm finished." Edgar had five daughters. They all shared a single laptop, and each one wanted it to do something different. At least once a month, he came by so Mercy could clean the cache, run adware to remove the endless popups the girls clicked on, and restore everything so the laptop would live to fight another day.

"Thank you. I appreciate it. Girls," he shook his hands at the ceiling, "always breaking things." As if on cue, a thunder of feet racing down the hallway echoed from the apartment above Mercy's. "So loud." He sighed. "I'll wait here." He settled on her sofa. That was when she officially panicked.

She was fairly certain he'd decided to wait on her to fix the computer because it would give him some time to exist in relative silence, something he probably didn't experience upstairs. She wanted to point out that it really wasn't fair to leave his wife to deal with all of their kids, but he was the landlord, and she wasn't stupid.

Glancing back toward her bedroom and offering a silent prayer to the patron saint of kittens, whomever that might be, she opened the laptop on her desk and worked as quickly as she could.

Music wasn't going to help her head, but it might save the cat, so she switched on the last playlist she'd been listening to. Her mind was uncooperative. It didn't seem to understand why she was trying to accomplish things when clearly her head was going to be hosting a migraine in the next few hours.

Another vibration of the bathroom door reminded her that she was going to have to get over it. Edgar seemed oblivious to the noise and happy to sit quietly and wait. Twenty minutes later, the laptop whirred back to life at a functional speed. She slumped in relief. "Okay. Good as almost new," she assured him.

"That was fast." He sounded disappointed by that fact.

"I'm just that good," she tried for a joke but needed him to leave.

"I should pay you or give you a break on your rent or something."

Mercy had no idea what to do with that statement, and he said nothing else. He should, but she doubted he would, so she just stared at him awkwardly. "Uh... I really need to shower."

"Oh, yes. Terribly sorry. Thank you for this." He lifted the laptop and headed out the door.

As soon as she got rid of him, she raced to the bathroom to free the kitten. He had left her a few wet messages on the rug as a reminder that he didn't care for being locked up. "Definitely need to get you a litter box." She cleaned up the room and gave the cat more tuna.

After locating some Motrin for herself, she settled with her own laptop to try to get a few things done before the pain and pressure set in fully. The screenshot of her own kiss of death was still on full display on the former revenge porn site. That sense of hope she'd experienced the night before rushed warmth to the center of her chest, and a grin formed on her features. She'd never hacked with a partner before. Whoever they were, she appreciated the help, not that she'd needed it. Her protégé wasn't as good as she was. Maybe they were still learning. It was cool they were after the same site. She wondered how long they'd been at it before she'd finished it off for them.

Loneliness had been her only companion for so long, she was certain normal people didn't get a thrill over digital interactions with nameless, faceless humans. But her entire world existed only in nameless, faceless interactions. It was the landscape she truly understood, a place where she knew the rules well enough to break them.

She opened her email and all of that warm, gooey, excitement over hacking with a partner quickly escaped her lungs in a hot breath. Why today? She'd been waiting to hear from her brother for weeks, after his last few cryptic emails. Now, he needed her help on the one day she was going to be at her worst.

Her little brother always managed to jump before he looked to see if there was anything that could catch his fall. Mercy assumed that was because she'd always been his safety net. According to their mother, he had too much of their father in him. The last thing he'd told her before he left Kansas City was that he'd taken some job where he would be out of town for an extended period of time. She assumed it must've been with a weapons development company. Julian could pretty much talk his way into or out of anything, so the job offer hadn't shocked her. She'd been a little put out that he'd abandoned her so readily, though. Hadn't they promised to stick together after their mother's death?

But just like always, Julian went after whatever shiny object he thought would make him a hero, with no regard for his sister. He'd figured out how to design some kind of drone radar system that he planned to sell to the military. He'd always been good at engineering and design, so Mercy could see how he'd be a natural fit.

It was her brother's need for praise and stupid amounts of money that irked her. He couldn't just make a quiet deal with the army or the navy or whomever you sold systems like that to. No, Julian wanted fanfare. He wanted bid wars and recognition. He must've gone off bragging to the wrong people. Someone had stolen the designs and, of course, Mercy was going to come to his rescue... again. Such is the life of Julian Valon's big sister. She knew her role. She'd been playing it since his birth.

The kitten meowed insistently and nudged Mercy's thigh with his tiny head.

"You need a name and some toys, but I have to do this for Julian first." That only got her another meow. The next email was from a retail site with several issues, including their shopping cart program. She'd pointed out several bugs in their security infrastructure and had offered to fix the problems, for payment of course. A girl had to live. They'd accepted her proposal.

She went back to Julian's email. He'd provided an actual server where his stolen designs were being stored, and he was certain they were going to be moving them that evening. His company was supposed to pitch the designs to their buyer the next day. She had a few hours to wipe the designs off of the thief's servers and return them to their rightful owners. Surely she could get it done before she needed to sleep off the migraine. After all, she was K155, the kiss of death.

Returning her attention to the kitten, she considered a name. The way his little ears stood on end, too big for his tiny body, gave her an idea. "How about Yoda? He trained Luke, and he's kind of adorable in his own way. We'll watch the movies later. They're completely amazing, except for that Jar-Jar thing, but I've decided it's a forgivable offense. Right now, I have to go steal something back for Julian. Pro tip—never promise to do favors for my brother." She spent a full minute playing with Yoda before shoving her laptop, iPad, and phone into her bag and heading out. For this particular job, she preferred to use public Wi-Fi. Just in case.

4

Smith pointed at Mercy's Honda. "She's turning there."

Voodoo spared him an eye roll. "Yeah, I can see that, since she's forty feet ahead of us. Calm your tits. Geez."

"What does that even mean? Calm your tits? It makes no sense. I would think that you, of all people, would prefer it if the tits were not particularly calm." For some reason, Smith felt like arguing, or complaining, or doing anything that got his mind off what he was about to do. He was beyond certain the FBI was monitoring her emails. Her brother was a viper, and he knew they were watching her. Julian was going to let her take the fall for him. That thought turned the coffee he'd had that morning into a solid block in Smith's gut.

Voodoo laughed at him outright. "Are you seriously nervous? Dude, you're like the computer whisperer. You can do this. Or are you thinking about doing something that might excite Mercy's huge..."

Smith interrupted Voodoo with some kind of unrecognizable threatening noise that vaulted from his mouth and cut the word "tits" off of the end of his question. "Do not say another word about her... attributes. Ever. Just don't. You got it?"

"Yeah, I got it. Never thought I'd see cool-as-a-cucumber Smitty Hagen so shook. Girl really gets you going, doesn't she?"

Smith refused to answer that. If someone had told him when he'd signed on to this mission that a woman existed who could make him feel this protective, intrigued, and horny all at the same time, he would've laughed. He was nearing forty. He'd never been even half this fascinated with any of the women he'd ever slept with.

Keeping Mercy from hacking the DoD didn't worry him. Keeping her safe from the FBI drilled tension throughout his musculature. Thinking about the more-than-ample swells of her breasts only served to thicken his cock until he swore he was choking. Christ, he wanted to feel the weight of them in his massive hands, to know the other lush curves of her body as she moved under his own. He longed to experience the soft heat of her skin melding into his. He wanted to feel her thick thighs wrapped around his waist, and to grip her full feminine backside while he drove himself deep inside of her. He was strung so tight he was going to blow, and he didn't have time for that.

He attempted to swallow down the hunger. This would be the first time he shared a space with her, not a close proximity of course, but she'd likely see him at the very least. He wasn't an easy guy to hide. He was removing the barrier between them. Thoughts of getting to talk to her had him hoping there'd be a need for conversation.

Mercy's car stopped at a coffee shop, and Voodoo circled once before turning into the parking lot to keep from alerting her that she was being followed. By the time they parked, she was heading inside. Smith studied her features. She looked more annoyed than frightened. Of course, she still didn't know the actual site her brother wanted her to hack.

With the precision of one of the greatest Special Forces teams ever to have existed, Smith and Voodoo prepared. They took position and alerted the rest of Tier Seven as to what was about to go down. Voodoo stationed himself outside the shop with views of both entrances and the cross streets.

Smith entered the shop, letting the coffee-infused air fill his lungs as he joined the line. The ambience was assaulted by the whir of the grinder and chug of steam from the barista station. He'd wondered for years why the world had to be so damn loud. He could barely hear himself think.

Three people separated him from Mercy. She wasn't so concerned about her brother's task that she'd decided to forgo a drink. That eased a little of the tension in Smith's jaw.

He rubbed his beard and pretended not to notice her. In reality, he studied every minute detail. The way she shifted the bag on her shoulder, the way she swayed her weight from one foot to the other. Impatient or nervous? He couldn't quite tell. She ran her fingers through her long brunette hair and rubbed the ends. He was fairly certain that was a nervous habit. Then she cringed and rubbed her temples. Was she in pain? That thought had him edging closer to her. He wanted to fix whatever the problem was. His fingertips tingled, anxious to rub away any ailment.

He bumped into the man directly ahead of him and the annoyed patron turned to shoot Smith a glare, only to change his mind when he took in his sheer size.

The urge to demand that she not follow through on her brother's plan welled in Smith's chest. Some primal longing had him contemplating throwing her over his shoulder and running out with her caveman style. If he took her to his home in Lincoln, she'd be safe, and she'd be his. He could wipe away her pain, and tuck her up in his bed, warm and content. There was no need for her to fear storms or anything else. He'd stand between her and the world and never allow anything or anyone to get to her. He would personally freeze hell himself before he let her brother get close enough to hurt her ever again. Half of one brain cell managed to remind all the others that what he was considering was called abduction. Jesus, what was wrong with him?

He smiled when he heard Mercy order herself coffee with extra cream, the way she drank it in her apartment. That's precisely how he drank his as well. In his experience, people who drank black coffee were either sociopaths or had parents who didn't love them enough or something.

The barista set her drink on the bar and bellowed out, "Mercy," as

Smith placed his order. If he'd had any doubts about her knowing which site she was going to try to hack, that quelled it. No one planning to hack the Department of Defense gave a barista their real name.

She smiled at the barista when picking up her coffee. It was one of those sweet smiles that made jealousy rush through him like a flood. He wanted to earn a smile. Just one. Anything to reassure himself that all of this wasn't about to blow up in both of their faces.

SETTLING at a table with her coffee, Mercy tried to pop some of the tension out of her neck. She had to focus. Julian needed her. Opening her laptop, she joined the coffee shop's Wi-Fi and rescanned the emailed instructions. "Julian, what have you gotten yourself into?" she huffed through her teeth. She frequently skated on the edge of legality with her hacking, but something about this told her she was about to take a walk on the dark side. How had these people even found Julian's designs? Who the hell had he been talking to?

Before she could determine the best way to get to the server in question, she lifted her head, and then lifted it a little more, in order to watch what had to be the world's most attractive male walking toward her. Holy wow. Everything about him was solid and substantial. Grizzly-bear sized with kind, patient eyes and a full beard. His thighs were the diameter of tree trunks, and his hands, dear God, those hands. He was carrying a laptop of his own. She swore one of his hands spanned the entire cover. Raw heat slipped into her belly. Utterly distracted by the giant, she forgot all about her brother. Her eyes took their own sweet time traversing the expanse of his chest and the thick ropes of muscles that comprised his arms. The leather jacket he was wearing couldn't conceal his sheer might.

It seemed impossible that all this time she'd been completely wrong about her type. The few skinny, whiny, pity-hounds she'd endured on dates in the last few years had all been looking for someone who'd replace their mother. Mercy refused. Either that or they were jealous of her computer skills and looking for dirt on her. Whatever it was, none of them had ever been able to crack the surface of the things she wanted in this life, the things she definitely needed. Suddenly, barrel-chested, bearded, and buff ranked directly above air and water in her hierarchy of needs. There was a hard edge to his gaze, a confidence maybe, coupled with intelligence in those gorgeous hazel eyes. It said he knew more than he let on in all circumstances. Blood flooded her cheeks as she thought of just a few of the things she'd like to experience with a man like that, if only he could read her mind, because she wasn't brave enough to voice them out loud.

When he passed her table, one of his massive thighs brushed her arm. The friction against her skin drew a slight gasp from her. He stopped and one of those hands gently touched her arm. "I'm sorry, ma'am. I didn't mean to bump you. Are you okay?" His eyes said he was truly concerned that he might've injured her. His fingers continued to caress her arm. His touch was shockingly tender compared with the enormity of his size. All of that and he came with manners, too. She wondered if he was always so polite. Maybe she'd been too hasty about giving up on humanity.

She managed to nod but couldn't remember how to formulate words. Several odd sounds escaped her lips before she produced, "I'm fine. You didn't hurt me. I mean, it's really... fine. The tables... they're...close together, and you're so... big." *Shut up, Mercy.*

"I'm glad you're okay." He squeezed her arm gently before walking away from her. Wait. Why was he leaving? Her arm needed to be touched some more, and she needed to hear that deep rumble of his voice again. Wasn't there some kind of law that if you bump into someone you have to tell them your name? If that wasn't a law, it should be. *Come back.*

He took a table at the back of the shop. She should've been embarrassed that she was still staring at him, but that didn't occur to her at the moment. The thick muscles of his shoulders rolled as he slid out of his jacket and settled in a chair that was entirely too small for him.

He gave her a half grin and winked before opening his laptop. Her heart fluttered out of her rib cage and landed in her throat. *You can't just keep staring at him.* Some portion of her brain tried to remind her of this. He probably still lives with his mother, or has no idea what a VPN is, and it's pretty much guaranteed he only speaks in sports statistics. He was likely some kind of lineman for a football team somewhere and did that thing where guys run toward each other and bump chests. Either that or he punctuated every sentence with the words *dude* and *bro*, or worse, *dudebro*. Nope. Not for her. Pretty to look at, but she had a job to do.

Eventually, she turned back to her own computer. Disappointment crashed through her, leaving loneliness in its wake. She was surrounded by people, but there was only one she had any interest in talking to, and she shouldn't want to talk to him. Being turned on was not a good reason to strike up a conversation. Besides, her head was starting to throb. When the vision in her right eye blurred, she tried to blink the sensation away. No luck. It only worsened until the sight in her right eye fractured completely, leaving her with an odd jagged hole in her vision. She had to save Julian before his designs were gone forever.

5

Smith's father was a four-star general. From his birth, Smith had only ever known the army way of life. It took almost no effort for him to berate himself for what he'd just done, in his father's tone no less. *You compromised the mission and your team, all because you let this girl get under your skin. She doesn't even know you. She is a target. You're supposed to turn her into an asset and nothing more. She cannot and will not ever be more than that. Voodoo is outside keeping your ass safe while you're in here putting your hands all over a target.* A fist of shame slammed into his throat. Disgust curdled in his veins.

Disobeying orders, engaging the target before the right moment, helping her hack another site. None of those were things he did. He was Special Forces, and it was damned time he started acting like it.

When he'd seen her staring up at him with her lips parted and her eyes roving his chest, he'd lost any sense he'd ever possessed. The need to interact with her in some small way had taken over. The need to touch her silky skin, to know her scent, to feel her heat had gotten to him like he was some horny teenager on the prowl.

Determined to right his wrong, he set up the camera, hidden inside the case of an external hard drive, so he could see exactly what Mercy was typing from his location. His team was counting on him.

Roman needed her so he could get to Julian. If her brother got his way, Mercy was going to end up in prison instead of him. Smith was the only man capable of preventing that from happening. He had to get his mind back in the game and get the job done.

Unable to keep his gaze from Mercy, his heart sank as she leaned her head into her hands and massaged her temples again. Something, besides what was about to happen, was clearly wrong, but there wasn't a damned thing he could do about it. She took a long sip of her coffee and poised her fingers over her keyboard. Smith matched her position and waited. Game on.

Her first attempt was to bounce the signal through a server in Hong Kong. He let that one go. On her next bounce to Toronto, he cut her off. If he moved too soon, she'd know someone was personally blocking her. He had to let her get closer with each pass to kill any suspicions that anything more than firewalls and port blocks were keeping her from those designs.

He controlled the space and the target. Time was the only unknown factor. He had no idea how determined she'd be to do her brother's bidding, or how long she'd try to get through. She was brilliant, after all. Eventually she was going to figure out that someone was watching her efforts, and he was the idiot who'd just made himself known in her world.

Frustration knitted her brow. He watched her jaw flex and her eyes close for a half beat too long. A chasm formed between the man he'd always been and the guy he wanted to be for her. Some fucked-up part of himself wanted her to succeed simply so she could feel relief and accomplishment. Certain that he was losing his mind, he let his training take over. *Team above individual. The hunter never the hunted. Fight hard. Fight now. Win or don't go home.*

Mercy made another attempt. This time she brought it closer to the intended target. She bounced to a server somewhere in Texas and then to a hotspot in Seattle.

It's fucking cold out here. How much longer? Appeared on Smith's screen. He ground his teeth at Voodoo's text and refocused. Back to

Houston. Somewhere in the Philippines. He cut her off at the bounce to Hartford. That was as close to D.C. as she was going to get.

My balls have icicles appeared in another text box.

Mercy was rubbing her head again and trying to reset, so Smith clicked on the texts.

Busy. Try underwear next time

That would disappoint women everywhere

Smith rolled his eyes. He was going to strangle Voodoo when this was all over. *Sympathy to your sac. Now do your job.*

Undeterred, Mercy tried again. Tokyo, Istanbul, Lyon. Smith ended it there.

He'd picked up lip-reading in Special Forces, which came in handy when interpreting the long string of expletives coming from her mouth. Her temper both humored and enlivened him. He'd never engaged a more beautiful challenge. But then, some douche he instantly hated approached her table and offered to buy her a refill.

She cocked her jaw to the side and shook her head, but then she cringed and rubbed her face again.

When she picked up her phone, frustration and fear fought for dominance in his gut. He couldn't make out the screen of her phone with his camera. Surely, she wasn't going to try to get in through her cell. Her fingers flew. His gut clenched. If she got through on her phone, he couldn't save her.

Heads up! We've got company. Get her out of there.

Smith scanned the parking lot from the window. Three black Escalades with government plates all pulled into spots near the front. Shit.

U nable to see without covering her right eye, Mercy tried to quell the rising tide of panic and nausea roaring in her stomach. How was someone blocking her attempts at every turn?

The migraine had stripped away some of her practiced caution. She wasn't going about this the way she normally would. She didn't even know the site Julian wanted her to hack. She was going in the back end through their servers instead of approaching from the front with knowledge.

A hard swallow did nothing to cool the hot singe of bile that coated her throat. She managed the few keystrokes required to access the site's home page.

A frozen fist of dread gripped her and then melted over her fevered skin. The exchange of temperatures made her sway as the nausea overtook her. She barely managed to read the site's pop-up:

You are attempting to access a U.S. Government Information System. The USG intercepts and monitors all communications on this network. At any time the USG may inspect and seize any acquired data. The accessor will be prosecuted to the full extent of the law.

"Oh God, oh God, oh God." Mercy wasn't certain if her words were a prayer or a curse.

At that moment, three men who looked precisely the way federal agents looked in movies entered the coffee shop.

Mercy closed her laptop and slipped her phone back into her bag. Her hands shook so violently she almost knocked the computer to the floor. The world blurred and tilted as the men slowly scanned the shop. She had to run. Her panic was subverted by pain. The pressure behind her eyes crackled outwards toward her skull.

Standing, she turned and faced a wall. Was there a wall there before? No, wait. It wasn't a wall. It was the gorgeous giant. She could barely make him out through her fractured vision.

"Mercy, my name is Smith Hagen. Julian sent me to keep you safe. The three men that just walked in are FBI. I know you have no idea who I am, but it's probably me or them. I'll take care of you, but I need you to come with me." She found his engine-rumble voice oddly soothing.

She blinked up at him and tried to bring his form fully into her shimmering vision. How insanely stupid was it to be willing to go with this Colossus of a man? She told herself it wasn't because he was gorgeous. He knew her name and Julian's name, so he couldn't be lying. Her brother must've known the danger he had put her in, and he'd hired the biggest guy he could find to protect her. That made sense. She and Julian had always looked out for each other.

The sharp peal of a fire alarm split the air. Every excruciating whir pounded blunt nails into her skull.

"That's my partner with our distraction," whispered the beautiful giant as he reached for her laptop.

She gripped the back of her chair as a cough overwhelmed her. *No. Please.* Her stomach roiled ominously. She pled with any deity in the universe, but she was denied. Bile flooded her mouth. Cold sweat dewed on her forehead. A cruel shiver vibrated through her.

Colossus leapt back when her body pitched forward, but he didn't quite make it. The remnants of her coffee and her morning bagel landed on his boots. "Oh no," she whimpered. "I threw up on the giant."

To her absolute astonishment, rather than running away, he calmly grabbed a few napkins from a nearby table, stepped around the vomit on the floor, and gently wiped her face. When he finished with her, he wiped off his own boots then gently lifted her into his arms. "Let's get you out of here, okay?"

Whatever Julian was paying this guy, it wasn't enough. Somehow in the midst of her world crashing down around her, she knew she was safe as soon as she was tucked against his massive form.

Too sick to help herself, Mercy pressed her face against his chest. Comfort and safety permeated her weary bones. She hadn't felt either of those things since before her mother's death. Just before her eyes closed, she was almost certain he smiled.

SMITH HAD TO FIX THIS. She was sick. He wouldn't allow it. She should never be sick. Her vomiting had drawn the agents' attention their way, but Voodoo had come through with the perfect distraction just like always. The coffee shop full of patrons had descended into chaos at the blare of the fire alarm. People raced toward the front doors, while the baristas frantically searched the kitchen to locate the source of the nonexistent fire.

With a few quick moves around other escaping customers, Smith scooted her out a side door and rushed to the waiting van with Voodoo inside. "I'll drive," he commanded, "you make her better. She's sick."

Voodoo chuckled. "Yes, sir," he taunted.

Smith had no idea why Voodoo found this funny. She was sick. He was the medic. He had to fix her now. How did he not understand this?

Tenderly, Smith lowered one of the middle seats and laid her on it. He shrugged out of his jacket and covered her with it. They weren't likely to get out of the parking lot without an FBI tail. As soon as the agents made their way out of the chaos, they'd be on them, and yet, her contented sigh made him smile. A sense of accomplishment filled him.

She whimpered when he was forced to make a hard right out of the parking lot. Panic seized him. He checked on her via the rearview mirror for what felt like the tenth time in as many seconds.

"Try to keep it steady, man," Voodoo instructed him unnecessarily. "You're not using, are you, Mercy?"

She tried to shake her head but couldn't quite manage it.

"No," Smith insisted. "She has a stomach virus or something. She threw up back there." Hackers were never users. The two didn't mix. Plus, they'd been watching her for weeks. She'd never used drugs. He knew Voodoo was doing his standard checks, but this time it annoyed him.

In a pained whisper, she explained, "Migraine."

Voodoo cringed. "Poor kid. Let's see what we can do." He pulled his old, black Special Forces sweatshirt from his bag, folded it into an odd blindfold, and laid it over her eyes.

"Thank you," made its way from her lips.

"Listen to me for just a second. I know it hurts. Everyone calls me Voodoo, so you can, too. I used to be an army medic. Special Forces, actually. That just means I'm damned good at what I do. I can give you something for the nausea and for the pain, but it's going to make you sleepy. You're in a van with two dudes you don't know, so I want to make sure you're okay with me treating you. Smitty here is about the nicest guy you'll ever meet, as long as you're not shooting at him. I save people. I don't hurt them. Are you okay with me giving you something that'll help?"

A bolt of guilt tightened in Smith's gut. Voodoo was working the plan. Be as honest as they could with her, so she'd ultimately trust them enough to turn on her brother. It was Smith who'd had to lie to her. If she let Voodoo treat her, it would only be because Smith had told her Julian had sent them. He'd known it would be the only way to get her to come with him, but now, he had to figure out how to undo the web he'd spun. The need for her trust tunneled through him. It was more than the role Tier Seven wanted her to fill as a target. It held more weight, meant more, maybe everything. It meant enough that it frightened him.

If she contacted her brother and asked about them, the mission was a failure, but more than that, he regretted that the first things he'd ever spoken to her were outright lies. He'd meant to bump into her, desperate for contact with her soft skin, so the only truth his apology held was that he never intended to hurt her. Self-hatred coiled in his gut.

Even if they managed to keep her from any contact with her brother, what would happen when Smith ultimately had to come clean with her? The way she'd tucked her limp body against his chest, and held on with all of her waning strength, compressed his lungs again. She'd fit in his arms like they were the pillars put on this earth to protect her. It made absolutely no sense, but the connection had been there. If Special Forces had taught him anything at all, it was that you could assume any necessary role for guerrilla warfare, but you couldn't lie to yourself. You knew when you were full of shit. He knew there was something between him and Mercy. There just wasn't a damn thing he could do about it.

"It's fine," she urged. "Thank you."

Voodoo smiled down at her. "That's my job."

7

S omewhere in the recesses of Mercy's mind, she suspected she shouldn't have agreed to being drugged by this guy. Had he said his name was Voodoo? A jolt of panic prompted her to get up and out of the vehicle, but she was finally warm under the other man's blanket-sized coat and ignored her survival instincts. Had he mentioned his name? She couldn't remember.

The lead weight of pain in her head slowed her thoughts and formed some kind of impenetrable force around the panic. She was only capable of understanding small, singular truths. The one that centered in her addled mind was that she wanted the other man to talk to her again. She wanted to ask him to hold her the way he had. For a woman who'd spent most of her life in fear, that feeling of security was a drug unlike anything the medic could ever give her. She longed to bury her face in the giant's chest and inhale that pine tree and leather scent that clung to his jacket. Maybe once they were safe, she could work up the courage to actually talk to him. Maybe.

She felt the medic's hand on her shoulder. "All right, this is Phenergan. It'll help whatever might still be in your stomach to stay there, and it should help with the dizziness, too. Do you think you can sit up just a little so you can take it?"

It took everything Mercy had just to lift her head. The medic, Voodoo, she reminded herself, slipped the cloth off of her face and braced her. He placed the pill on her tongue and held a water bottle to her lips. More thankful for the water than the medicine, she downed a few sips and then drank more. Another round of dizziness swept through her, and her body went simultaneously hot and cold. "Oh no," she whimpered. The medic really was good at his job. He had a barf bag to her lips in half a second.

"Close your eyes, sweet pea. Focus on the last thing that made you feel happy. Just one thing. Focus everything you've got on that," his smooth, steady voice guided her. She heard him tear open a package and then felt a cold wipe on her face. Julian definitely wasn't paying these men enough. After a few deep breaths, she laid back down, thankful she hadn't needed the bag.

The last time she'd been truly happy. Whenever she tried to focus on something like that, for whatever purpose, she always chose what she wanted for the future since her past didn't have all that many great memories. She'd picture a house, complete with stairs and a fireplace, that was all hers, one she could keep. Her mother never made much money, so they moved around a lot as kids. What she wanted for the future was a job that didn't require a daily scrounge of the internet and someone who liked talking with her. Maybe even someone who understood her, assuming that someone even existed, which she wasn't entirely sure about. She probably wouldn't ever have any of those things, but it was always nice to think about them.

But those wishes didn't come to her as, once again, vomit ransacked her stomach and climbed a ladder to her throat. Remembering Voodoo's prompting for keeping the contents of her stomach where it belonged, she tried to refocus. The moment she chose this time was probably even more ridiculous, but desperate times called for desperate measures. She recalled exactly what the giant's arms felt like as they cradled her. The precise way he'd smelled just the way men were supposed to smell, at least in her dreams, and the soothing timbre of his voice. Slowly, the wave of nausea eased its vicious grip.

"That's it," Voodoo continued his encouragement as he placed the sweatshirt back over her eyes, which was a gift like no other. The sunlight was brutal. "All right, the strongest pain killer I carry on me is Ketorolac. Think of it like Aspirin on steroids. By the time you wake up, the headache should be gone. Little pinch, and I'll let you sleep."

Mercy didn't fully understand what was about to happen until she felt the quick slip of a needle in her arm. Oddly, the shot did more to reassure her that these were good men. It clearly wasn't the first time the army medic had given a shot. She'd barely felt it. He really was good at what he did. With that thought, the medicine seemed to surround the pain and submerge it.

She tried to stay awake. She wanted to hear the other man talk again. She wanted to be able to focus on his voice. As if he could hear her mental imploring, the last conscious memory she had was of him asking, "That any better, sweetheart?"

The ability to nod came back to her so she moved her head against the seat, and then a fog filled her brain and whisked her somewhere else. Her eyelids weighed more than the rest of her body. She couldn't lift them to blink, so she left them closed and drifted off to somewhere away from the pain and the fear.

"Is she going to be okay?" Smith demanded as soon as Voodoo's ass hit the seat beside him.

"I'm only taking all of your shit because I know you have a raging hard-on for our hacker refugee, but come on. I took out your appendix in a hut in Herat and had you back in your boots the next day. I think I can handle a migraine."

That was true. Smith barely even had a scar from the emergency surgery, but the panic over her being sick wouldn't give him peace. "Shut it," he snapped before glancing back to see if Mercy had reacted to Voodoo's crude announcement that he was attracted to her.

"Relax, she ain't hearing anything right now. Do you have a plan for bedding her? Like I said, I could help you come up with something."

An annoying shard of pure heat stabbed through Smith at the thought of taking her to his bed, cradling her under him, protecting her, and sating a hunger that had ridden him hard for too many years.

"We are not having this conversation, ever." Another check of the rearview mirror revealed nothing out of the ordinary on the road behind them, but that did nothing to soothe him. Better to see your enemy and know what he's doing than to have no idea where he is or what he's up to.

"Fine," said Voodoo with a smirk. "Have you let T and Roman know we have her?"

"Not yet, and I still don't see our tail."

"Could be good. Could be bad. Maybe they didn't get out in time."

"They're the FBI. They're out there. I just don't know where yet."

"Are we heading south now?"

"Unless I'm told otherwise."

T-Byrd had arranged a safe house for them down in Oklahoma, in a small ranching town where one of Tier Seven's best contractors lived.

"I'm not telling you otherwise, but I am saying she isn't going to be able to go all the way to Maddox's today. We're gonna have to stop somewhere, get some fluids in her, and get her in bed for a few hours. From what I saw, she didn't have anything but a cup of coffee and a bagel before she left her apartment. She's going to get dehydrated quickly. I have flush syringes and saline bags with me, but I'm not risking an IV in a van."

That same protective, possessive instinct continued to hammer at the base of Smith's skull. She divided his body into two distinct camps—guilty and horny.

But he wasn't an idiot. Julian was her only living family, and she'd already put herself in danger to help him. It didn't take a genius to see that there wasn't anything she wouldn't do for her brother. Smith was going to have to continue lying to her, and ultimately, that was going to blow up in his face. He'd thought finding terrorists in the mountains of Afghanistan was tough. That was nothing compared to this.

Keeping Mercy out of the hospital was crucial for their mission. Keeping her healthy and comfortable was necessary for him to continue drawing breath. My God. What was this girl doing to him?

Voodoo interrupted his panic. "I still think you need a plan. Don't overthink this one. If you're into her, do something about it." After that, he brought his phone to his ear to call Tier Seven and announce their success with the first part of their assignment.

Smith ground his teeth. He didn't have the luxury of having women eagerly line up to climb under him the way Voodoo did. He swore the medic could walk into a bar, flirt and grin, and then walk out with the woman of his choice. Smith had never experienced anything like that. He wasn't certain he wanted to, but it would be nice to not frighten women.

They were often intimidated by his size, and that killed him. He wasn't some monster prowling the local nightlife to find a victim to steal back to his cave, unless, of course, that whole caveman thing got her going. He was nothing if not adaptable. Hell, if Mercy wanted him to play some kind of porn star repairman for her, he'd be down at the hardware store picking up a hard hat and tool belt.

He listened to Voodoo's half of the conversation with Roman for a few minutes to wipe away thoughts of just what might make Mercy Valon tick. "Shit, man. Neither of those things are what we needed to hear. Are you heading to Texas?" A thousand thoughts as to what Roman might be sharing racked in Smith's head, each one worse than the one before. "You know we'll keep her safe. You go get our contact out. We're probably going to drop off the grid once we stop, but we'll let you know where we are when we can."

"What now?" Smith asked when he ended the call.

"Davis Wakefield missed his contact time this morning. Roman thinks he's been compromised." That explained why Roman was going to Texas. Davis Wakefield was the DEA agent embedded deep in the Castellas cartel. He'd been feeding intel to Roman for months.

That's how they'd learned about Mercy, when Julian showed up at the cartel compound requesting a way to join.

"Who's Roman taking with him?"

"Rio's team. If anyone can get him out, they can. T ran checks on all of the photos I took of the coffee shop. It's not just the FBI who followed her this morning. One of her brother's associates was in there as well. He had to have seen you leave with her."

"The guy who asked if he could buy her a refill." Smith knew instantly. He was certain Mercy got hit on whenever she went out, but that guy was after more than her number. But why would he make contact with her before she'd successfully acquired the designs? She was useless to the cartel until she had those. Davis had been clear that they were only interested in her for her ability to access secure servers. The question tumbled through his mind as he drove them away from Kansas City until the answer shimmered in the periphery much clearer than he could stand. *Because I did.* Fuck. Her brother's man made an appearance because Smith had first. If a spy was that blatant, it meant he wasn't worried about being made. Was it a warning for Smith? Or for her? Had his cover been blown? He had no way of knowing. For a moment, he thought Mercy wasn't the only one who was going to be sick.

Dammit. He had to get his head straight. Both of their lives depended on it.

8

Two jet-black Escalades appeared in Smith's passenger-side mirror. His breaths came a little easier. "FBI on our four. Quarter mile back." Missouri being flatter than a pancake was certainly helping him spot a tail.

Voodoo checked the mirrors. "Thank God. I was lying before when I said it could be good they weren't behind us. I like 'em where I can see them."

Smith grinned. "Let's show them how Special Forces plays chase."

Voodoo chuckled as he pulled up a map on his phone. "In another mile there will be four exits in a row. Can't ask for better than that. Thirty or so miles after that there's another cluster. We need to lose them sooner than later, so we can get her some food."

At the second cluster of exits, they could drive for a while and find some out of the way motel. Heading for a major city wasn't a good idea. The FBI had friends everywhere. Unfortunately, so did the Castellas cartel. They ran drugs from Houston all the way up to Omaha, gaining more contacts, hitmen, and resources with every passing day. "All right, I'm going to attempt to get them to believe that I'm taking the first exit in the next cluster, but I'm really going to take the second. If they don't get off at the first, we'll get back on using the on ramp after taking the second and keep going. Eventually, we'll lose them."

"Let's do it." Making certain their tail saw him, he signaled and changed lanes toward the first exit. When they followed his movement, he flew past the exit ramp like he'd just noticed them in his mirrors. For a moment the tail disappeared from vision, but that was the whole idea. A few seconds later, they reappeared. He took the second exit.

Flooring the van, Smith stayed on the exit ramp allowing it to lead him directly to the on ramp that would take them right back onto the highway. Now, they were just a little farther down the road. Angry drivers cut off by the black SUV let loose a blaring horn chorus, assuring Smith that the FBI had made the second exit. He shared a quick grin with Voodoo as they pulled back onto the interstate. With any luck at all, they'd missed the fact that Smith and Voodoo hadn't actually exited. The FBI could skulk around whatever town they'd just passed for a while. By the time they figured out Tier Seven was second to none, Smith would have them hidden away for the night.

Mercy's soft groan gripped him by the short hairs. He shot a pleading look at Voodoo who was already in motion. "I got her. You drive."

Leaping back over the center console, he pressed his hand to her forehead. Some bizarre feeling swiped through Smith. What the hell? He tried to deny the snarl of huffy frustration and jealousy low in his gut, but it was there. His hands itched to hold her. If she had a fever, he wanted to know. He wanted to be the one to make her feel better. The need to be the one to solve problems for her clawed over his muscles yet again. He called himself an asshole for good measure.

"Can you drink some water for me?" Voodoo soothed. Smith almost drove into a Buick directly ahead of him as he watched her struggle to sit up and drink. He braced for the worst when she started to cough, but Voodoo coaxed more water down her throat and then resettled her. Five minutes later, she was fast asleep again. "If she keeps waking up to drink like that, we can go further," he explained as he crawled back into the front seat.

"We have to make certain we don't have anyone else following us before we make it to the Oklahoma line. I'm not drawing a map for *them* directly to Holder County." He had no idea how much Mercy was hearing or understanding. No need to frighten her by giving out more information than was necessary. For a brief moment, that eased the guilt over his earlier lies.

THIS WAS the best dream of her life. If only that annoying tug of pain behind her eyes would take a hike, Mercy would have gladly slept for eternity. She decided the eye ache wasn't all that bad anymore, anyway. Nothing was perfect. She could deal as long as this dream kept going. With a grin, she tucked herself tighter into the strong arms cradling her. Correction, being held in his arms was actually perfection even with the remnants of pain. Yep, best dream ever.

The distinctive clicking of a keycard sliding into a door lock interrupted the dream. But when a blast of humid air laced with stale bleach diminished the heavenly aroma of man and leather, she wondered if perhaps this wasn't a dream. She couldn't recall ever dreaming up smells before.

"This place is a dive," the owner of the arms surrounding her whispered his irritation.

"It's an hourly motel. What did you expect? It's clean. That's something. What do you care, anyway?" The distinctive sound of the other male's voice had her blinking her eyes open. If the giant hadn't been holding her, she was certain she would have collapsed under the crushing weight of reality as it rushed over her. Julian, the FBI, the designs. All of it swept her up in a tidal wave, ripping the air from her lungs.

"She shouldn't have to stay somewhere like this," the giant huffed.

Still not quite certain how one was supposed to behave when they were running from the FBI, she gave in to her first instinct. Her fingertips stroked over his thick beard. It was softer than she'd imagined, a complement to the soft heat in his eyes. When he looked down at her and smiled, she sank her teeth into her bottom lip and allowed herself one more trace over the angles of his face, still evident even with all of his facial hair. "It's okay. I know you're doing this to keep me safe. I don't care where we stay." She had just enough sense not to include the words *as long as you stay with me*.

He settled on one of the beds with her still in his arms. She wasn't going to complain.

"How are you feeling, sweet pea?" the other man asked. When he came into her line of sight, she recalled his name.

"I'm okay. Did you say your name was Voodoo?"

He grinned. "Yep. The drugs I gave you aren't that good. Whatever you remember is likely what happened."

That wasn't what she wanted to hear. Her focus readily returned to the giant. She stiffened in his arms, and panic formed in his compelling eyes. "Are you okay?"

"No, because that means I actually did throw up on you. Oh God. I'm so sorry." Mercy squeezed her own eyes shut, blocking his gorgeous form from sight. Though it was cruel, it was a suitable punishment for barfing on him.

His throaty chuckle slipped and slid over her skin in a pleasing caress. "Believe me, I've had much worse on me before. Besides, you had good aim. Just got my boots. Don't worry about it. Uh... do you want me to lay you down?"

No. Not really. Would you mind holding me like this forever? The phrases danced on her tongue, but she'd already embarrassed herself thoroughly with the men her brother had tasked with keeping her safe. Since she'd buried her face against his broad chest and was clinging to his shirt, she knew why he'd asked. She told herself there really wasn't a need to make this situation worse on him.

Besides, she could take care of herself when she wasn't crippled with a migraine from the depths of hell. They'd never believe that if she stayed tucked up in his arms for the entirety of this... *adventure*. Surely that wasn't the right word, but telling herself she was on the lam conjured up men in pinstripe suits and feathered hats, with cigars, and incompetent lackeys that went by the name of Morty. She scolded herself for her lack of knowledge of how to run away. Escape and evasion online happened to be her specialty. She'd never imagined that she'd need to know how to do it in real life.

"I'm okay," she didn't sound quite as confident as she would've liked. When he realized that she was attempting to stand, he gently helped her to her feet. The room seemed to shift at an angle much too quickly while she remained still. Her eyes closed, and she swayed. Before she could face-plant on the cheap carpeting, he had her back in his arms. This time he stood and laid her on the bed. Concern tensed in his gaze as he stared down at her.

"We've got to get some food in her." Urgency flooded Voodoo's tone. "I'm not ready to try a protein bar or an MRE on her stomach. Can you stay with her for a few? I'll see if I can find some drive-through chicken soup. Roman has us a new car that I need to pick up as well."

Roman must've been a friend of Julian's. Maybe that was how her brother had learned how to hire security guards for her. No matter how many times she tried to make sense of the situation, none of it would compute in her head. How was this suddenly her life?

"Yeah, we'll be fine. You go on."

"Where are we exactly?" She needed some point of reference. A dot on a map would at least provide her gravity while her world spun much too quickly.

The giant shared a quick glance with Voodoo before he returned his gaze to her. "We're in a tiny town in the middle of Kansas. There's a gas station, a couple of restaurants, three traffic lights, and this motel, but that's about it."

"I don't remember what you said your name was," she admitted next and managed to refrain from informing him that she'd been calling him the giant.

For a man with that much bear-like height and muscle, his smiles were almost painfully tender. "There was a lot of chaos when I introduced myself, but my name is Smith."

Smith and Voodoo. So, clearly she wasn't being given first names or even real names. Smith had to be the fakiest fake name ever. That, more than anything else, cemented the danger of their current situation in her mind. They'd done nothing but help her ever since they'd rescued her, but caution and a distinct wariness crept through her weary muscles. She didn't know them, and no matter how good it felt to be near Smith, or whatever his real name was, she needed to remember that. They were armed, she could see pistols on both of their hips, and they were helping her run from the FBI. Until that moment, she would've sworn that the FBI were the good guys. That left her with one distinctly uncomfortable conclusion—the men helping her were not.

9

Smith despised the fear that had permeated her eyes. He was scaring her. He reminded himself that she should be frightened, just not of him. Standing up from the bed, he ordered himself to the far corner of the room to give her space. He couldn't bear the tense set of her entire body when she looked at him anymore, anyway.

"I'm sure Voodoo will be back in just a minute." That would probably make her feel better.

She forced herself to a seated position on the bed, and it took every ounce of raw power he possessed not to help her. "Thank you for rescuing me," spilled from those gorgeous lips, but that wasn't what she wanted to say. She still wouldn't look him in the eye.

"Mercy," her name threaded to a low whisper. Her gaze flickered up to his finally. "Ask me whatever you need to know. I didn't mean to scare you."

That coveted gaze he'd had for a split second fell to the polyester bedspread. She cringed at a circular stain and scooted away from it. He cursed Voodoo again for picking this dumpster of a motel, not that they'd had many options.

"How did you know I was scared?"

'I've been watching you for weeks' was decidedly not the right answer. "I've always been pretty good at reading people. Special Forces enhanced that ability." There. All of that was *true* even if it wasn't exactly the truth.

Her head lifted. Defiance glimmered in her eyes now. That was better than fear. Anything was better than her being afraid of him. "Well, I mean, I'm running from the FBI for doing something I didn't even intend to do, which was so stupid on my part. I don't know where my brother is. He told me not to call him, but he sent you to take care of me, even though I can take care of myself. So, yeah, I'm kind of terrified right now and also pissed at myself. Sue me."

He tried to quell his grin but didn't quite manage it. "I'm glad you're feeling well enough to be mad, honestly. You had me worried."

That seemed to confuse her more than anything. "Honestly?" She rolled her eyes, but clearly her headache hadn't improved enough for that task. She clutched her forehead again. "You won't even tell me the name of the city we're in or your real name, so forgive me for not thinking you're doing anything honestly."

Desperate to prove himself, Smith yanked his wallet from his back pocket. "We're in a town called Pony Express." He held up a brochure from the desk in the room with the town's name splayed on the cover. "And Smith is my real name. Smith Gerald Hagen, after both of my parents." Tossing the brochure away, he marched toward her, pleased that she didn't duck away from him, and showed her his license. "I wasn't lying to you." *About that.*

She took his wallet from him and studied the ID. Guilt shadowed her features as she handed it back. "So, Smith is your real name?" She folded her legs closer to her body and gestured for him to sit down near her. "I thought you were just bad at coming up with aliases or something."

Relief flooded through him. He eased down on the end of the bed. "I know it's a weird first name. My dad wanted me to be a junior, but my mom hated the idea. My father was serving in Korea when I was born. The story goes that Mom was so angry he didn't make it back for my birth she decided to give me her maiden name for a first name and to call me that." He shrugged.

And there it was. He officially earned himself one of her sweet grins. "Thanks for telling me the truth. That means a lot to me. My mom didn't even have a good reason for naming me Mercy, or at least she never told me if she did. I definitely get having a weird first name." Her mouth twisted in consideration.

"Just ask me," he prompted.

"Please tell me his mother didn't actually name him Voodoo because that would be even worse than Mercy."

It was odd to be laughing in a shithole of a hotel with a girl he was helping to evade the FBI. Roman had ties to enough senators and higher-ups in the NSA to get Tier Seven out of trouble if this went badly. She didn't have that luxury. At that moment, he chose not to think about all the complications and pressures involved in this. Laughing with her was a hell of a lot better than just watching her through a lens.

"His first name is Vince, but no one calls him that. I'm not sure he'd even answer to it if you tried. If he were here, he'd tell you he earned the name Voodoo by having magic fingers. He was the best medic the army had, so that's the truth, but you and I both know that's not how he means it." Smith continued to tell her entirely too much, more than she would ever possibly want to know. Those inquisitive eyes, so quick to cast doubt, served as some kind of truth serum to his soul. "And I like your name."

"You do?" Disbelief dripped into her tone.

"Yeah. Has no one ever told you that before?" He found that hard to believe. Everyone he'd ever met had an opinion on his name.

"Not that many people know my name." She shook her head as if that would free her from whatever thought continued to plague her features. "So...were you in Special Forces with Voodoo?" She seemed pleased with that question in particular.

He paused to keep from demanding that she tell him whatever

she was thinking and forced himself to answer her question. "Yeah. Back in the day. He's a great guy ... despite his insanely high opinion of his skill set."

Her quick laugh was almost haunted now. Unable to help himself, he eased closer to her in the bed longing to gather her back up in his arms.

"My dad was in Special Forces," she explained.

Smith swore there was an audible record scratch in his head at that declaration. Her father had been murdered in a hit ten years prior by his own underboss, Javier Marino. He'd gotten mouthy about his dominance and invincibility, and Marino had set out to show him that he had more security breaches in his administration than he thought.

Searching Mercy's beautiful face for any sign that she knew she was lying, he schooled his own features. "I'm... sorry for your loss," he pressed out.

Her lips folded under the weight of her teeth as she shrugged. "Thanks, but I never knew him. It's hard to miss something that was never there. He was always gone when I was little. I mean, you must know how Special Forces soldiers aren't ever allowed to go home. Like you said about your dad not being there when you were born. I've seen a few pictures of him, and the letter the army sent my mom saying he'd been killed. That's really all I knew of him. My mom didn't talk about him that much."

There were so many things wrong with her story he didn't know where to begin. Special Forces soldiers definitely went home on occasion, typically on a nine-month cycle. They all knew their children, and the army never sent a letter when a soldier was KIA. The entire story was a fabrication. Based on Mercy's expression, she believed the whole thing without question. He wondered who'd come up with the lies. Either her mother had crafted them, or she also believed them. Julian had to have known the truth. He'd sought out his father's old cartel three months ago.

Another boulder of complication affixed itself to Smith's shoulders. His heart ached for all she didn't yet know, all she'd ultimately have to learn. Perhaps the worst part was that he was likely going to have to be the man to tell her.

10

It was always odd to discuss her father with anyone other than Julian. Missing a void in your life leaves plenty of room for confusion. You can't erase an absence. Mercy told herself the confusion was why she was feeling so safe in Smith's presence, and why she wanted to keep talking with him about most anything.

But thoughts of Julian intruded on her plans to keep Smith talking. "Oh my gosh. My computer. Did I get it when we ran out of the coffee shop? I can't remember. Julian might email me."

If she wasn't mistaken, she thought she saw a quick tense of Smith's square jaw. "I got it for you." The mattress leaned and shook as he lumbered off of the bed, dug in his bags, and retrieved her laptop.

Her mind instantly provided thoughts of what it might be like to be pressed into a mattress by his impressive body, how heavy and hard he must feel. Despite everything wrong in her world, she allowed herself another long visual inventory of him. The impressive span of his shoulders was probably equal to a dozen of her hands. She wished she could run her fingertips over every rope of muscle and discover just how many of her hands it took to cover his Goliath-sized form. Her eyes trailed to his zipper line, and her tongue automatically darted out over her lips. Whatever drugs Voodoo had given her may not have affected her memory, but they were doing a real number on her good sense.

Heady relief tumbled through her when he handed over the laptop, but she still wanted him to sit near her again. The absence registered far more than was logical and certainly more than was intelligent.

"I doubt Julian will contact you. He knows things went south. You need to be aware that the FBI is monitoring your emails."

Terror stitched itself along every nerve ending in her body, but fury knotted in her gut. She clung to the fury over the fear. Fear had no solutions. Anger could at least be discussed and eased. "That's impossible. You may not know this, but I'm one of the best hackers out there. I would know if someone was monitoring my emails."

Was that a smirk on his face? "So, three federal agents just happened to know which coffee shop you were going to be at and what you were going to be doing today. Have they been showing up anywhere else you've gone lately?"

She shook her head. Hot dread slithered to her throat.

"That's what I thought. They're good, but no one's that good. The FBI employs some of the best hackers out there."

He didn't state the obvious conclusion, which she supposed she appreciated. Clearly, the FBI employed hackers who were better than she was, so now she was screwed. She shoved the laptop away from her on the bed without opening it. "I don't understand any of this. How did Julian get involved with this whole thing? When did the government start stealing designs from weapons companies? None of this makes sense. How did he find you? I mean... when did he figure out that I was going to be arrested? My brother and I have always looked out for each other, but it's usually me looking out for him. If he'd thought I could get in trouble for getting his designs back, he never would've asked me to do it."

≈

THERE WERE NONE SO BLIND....

Smith hated Julian Valon more with each passing moment. Of course she was loyal to her brother at all costs. Smith got that. If someone had told him Hannah was working with a drug cartel and trying to steal something owned and operated by the Department of Defense, he would've laughed and then ground them into the pavement for accusing his sister of something so despicable.

It was with that realization that the next few lies came a little easier. If he told her the truth, she'd run. It was penned in every fearful glance. People were never more dangerous than when they were afraid. Fear-driven defiance was something she could latch on to at any moment.

He had to earn her trust, so that when the time was right he could reveal her brother for what he really was—a dirty lieutenant in the Castellas cartel, following right in their father's footsteps.

Showing his hand too quickly would crush her. Her father had been as far from a hero as you could get, and her brother was no better. She couldn't bear the weight of the truth without something to keep her upright and moving forward. He wanted to become that foundation for her, so he had to play this hand he'd been dealt with extreme caution.

Drawing a deep breath, he weighed each of her questions and started with the things he could answer truthfully. "I was hired by the DEA to keep you safe, through a CIA operative who works with us at our security firm, Tier Seven. We've been monitoring your movements. I need you to know that I would never let anything happen to you. I promise you that." Then he spun the web of lies that ultimately would be what kept her safe, at the cost of him ever being able to have a chance with her. "Your brother is aware I was tasked with watching out for you. I don't know how *his* designs ended up on their server." The plans she'd been trying to steal had been designed by an air force defense contracting firm, not her brother. Drug cartels were desperate for the new drone radar designs because the DEA was catching mules with drone technology faster than they could replace them. For once, the good guys were winning.

"Wait, the DEA hired you to keep me safe? I thought they were the drug part of the FBI. What do those designs have to do with drugs?"

"Drug Enforcement is an entirely different entity from the FBI. Different tactics. Different goals."

"Well, then, could the DEA just tell the FBI to back off if they don't want me in prison?"

"Unfortunately, it doesn't work that way. If the FBI catches you, which isn't going to happen on my watch, the DEA could potentially get you a lesser sentence as long as you did what they asked. But that would be about as kind as they ever get."

"So, I'm only worthy of saving if I'm doing something for them? Like hacking something. I'm good, but I don't know if I'm that good. I don't understand what I could do for the DEA. I don't know anything about drugs. I'm just... me."

Smith had no idea how someone like her could ever deem themselves unworthy, but he intended to do something about it. His fingers still ached to feel the warmth of her skin, so he went with it. Catching her chin in his palm, he lifted her face until their gazes met. "Who gave you the idea that you're not worthy of saving just for being you?"

Her breath caught as she stared him down. He could feel the quickening thrum of her pulse at her throat. Her pupils stretched to cover more of the deep green in her eyes, and her tongue darted over her lips again. He'd had extensive training noticing all of the details that the average human thought were insignificant. Her body spoke much louder than her voice. Almost everyone's did. He never made a bet he didn't know he would win, and he would've let it all ride on the fact that she was aroused by his caress and his vow.

Her long eyelashes shadowed her eyes with her quick blink as she tried to dispel the flow of electricity between them. Before she could respond, Voodoo busted back in the door. "We've got to go. Now."

Smith was on his feet. "Who?"

"FBI. They were at the gas station when I was pulling out of the drive-through. They're just arriving. We need to move."

"Did you get the new car?"

"No. T called in a few favors and got us a pilot instead." Voodoo grabbed Mercy's bag, shoved her laptop back inside, and then got his own pack. "There's a private airfield about thirty miles east of here. She's flying in now. We'll have to leave the van there. Even if they find it, they'll have no idea where we're going."

Smith shook his head. "I doubt they'll look that far. They're just driving through checking hotels in nearby towns. There's no way they got here so quickly if they're really doing quadrant searches."

He leaned to scoop Mercy back up into his arms, oddly thankful for another excuse to hold her, but she shook her head. "I can walk. I'm fine." She did manage to stand on her own though she drove the heels of her palms into her temples for a quick rub. "Let's just go. I've got to get to Julian somehow. This is insane."

Special Forces teams didn't even have to make eye contact to know when they were thinking the same thing. Smith knew he and Voodoo were of one mind—if she got in contact with her brother, all hell was going to break loose.

11

None of this made any sense, but remaining in place until she figured things out wasn't an option. Forcing her feet to move, she weighed everything Smith had told her. Between the headache, the pain meds, and the gruff tenderness he somehow managed in both his touch and his voice, she'd had a hard time paying attention. When he touched her face, she swore all of the terror and noise in the world gave way to peace.

Pain vibrated through her skull as she rushed out to the van between her two protectors. They watched over her like she was set to detonate at any moment. When her stomach gave an odd roll and bile ascended up her chest once again, she must've cringed. Smith lifted her back up into his arms. "Just let me carry you. Taking care of you is my job."

Torn between feeling indignant that she was being carried like an infant and elated that she was back in his protective embrace, she consented. He seemed to want to, and it wasn't that far to the parking lot.

The only obvious conclusion was that Julian was somehow working for the DEA. That had to be why Smith and Voodoo had been hired to rescue her, and it explained where he'd been for the past few months. Why he rarely called her and only communicated in quick emails. And why he couldn't tell her where he was. Maybe he'd been recruited by them the same way the CIA hired the hackers who'd performed well at the DEF CON hacker convention a few years back. Dread coiled low in her belly when she began to process that her brother may have taken a job that would put him in constant danger. It had always been her job to keep him safe. What if she couldn't now?

Mercy knew why Julian would've jumped at the chance to work for some government agency. He'd always wanted to be a hero like their father. Their mother had flat-out refused to sign the paperwork for him to join the marine corps when he was seventeen, even though he'd graduated early. For a while he'd played with engineering and design, letting the money he made soothe the absence left by their father that they both existed inside of, but it wasn't enough. That's why he always wanted more. He hadn't even given her the opportunity to talk him out of it. Probably because he knew she would try.

The rolling slam of the van doors shook through her. Voodoo handed a cup of soup back to her. "Think you could drink it while we roll? We need to get something in your system. You can wait until we take off, but I don't know what we're flying out of here. Might not be any easier on the plane."

"I'll try," she offered. It took her a few minutes to realize she was starving, which she supposed was a good sign. With every sip she managed, terror compounded in her chest. She had jobs to do, clients waiting on her work, and other sites that deserved to be sabotaged. "Wait!"

Smith and Voodoo both jerked around to see her, despite the fact that Smith should've been looking at the road ahead of him.

"I can't just fly away. Where are we even flying to? I have to go back home. Yoda's there." Pretending the FBI didn't know where she lived was too appealing to ignore. At home she could hide herself away again, go back to life within the safety of her four rented walls.

Smith settled back in the driver's seat. "Yoda is...?"

"My kitten."

He nodded like he'd been expecting her to say that. "You can't go back home. They're watching your apartment. The FBI would be all over you, but I have a friend who owes me a lifetime's worth of favors. He can get in, get your cat, and get out."

She let that idea coast down to her stomach along with another sip of soup. "Wouldn't the FBI see your friend, too? I don't want anyone getting arrested because of me."

Her protectors both chuckled. Smith shook his head. "Trust me, he can get in and out, and no one will ever know he was there."

"So, what? Your friend is a ghost or something?"

Voodoo snorted. "Jesus, if Griff ever hears her call him that, we won't be able to live with him."

Smith brought his phone to his ear.

GRIFF SKIPPED any kind of greeting and dove into conversation, which was standard for them. They'd been best friends since Special Forces training. "The FBI and a drug cartel on your tail. Do you ever think we'll get sick of this shit being a day at the office?"

"Nah, it's just a thing," Smith provided the expected response, former SF Team Seven's answer to most everything.

"I hear that."

"Hey, you remember how you dated my sister without me knowing for years and then married her without me being there? And then how I didn't beat the piss out of you?"

Griff huffed audibly. "To be fair, you did try."

"Yeah, but I didn't."

"I do seem to recall that, and I have a feeling I'm about to pay for it all. Still worth it. I'm just trying to figure exactly how fucked my day is about to become."

"I need you to drive to Kansas City, break into Mercy's apartment, and rescue her kitten."

Smith couldn't help but laugh as a long string of expletives spewed from Griff. "You want me to fucking make a six-hour round trip to Missouri, break into an apartment the feds are actively running surveillance on, and rescue a cat?"

"Are you telling me you can't do it?" Smith challenged. He knew how to get Griff Haywood to do what he wanted.

"Fucker, one day that shit isn't going to work on me."

"I seriously doubt that."

"Oh, here's a good question. Do you remember what you said to me after you tried to beat me shitless?" Smith was already laughing. "You said, I hate you so fucking much right now. Well, bro, the feeling is currently mutual."

"Just get down there, and get the cat. You can hate me later."

"Fine, but if I bring this thing home, Hannah's gonna want one. You know I can't ever tell her no."

Smith grinned. "When I get back, I'll drive you to the shelter. Hey, I'll even text my baby sister some cat videos for the next few days while I'm gone. You know, to help."

"You do that and when you get home, I'll get her to come up to the office so we can try out my desk nice and loud, or maybe the wall between our offices. Better yet, while you're gone we could just use your desk. I'll leave my ass-print on the glass for you."

Smith narrowed his eyes. "You know, Mom and the General were thinking about spending an entire month this summer in Lincoln. They were going to get an Airbnb, but I think I'll just tell them you and Hannah really want them to stay with you." Griff grumbled out something unintelligible, so Smith continued to up the ante. "A whole month. Dad still plays reveille at sunrise every morning before he goes on his run. I'll tell him you'd love to run with him. What good son-in-law wouldn't want to do that?"

"I'll get the damned cat. You keep your mouth shut to your parents about staying here. And after this, I owe you no favors."

"Years, man. You dated her for years behind my back."

"You know, I do this thing with my hips that Hannah loves. She makes this noise..."

"Hang on, incoming call, probably from Dad," Smith sniped. "Go get the cat, and be careful while you're in there. It means a lot to her, and don't get caught. I don't have time to break you out of a federal prison."

Griff grunted like the very idea that he might be caught was preposterous. "Yeah fine, I'll get her cat. The way Voodoo talks, it sounds like you'd prefer to be the one rescuing her pussy."

"I'm hanging up now."

"Hey, if you get the opportunity, go for it, man. Maybe it's all of those Oprah soul things your sister's been making me watch, but I want good shit for you. You deserve it."

"Thanks, and since you're doing me a favor, I won't call *you* a pussy for what you just said."

"Fuck off."

"I love you, too, and you and my sister stay the hell out of my office." Equilibrium and ease settled through him as Smith tossed his phone in the console. It had far more to do with the fact that Mercy was seated behind him, trying to hide her giggles from his half of the conversation, than from talking with Griff. "He'll take care of Yoda. Don't worry about it."

She bit her lips together and nodded. "Thank you," finally escaped the trap of her mouth along with a chuckle. "I take it your friend married your little sister."

Smith grinned. "I've never seen Hannah so happy. Most of me doesn't care anymore, but it's still fun to harass him about it."

12

M ercy had no idea how Smith had deduced that Yoda meant the world to her, just because she'd freaked out about leaving. Being understood was a heady thing. She prayed he hadn't picked up on how insanely attracted she was to him. She was certain she should be frightened of the FBI and all of the things she didn't fully understand about this, but the fear was subdued by the assuredness that rolled off of him in waves.

He would keep her safe. He'd already proven himself repeatedly. She just had to trust him, even though she was fairly certain he was keeping something from her. Deciding to delve into that later, when they were somewhere that the FBI wasn't, she drew another long sip of the soup and let the calories ease the gnaw of hunger in her belly.

"Shit," Smith spat after glancing in the rearview mirror.

Mercy's heart leapt to her throat. She spun to see out the back windows. Her head protested the rapid movement, and her vision blurred. "What's wrong?"

"They just spotted us. They must've left the gas station and gone straight to the hotel."

The van lurched and then rapidly picked up speed. Smith must've floored it. "Call T. Tell him we need to get where we're going without a flight plan being filed. See if he can call in a few favors from the FAA. Then call Wildcat. Tell her we're coming in hot and need to be in the air as soon as we arrive."

"On it," Voodoo immediately brought his phone to his ear.

Mercy wanted to ask who T and Wildcat were, but the entire endless day seemed lodged in her throat. She couldn't speak around the confusion. The van jerked to the right as Smith managed to pass two cars ahead of them, putting more space between them and the tail. She dug her short fingernails into the armrests of her seat and willed all of this to be some kind of horrible nightmare.

When Voodoo finished his call, he returned his phone to his pocket and grimaced. "T says the feds just busted into Tier Seven. He can't call the FAA right now, but he said she knew what she was doing."

Smith's grimace matched Voodoo's. "How's he going to get rid of the feds?"

"Roman's taking care of it."

A high-pitched squeal from their tires ripped through her eardrums and echoed against her skull. It was getting even harder for Mercy to keep a register of the names they were saying so she could remember to ask Smith about them later. Keeping her mind busy was key to her not completely freaking out. Telling herself that there would be a later when they could talk was necessary as well. They were going to get away. They had to.

Despite sirens of warning ricocheting against her skull, she clung to something akin to inevitability. There was something about Smith and her, maybe. She could recall no other time in her life when she'd reacted this way to anyone, much less some mountain of a man comprised of equal parts brute force and tender care. There would be more time for her to figure out her own reactions. More time to analyze and to reach some kind of understanding. She had to believe that.

The back of the van fishtailed as he made a rapid, unplanned turn onto the grass, but Smith kept it under control. A slight shift of the muscles in his cheek was the only physical sign he gave that things weren't going well. Did anything ever throw this guy?

She turned, more cautiously this time, to stare out the back again. A moment of relief flooded through her when, after gaining ground on them, the Escalade missed the turn.

"Change of plans. We're going in on foot," he announced.

"I was just thinking the same thing," Voodoo concurred. "They aren't gonna want to get their loafers dirty."

A flicker of a cocky smirk formed on Smith's lips. "If they want to chase SF, they should've worn boots." Mercy's stomach stirred with something far more pleasant than the soup but every bit as hot at his expression. Somehow, his confidence both soothed and enlivened her, all while her own bodily reactions continued to confuse her.

Voodoo made quick work of securing his medical pack. "You sure you're good with her for a half klick?"

Mercy had no idea what that meant, but Smith rolled his eyes and Voodoo laughed. She wished anything made sense. The motor protested with a choked whir, irritated at being forced to travel on rough earth rather than pavement. Still studying Smith's features, she wondered if the narrowing of his eyes was how he willed something to happen.

She had no more time to consider before he slammed the van into park under a thick outcropping of trees. He grabbed his pack, threw open the door, and had her in his arms in two seconds flat.

"I can walk." She wiggled in an effort to put her feet on solid ground.

"We need to move fast, and ...I like holding you." That same muscle shifted in his cheek. Surely, he'd only said that because he didn't want her to feel like such a burden. Despite everything bearing down on top of them, Mercy's stupid brain latched onto his vow like it was really the truth.

He darted under the canopy of cypress trees and took off at a heated sprint, as though she weighed nothing at all.

∾

REGRET NIPPED at Smith's heels as he whipped and darted through the landscape avoiding the mud to keep from leaving boot prints. His only prayer was that she'd somehow forget he'd just informed her that he liked holding her. Jesus, she stripped away every ounce of his practiced reserve. Mistakes were not an option, and he just kept making them with her.

Adrenaline-spiked awareness shook through him as his tendency to stare down at her almost made him race headlong into a tree. Terror buzzed up his spine at the thought of her being hurt while in his arms. He lowered his head and cradled her tighter, protecting her from the claw of a low branch as he bore right around the cotton-woods. The sting on his temple marked the scratches he'd received in the encounter. Since it was his own distracted stupidity that had caused the injury, he'd deserved much worse.

Her hand bounced against his face as she reached to ease her fingers over the red scrapes. Her touch made him far more breathless than his sprint.

"You're bleeding." Devastation cast her tone.

"I'm fine."

Voodoo surged ahead and held back another limb for Smith and Mercy. "He's had worse, trust me. I'll bandage it up when we get where we're going."

It took every available brain cell he possessed to stay focused on the mission at hand with her sweet little body bouncing against his chest with every footfall. An onslaught of need threatened to drown him as the friction of her lush tits moved to the rhythm of his body. God, he wanted to feel her curves move in far dirtier ways, to watch her tits dance all for him with every pounding thrust, to incite friction between those thick thighs as he slammed his cock into her hard and fast.

He was actually impressed with himself that he'd even noticed the flash of concern in her eyes at Voodoo's comment. Yeah, he'd had a hell of a lot worse, but it wasn't something he wanted her to worry over. Given the nature of his current thoughts, she should be back-handing him, not fussing over him.

The distinctive echoes of footsteps behind them reached through the low roar of a motor just ahead. Faster. He had to move faster. Certain he was holding beauty personified in his arms, he encountered another sight for sore eyes as he spotted Wildcat leaned up against her personal Cessna Skywagon giving them her signature smirk. They tore off towards the clearing.

"This doesn't look much like a chopper, Kitty Kat. You sure you can get it off the ground?" Voodoo harassed as Smith set Mercy on her feet.

Wildcat's smirk turned into a full-faced grin. "Shut your face, Grimaldi, I could fly a boat with an outboard and a rubber band, and you know it."

Voodoo laughed as he climbed onboard. "Retract the claws, girly. I'm just teasing you. You know we love you."

"You better. Are you going to introduce me to your tagalong here, or is Smitty just going to stow her under his seat?"

Rolling his eyes, Smith helped boost Mercy into the back seat. "We'll make introductions in the air since the FBI is headed this way." His shame over his actions and reactions to her did nothing to keep him from letting his hand drag over the tight curve of her ass as she climbed up into the Cessna. It was all he could do not to squeeze the supple flesh. *Dammit, Hagen. What the hell is wrong with you?* An apology hung on his dry tongue, but heat bloomed across her features as she turned back to stare him down. Shock and intrigue mixed in an intoxicating dance in her soft-green eyes. She'd been pale most of the morning. The pink glow of her cheeks twisted him in knots. "Uh... sorry," he pushed the words past the hunger in his throat.

"It's okay," she assured him. "Thanks for helping me. I feel terrible that you're having to do all of this."

He should've reassured her by reminding her that she was just a job, but he'd lied to her enough for one day. Her safety meant far more to him than any other security job he'd ever been assigned. For a moment, he allowed himself to wonder if her safety meant more to him than his own.

13

Mercy's mind began to formulate some kind of spreadsheet. He had definitely said that he liked holding her, and she was pretty sure he could've gotten her into the plane without touching her rear end. But maybe he couldn't have. She didn't know. Was that how men acted if they liked you? Was it okay if he liked her? What would Julian think if she kind of had a thing for the bodyguard he'd hired for her?

She shook off the perplexing questions. She didn't have time for them, and she'd never been liked by a man before. As far as she knew, she was reading this all wrong. He was probably just being nice and trying to reassure her.

There was a plaguing murmur somewhere deep in the recesses of her mind that reminded her of the sheer number of romance novels she'd devoured. Reading about other people falling in love was her substitute for ever risking something so terrifying in real life. In almost every book, the hero had acted kind of the way Smith was acting.

She tried to discreetly check his eyes. It seemed that whenever the hero was about to have sex with the heroine, his eyes somehow got darker. She didn't really understand how that worked, and

Smith's eyes still looked perfectly normal. Clearly, he was just trying to make her feel better. Prickly disappointment joined that odd wash of heat she could still feel in her cheeks.

No. She didn't have time for this. She was just still loopy from those meds, or the whole insane situation was getting to her or something. Besides, the far more pressing concern was that she was in an airplane not much bigger than that van they'd been in a few minutes before, and it was somehow going to go up into the air and take her someplace. If she hadn't existed almost entirely inside her apartment for so long, she was sure she wouldn't find this both terrifying and thrilling. God, how had her life become nothing more than a keyboard and screened reality?

She missed Yoda.

Suddenly, the plane was speeding down a long grass path, straight towards a thicket of trees in the distance. They picked up pace constantly. The trees were right there. How did the pilot not see them? They were going to crash.

Her heart pounded a frantic SOS and a yelp tangled in her chest. Her tiny hand instinctively gripped Smith's much larger one as the trees rushed toward them. Her throat felt much too large for her neck. She squeezed her eyes shut. Smith enclosed her hand entirely in his own and gave her a reassuring squeeze. Suddenly, the plane lifted off the ground, missing the trees and climbing out of the danger that had previously threatened to engulf them.

Smith's massive form loomed closer, his hot breath caressed her ear, and he steadied her with that soothing rumble of his voice. "Ever flown in a small plane?"

She shook her head. She'd never flown in a jet either, but admitting that made her feel even more ridiculous for being frightened.

"What did I tell you back in the hotel room?" He kept her hand cradled gently in his own and stroked his thumb up and down in her palm, soothing her. She tried to remember what he'd just asked. Somehow the motions of his thumb were scrambling her brain. Why did that feel so good? He'd told her that Julian was working for the DEA. No, wait. He hadn't actually said that. Ugh, she couldn't remember. Rescuing her once again, he smiled. "I swore to you that I'd never let anything happen to you, and I meant that. Wildcat's the best chopper pilot the army ever had. We're gonna be fine. I've got you."

Her stomach dislodged from its correct location and cascaded downward to somewhere near her knees as a tingle of thrill danced along her spine. She called herself an idiot for being frightened in the first place. Smith was there. She would be fine.

Once, when she was little, one of her mother's boyfriends, Paul, had taken them all to the fair over in Johnson County. Julian had taunted her for not wanting to ride the Zero Gravity ride. When Paul joined in the harassment, she'd finally relented, more out of embarrassment than anything else. She hadn't hated it as much as she'd thought she would, and it had shut Julian up, which made the whole thing worth it. This was similar, and yet different. Better and worse. No one had been trying to arrest her back then, and her brother had been perfectly safe at the fair that warm summer day, but then again, Smith hadn't been there either.

His presence dominated most of the seat they shared, pressing her thigh to the warmth of his own due to the lack of space. He was so substantial, so solid, it made no sense that just a few hours ago, he hadn't existed in her world. It was almost as if a mountain had moved to keep her safe in its shadow.

She'd intended to ask where they were going but, "Why is her name Wildcat?" came out instead.

The pilot's brown hair swished along her shoulders as she turned back to flash a quick grin at Mercy. "Wildcat's my call sign. I'm Catarina Corvallis, pilot extraordinaire, and Tier Seven's preferred emergency airborne Uber at your service. Don't let these twat-wads intimidate you, sweets. They're both full of shit most of the time."

Did she sound intimidated? Crap. She probably did. "I'm not intimidated," Mercy tried and cursed her own voice for shaking. "I think they're nice." There, that was moderately better.

Wildcat laughed. "Clearly, she's been with Smitty more than you." She elbowed Voodoo in the seat beside her.

He mocked offense. "Hey, I'm nice, too."

"Nicest player in Special Forces, right?"
"Yeah... but still nice."

SMITH ROLLED his eyes and wished the two of them would shut up. Voodoo had probably hit on her at some point, and she still wanted to harass him about it. Their taunting each other was distracting him, and he wanted to memorize the tender weight of Mercy's hand in his own. She still hadn't removed it from his grip, not that he'd given her much choice. His breaths came easier as long as her hand was in his own.

Mercy leaned in even closer, bringing her face an inch or two from his own. Those full, pink lips were right there, but he knew they might as well have been a hundred miles from his own. They weren't his to kiss. That knowledge didn't stop his cock from thickening against his thigh, so ridiculously anxious for her that Smith knew he should be ashamed. He felt her breath in every single whisker of his beard. Finally, she spoke. "Where are we going?"

Had he really forgotten to tell her that? Poor thing. He wasn't sure if she really trusted him enough to let him put her on an airplane without giving her their destination, or if she was just too sick to put up much of a fight. "Good friend of ours, his family owns a massive cattle ranch down in Oklahoma. I think they probably own half the state. We'll be safe down there until... Julian gets everything figured out." Her inquisitive gaze was locked on his so earnestly that guilt racked in his gut. The lies burned like battery acid on his tongue.

"How long do you think it will take for Julian to get everything figured out? Shouldn't we be doing something to help him?"

Urgency perforated her tone. That fist permanently lodged in his gut twisted hard. "He'll be fine. He has help. Our job is to keep you safe. You're all I'm worried about." That truth from his mouth eased the singe of acid.

She turned her head from him, robbing him of those eyes. Their absence stung. She muttered something about just being a job, and what was he to say to that? Not a damn thing. That was all she would ever be for him, other than in the recesses of his own fantasies, which were on his mind far too often when she was in his presence. Her being a job was the way it was supposed to work, but he hated that fact more and more with every passing millisecond.

Eventually, the adrenaline subsided, and the meds took over again. She slumped against him and fell asleep. Her neck was craned against his bicep. That couldn't possibly have been comfortable, and he was already walking through hell so he figured he might as well enjoy his trip. He tried to discreetly adjust, so he could cradle her head on his chest to keep her warm. When she stirred, he panicked until she readjusted all on her own. Fuck him, she wiggled that cute little ass further back against the plane and laid her head in his lap.

It wasn't until that moment that he really understood the multiple rings of hell. Her lying on him had been heavenly, a taste of the fantasies he'd had about her for weeks. The fact that he could never experience them made them hellish, but that was nothing compared to listening to her contented sigh with her mouth mere inches from his cock. He covered her with his jacket and brushed her hair away from her face, no longer certain if he was being a gentleman or an asshole. She snuggled closer still, and that was all that mattered.

A smirk rapidly formed on Voodoo's face when he glanced back at them. He made no effort to hide his chuckle. "Bet I know what you're thinking about."

"Fuck off," Smith huffed, but he couldn't summon any fight to fuel his fury. She was content in his lap. By the time they landed in Holder County, he'd likely have to see a doctor because if you had an erection for more than a few hours wasn't that what you were supposed to do? For now, he'd deal with it. Laying his head back against the seat, he allowed his eyes to close, too far gone not to indulge himself. The fantasy flickered to life in his mind without him consciously deciding to allow it.

The fingers of his right hand threaded through her hair and pushed her to her knees. His left hand stroked his cock. Her eyes danced to the move-

ment of his hand. She licked her lips. 'I know what my baby needs. Say please,' he ordered.

'Please,' she readily complied.

He dragged the slicked tip over her lips covering her mouth with the precum seeping from his slit. Her tongue darted over his head, hungry for a taste of him. 'I'm not always such a nice guy,' he warned.

Her eyes heated and glimmered at his warning. 'Good.' The single word whispered over the wet tip of his engorged cock was a hot lash of pleasure that threatened to destroy him. He tightened his grip on her hair.

'When I have you like this, nothing about me is nice. You make me need you, and now you'll pay for how fucking hard you make me. I ache. You're going to take good care of me this time. Say you understand.'

A deep, shuddered breath shook those drool-worthy tits wrenching a bellowed moan from low in his gut and another slip of his control. "I understand. Please, I need it,' she whimpered out a hungry plea.

He sank himself deep into the velvet sanctuary of her mouth.

14

Still dazed from her nap, Mercy sat up and tried to stretch out in the lack of space. She studied Smith's expression, but she didn't fully understand it. He looked kind of like he was in pain. Had she done something to cause that? "Sorry I fell asleep on you. You should've woken me up."

The pain in his eyes coupled with shock and some other emotion she couldn't quite read. "You didn't do anything wrong. Don't apologize. I'm glad you slept."

Then why did he look like he was in agony? She turned her attention to the fading sunlight outside the windshield while Wildcat guided the plane down underneath the thick cloud cover toward the ground. She couldn't look at Smith anymore. He was too kind and entirely too handsome, and she just kept making a fool of herself.

Clouds were something she understood, so she focused on those instead. When she was a kid, she'd stare up at them and try to identify shapes. She would spend hours making up stories about one cloud befriending another, but she'd never seen them from up above. Perspective was everything. She allowed herself a moment to wonder what her life looked like from the outside in. Probably just as boring and awkward as it was from the inside out.

As the burnt orange scattered into every possible shade of a sunset, from the brightest blue to pure white, the weight of the world settled on her shoulders with brutal force once again. Smith might've only been worried about her, but she had to take care of her brother. He was all she really had.

The designs had surely been moved to another server by now. She assumed if the DEA would go to all the trouble of hiring Smith and Voodoo to look after her, surely they would keep her brother safe as well. Defeat sank through her, bringing an icy chill of dread to the blood rushing through her veins. There had to be something else she could do to help Julian. She just had to figure out what that might be, and, most importantly, where he was.

Before she could contemplate further, the bounce of the plane against the grass yanked a quick gasp from her lungs. Smith smiled again and squeezed her hand. She readily latched their fingers together this time, thankful for the comfort of his touch. Its reassurance was intoxicating.

"One more bounce, then she'll set it down," he assured her.

Clearly, this wasn't his first flight. Of course it wasn't. He wasn't afraid to live. He was Special Forces. He probably wasn't terrified of anything. Ever since her mother's car wreck, she'd spent the whole of her existence focused on keeping herself and her brother safe. The days before the funeral, she'd been certain she was being followed. Someone was watching her. As the weeks wound on and she'd cried until her body had no more tears to offer, she'd almost come to expect that feeling every time she ventured out of her apartment. She found more and more excuses to stay home. She told herself she was insane. Who would be interested enough in her life to ever follow her? And when she'd finally convinced herself that it was nothing more than a product of her grief, she'd met Edgar's wife, Sophia, at the market. Mercy had been so lonely she'd told the woman all about her mother's death when she'd asked if she was okay. Sophia had insisted that Mercy move into their building, an apartment that she wouldn't associate with her mother. Sophia had been right. Once Mercy had moved, the feeling of someone's eyes on her at the video game store, the bookstore, and the gas station had subsided.

As the plane rolled over the endless grass field, she ordered herself to remember that she'd always been prone to allowing her imagination to get away from her. Her mother used to scold her for daydreaming in class, not that she'd really needed to pay attention, but that wasn't the point.

All of her confusing feelings about Smith were nothing more than a way to process what was going on. She had to remember that. He was just being nice. Isn't that what she'd been told by both Voodoo and Wildcat? Smith was the nicest guy you'd ever meet. That's what they'd said, and he'd proven them right over and over again.

The collar of his jacket brushed against her jaw. Unable to help herself, she inhaled that scent of him, all leather, pine trees, and man. No one like him would ever be interested in her anyway. She didn't know how to do all those things normal women could do. That's why she was still a virgin after all. Coy grins and flirtations were all some kind of strange computer language she hadn't yet learned. She couldn't even apply mascara without it ending up on her nose or in her hair. On her last date, the guy insisted that they split a burger and fries since she really should be losing some weight. And no man ever wanted to date a woman who could outmaneuver them on a computer at every turn.

The plane jerked and bumped along the ground until it finally stopped. Oklahoma. It was only a few states away, and yet it was another place she'd never seen. Voodoo opened the door and turned back to Smith with a nostalgic grin. "Every time I get out of a plane, I have to remember not to go face first."

Wildcat laughed. "If you two are looking to relive your glory days, just let me know. I'll take you up. If you manage not to piss me off, I'll even make sure your chute's attached."

"See, I knew you loved me."

Mercy tried to understand what exactly was being discussed. Did Smith really used to parachute out of planes? An odd string of panic pulled taut in her midsection. She supposed that feeling was normal given the circumstances, but she hadn't felt anything like that until she considered Smith free falling to the ground. Still woozy from either the medicine or his close proximity, Mercy's gaze sought his as his friends harassed each other. He shook his head gently and winked at her, giving her heart a disconcerting flutter. She really needed to get a grip.

Smith cleared his throat. "If you don't get out of *this* plane, you won't need Wildcat to take you up. I'll chuck you out face first."

Laughing, Voodoo spread his arms and jumped the three feet to the ground. Smith followed, without the theatrics, and then turned to catch Mercy as she tried to jump down as gracefully as he had. She cursed her lack of height again. She'd been doing that most of her life.

Smith caught her and gently lowered her to the ground, smiling the whole time. Why couldn't she just read his mind? That would make everything so much easier. Instead of wishing for the impossible—like the two of them ever being more than protector and protectee, if that was even a thing—she took in the surrounding landscape. The warm breeze ruffled through her hair as she spun all the way around. There was nothing but peaceful prairie land on all sides. Her breaths came a little easier, and that tight fist of dread that had knotted in her belly eased its grip.

Smith hadn't been kidding. Wherever they were, whoever this land belonged to, it did look like they owned half of the state of Oklahoma. When she heard the sound of an approaching engine, she turned back to see three cowboys on a Gator, pulling up in front of them. They definitely completed the picture.

Instinctively, she stepped closer to Smith as the men got out of their ride. His arm lifted as if to wrap it around her, but he seemed to think better of it and shoved his hands in his pockets instead. "Uh, Mercy, this is Maddox Holder. This is his family's ranch." He gestured to the shorter of the three men, not that any of them would really qualify as short.

Maddox grinned at her and offered his hand. "Ma'am. This is my cousin, Ford, and my brother, Cole. Guess we're the Holder family welcoming committee, so welcome to Holder Ranch. If you need anything, find me or somebody that looks like me, and they'll take care of you. Can't sling a wet towel out here without hitting a Holder, so you'll be fine. Mama's been up at the house most of the afternoon getting it ready."

Smith smiled at him. "We appreciate this, Mad-dog. Make sure your mom bills Tier Seven for all of her work."

Maddox laughed, and Mercy wondered if Smith had any friends who didn't have nicknames. "Mama would no sooner bill y'all for this than she'd skin a cat."

Ford, definitely the oldest of the trio, chuckled. "Aunt Liz likes it when people are on the ranch. She thinks it makes these two act like they have some couth. It doesn't. There's no helping them, but I ain't gonna mention it to her."

Everyone's laughter was cut off when Wildcat climbed out of the cockpit shooting daggers at Maddox with her eyes.

"You still pretending you know how to fly a plane, Kitten?" he sneered.

"Watch it, Mad-dog, don't let your mouth get too big for your muzzle," Catarina came right back.

Everyone else took a step back to avoid the invisible sparks of electricity that sizzled between them. Wildcat and Mad-dog seemed to both hate each other and to be magnetically drawn toward the same location. Maddox took another step. Challenge lit in his eyes, daring her closer.

She met him step for step. "Heard you got out. Probably good. It would've sucked if you'd retired when your age was higher than your ASVAB score."

Maddox grinned. "Aww now, kitty cat, that really the best you can come up with? Come on, now. Try a little harder. While you think on it, I'll get you a ball of yarn to play with, since you like everything with strings."

"Kiss my ass, Maddox."

"Believe I already did that. As I recall, you thoroughly enjoyed it."

Ford cleared his throat and smacked Maddox on the back of the head. "Jay-sus, you two either need to fuck it out or go sit in the truck. Either way, save it for after we get them up to the house."

Smith leaned down to whisper in Mercy's ear, "Not sure what happened between them, but you know that expression about cats and dogs?" Mercy nodded. "Pretty sure it came from Wildcat and Mad-dog. Every time I've ever been around them, they're like this."

She didn't have time to giggle before Ford was escorting them all to the Gator.

"So, that's Catarina, huh?" Cole whispered to his brother as they climbed in the back. "All your bullshit for the last few years suddenly makes sense."

"Shut up," Maddox snapped.

15

Maddox's mother met them at the house they'd be using for the foreseeable future. The small, three-bedroom ranch house would suit their needs perfectly. Smith tried to remember his manners while he thanked her for stocking the house with food, but his mind was mired in that damned fantasy playing on repeat in his head.

Even the vast landscape of Holder Ranch, that usually settled him, did nothing to relieve the guilt and tension of having her so close but not being able to do anything about it. Smith found himself watching her take in the ranch instead of enjoying the picturesque views himself.

"Your ranch is beautiful, Mrs. Holder," Mercy was almost gushing. Smith loved that she seemed to have loosened up. "Thank you for letting me stay here. I'm sorry about all of this. As soon as I can find my brother and get this all straightened out, I'm sure we'll be out of your hair."

Liz Holder glanced from Smith to Mercy and back again. There was a knowing grin on her face. "Oh, honey, Maddox might be one of the only Holder boys who offers up the ranch for a safe house, but that don't mean I don't love having you all here, just the same.

No need to apologize, and no need to rush home. Seems to me that the good Lord puts us right where we need to be, right when we need to be there. You never know what might happen on Holder Ranch. Things have a way of working out just the way they're supposed to here." She wiped her hands on a kitchen towel and then mopped up a few drops of water from the laminate counter-tops. "Now, there's three kinds of homemade soup and sandwich fixings in the fridge. Just need to heat them up. I stuck some eggs and things for breakfast in there, too, but you're all welcome up at our house or any of our houses anytime for any meal. Leigh brought down a meatloaf and her broccoli chicken casserole. Maddox don't care for her casserole, but my son tends to avoid things that would be good for him. I'd say he's as stubborn as a bull, but there ain't ever been a bull more stubborn than him. Now," she grinned, "can I get you anything before I go? You all look dead on your feet. You need to get some food in you and then get to bed."

Smith agreed with her on both counts and chuckled at Mrs. Hold-er's assessment of her own son. "Thanks again for all of this. If Voodoo or I can do anything to help while we're here, don't hesitate."

"Son, don't let my husband hear you say that. He'll have you up before the sun working cattle. You just take care of sweet Mercy here, and y'all relax. Ain't nothing that needs to be done that won't get done."

The words *taking care of Mercy* should not have elicited the thoughts they produced. He wanted nothing more than to take care of every single thing she might need or want or desire. All he needed was for Mrs. Holder and Voodoo to leave them alone. He wanted that so badly it seemed like a good idea. Clearly, Maddox wasn't the only stubborn one.

"There's a list of our cell numbers on the desk in the living room if you need anything." Mrs. Holder continued to speak. Smith managed to catch a few words here and there. Now that he knew she was safe, Mercy's proximity took up most of his focus.

Uncertain if he'd managed to tell Mrs. Holder thank you and

goodbye, he realized she'd whisked out the back door when he heard a truck engine roar to life.

Voodoo entered the kitchen and stowed his med pack on the counter, still sporting that smirk he'd been wearing for most of the day. "Are you two good?" He leaned down to look in the fridge. "Thank God there's food. You need to eat something else, Mercy, and I need to be alone with this meatloaf." He extracted it, turned, and shoved the entire pan into the oven before he cranked up the heat. "How about some toast? That'll get some carbs in you and be easy on your stomach."

"Toast is... fine," she agreed, but her eyes never left Smith's, and damn if that didn't twist him in knots. He wondered what she saw there and prayed she couldn't tell how badly he wanted her. If she could see even half of what was on his mind, she'd run away and never look back.

MERCY INHALED two pieces of toast and chicken soup. It tasted so much better than what Voodoo had provided her back in Kansas. She even considered a third bowl, but since she'd already embarrassed herself several times that day, she was desperate to avoid a comment about eating too much from either Voodoo or Smith.

Then again, they were both holding forks over the casserole dish of meatloaf. It seemed they were prepared to battle over it, if one tried to take too much. When Smith noticed her empty bowl, he set his fork down. "Here, I'll get you some more." Voodoo's grin said he considered that a white flag of surrender, and he transferred another hunk to his plate. "I want more of that," Smith barked as he refilled Mercy's bowl and brought her another slice of the fresh-baked bread.

"I really shouldn't," Mercy forced the words from her lips even though she was half-starving.

"Why?" He placed the piping-hot bowl in front of her. "You need to eat."

"I ate a bagel before my whole world got turned upside down."

Voodoo shook his head. "If you didn't keep it down," he swallowed the bite in his mouth, "it doesn't count. Eat. I'll be able to relax if you can keep some food in you."

She didn't want to be any more of a problem, so she didn't argue. The soup sated her taste buds and soothed her stomach even more than the ranch itself. She hoped she'd be able to explore a little the next day, and then realized how odd that thought was. She never voluntarily left her apartment. How had so much changed in less than twenty-four hours? As long as her brother was safe and whoever was trying to steal those designs didn't do anything horrible with them, she wondered if her life at that moment wasn't better than all of the months before.

After she ate and helped Smith clean the dishes, she escaped to the back bedroom. Taking inventory of her body, she tried to figure out what was the most pressing concern. Turning to study herself in the dresser mirror, it was immediately apparent that a shower and a toothbrush would be ideal.

There was a stack of T-shirts on the bed that must've belonged to one of the Holder girls. She selected a stretchy V-neck and prayed her cleavage wouldn't spill out of the neckline. She never quite knew what to do with her boobs and keeping them contained was sometimes a challenge.

Checking the hallway for either of her male roommates, she escaped to the bathroom without seeing them. She was simultaneously relieved and disappointed, but she was growing accustomed to existing in a general state of confusion. She both wanted to see Smith and to be alone with the chaos of her mind.

Waiting for the water in the shower to warm up, she scoured her mouth with the provided toothbrush and toothpaste. She brushed until the chalky-mint flavor rid her tongue of every horrifying thing that had come out of her lips that day.

She shed her clothes and stepped under the spray of water, watching as it diverted into streams down her curves and puddled at her feet. She wiggled her toes in the water, weighing the things she could control versus the things she could not. Being attracted to

Smith didn't seem optional. No woman with functioning eyes wouldn't be attracted to him, and if they'd ever felt the strength of his arms or the security of his embrace, they'd be just as far gone as she was. Still, she needed to remember that he was only keeping her safe and taking care of her because it was his job.

Not worrying herself sick over her brother wasn't an option either, but there wasn't anything more she could do to get the designs without getting all of them in even more trouble. She was a runaway felon at this point. The soup that had soothed her earlier turned to liquid concrete in her stomach and then hardened to encase her throat at that realization.

When she finally made herself get out of the shower, she ran a towel over her hair and pulled her jeans back on. She scrubbed her hands over the mirror to rid it of the steam so she could see just how tight the T-shirt was before facing the world. She tugged the neckline up a little higher, but the shirt was far more figure-hugging than she was comfortable with. Oh well. Not like anything else that day had been the norm for her. The shirt went right along.

Telling herself she was being ridiculous, she opened the door and followed the steam as it spilled into the hallway. She found Smith and Voodoo sitting on the couch both staring at Smith's laptop screen. He stroked his hand over his beard, considering something. Mercy watched the movements of his hands. How was he so sexy just stroking his beard? "I still can't take that cliff. I've been stuck here for days. They've got torpedo boats on the island, and the alliance controls the shoreline. I could try a shockwave in the ocean, but it won't take out enough of them. Any ideas?"

Voodoo rolled his eyes. "Dude, why are you asking me this? I don't speaky the geeky. You need to stop playing Rex-whatever-this-is and to go get laid."

But Smith was no longer paying attention to his friend. His eyes were locked on Mercy. If she were any good at understanding men, she would've been able to determine if that was appreciation or lust in his eyes, or if it was just that she'd startled him from his game. She was thankful for the heat that continued to cling to her cheeks from the shower. It disguised the fevered blush that crept up from her neck.

"Are you playing *RexArmis*?" She rushed to the couch, anxious to help. "Wait, are you trying to take Whiton's Cliff and Dunbar Island?"

Smith nodded. "Yeah, but there's no way. I don't have enough manna." Disappointment tugged at his tone. "I'm going to have to do another skirmish, and my shield is fractured."

Finally, something she understood. She wiggled into the seat on the other side of Smith. "You don't have to do that. I can get you through. There's a drop from the cave you passed back in Midlands. You have enough manna to defeat the dwellers there, and there's a healing potion for your shield on the island. I'll show you."

Voodoo leapt from the sofa. "Great. You two play creature war. I'm going to bed."

"Wait, Voodoo," Mercy remembered what she'd wanted to tell him. "Thank you for taking care of me. The medicine you gave me really helped. I've never gotten over a migraine so fast. Sometimes, they take me out for days."

He gave her an impish grin and looked a little uncomfortable with her thanks. "That's my job, sweets. Do you have any idea what triggers the headaches? I might could come up with a way for you to avoid getting them."

"I'm pretty sure it's stress. I didn't start getting them until after the car accident. It was an older car, and my head hit the passenger side window. I had a concussion. But I mean," the end of the story always robbed her of breath, "my mom was killed in the accident so... I guess I was lucky, right? I mean... that's what Julian always says." The noose of devastation cinched around her neck. Smith's hand closed over hers keeping her grounded there beside him. His touch prevented her from being jerked back in time to the day of the accident. She focused on the gentleness of his grasp and the security of being beside him to keep the tidal wave from crashing over her and dragging her into the depths again.

Voodoo sat back down on the edge of the couch. "You know, we both have a whole hell of a lot of experience being the ones that survived something. We get that being told you were the lucky one doesn't mean a damned thing when there are days you'd give most anything to be able to trade places with the person in the ground."

"You do?"

"Yeah, we do. I'm gonna hit the sack. Why don't you ask Smitty about it some time?"

She turned her gaze to Smith, when the door to Voodoo's room closed, not certain if she should ask him about what had happened. Every angle of his handsome face was cast in sorrow. She knew that look well enough not to doubt what she was seeing this time. She'd worn the same expression on her own face for the last two years. Later. Maybe later she'd ask him about what Voodoo had said.

Placing her other hand on top of his, she let her fingers graze over the slight hair on his knuckles. His blinks lengthened at her touch. He didn't have to talk to her, and she'd prove it to him. "Want me to show you the cave?"

Relief eased the tension in his eyes. "Yeah. That'd be great. And... uh, maybe I'll tell you about... all of that some other time, okay?" He choked out the offer.

"You don't have to. I understand. But if you ever want to, even after I'm not causing you so much trouble, just give me a call."

"Hey," he caught her chin in his hand, "you're not causing me any trouble. Don't say that."

Electricity tingled from his hand to her face. The air between them seemed to take on its own pulse. She couldn't even blink, that would've robbed her of the unmistakable hunger in his eyes. When his thumb moved delicately over her cheekbone, the air she'd trapped in her lungs escaped in a gasp. Instinctively, she leaned closer. His gaze roved over the low neckline of her shirt and then returned somewhere between her boobs and her eyes. Her lips. Oh God, he was staring at her lips. What came next? Were you even allowed to kiss your bodyguard? Her tongue darted over her bottom lip. If they *were* going to kiss, she didn't want them to be dry. A harsh grunt escaped from his throat. Her blood raced through her head, pounding in her ears.

He leaned closer still. His hot breaths caressed her mouth. Her heart dipped into her belly. She wanted to beg him. Just another inch, maybe two and...

A shrill ring from the cell phone in his pocket shattered the moment.

16

W ishing he could crush his phone in his fist, he managed to get the damned thing out of his pocket, certain the motion had directed Mercy's eyes to the outline of pure need through his jeans. He blinked away the haze of lust that clouded his eyes and his good sense. What the fuck was he thinking, anyway? He could not kiss her.

"What?" he finally answered Griff's call on the fourth ring.

"We need to talk." His best friend's grave tone ripped the remaining hunger from his chest.

A hundred horrible scenarios lit through his brain. His sister, his parents, Griff himself, T, T's baby that was due in a few weeks. What if something had happened to one of them? Jesus, he'd been sitting there about to take advantage of the woman he'd been tasked to keep safe, and all of the people he needed in order to remain sane could've been hurt or... worse. He couldn't lose anyone else. He wouldn't survive it. "What's wrong?" He tried to maintain control, but his voice betrayed his efforts.

"I've got the cat. Well, actually, I'm at one of those twenty-four-hour emergency vet clinics. The vet has the cat, but she said he'll be okay after the surgery to repair his hip. It was bad. The thing was barely moving when I got in, and the apartment was destroyed, man. They went so far as to slash her mattress and drive the knife through the sheetrock to shred it. Every fucking wall. Must've been big moth-erfuckers, too, because they pulled apart her desk, board by board and ripped the springs from her sofa. I'm guessing at least half of her stuff was taken. There was nothing methodic about it either, except for the way they got in. The door showed no signs of being forced. Whoever picked it did a hell of a good job. Other than that, this isn't someone who was looking for something specific. You and I both know the feds didn't do this. This is some kind of message from the cartel or something. They wanted Ms. Valon to know they are pissed."

"Damn," escaped Smith's mouth in a breath. How the hell had someone other than Griff broken into her apartment with the FBI watching it? Unless the FBI had given up on the apartment now that they knew he had her. That made no sense. They'd at least leave someone to watch it, in case Mercy reappeared there for some reason. The fucker in the coffee shop. He'd seen Smith take her. This had to have been the cartel's retribution for her escape.

"Damn is putting it mildly, and Roman has eyes on the Castellas compound down in Fort Worth. He's seen her brother a few times. He says something is definitely up. They're packing up to go somewhere else. If her shit-sack of a sibling ordered somebody to do this to his sister, I'd like to personally whip his ass. Wakefield still hasn't made contact. If you ask me, he's no longer with us. Roman says the guy was one hell of an operative and not to assume. Guess we'll see. Give my apologies to Mercy, and you might want to tell her she doesn't have anything to come home to, just to prepare her."

"Yeah, I'll figure out some way to do that." He could also figure out some way to set himself on fire, but that didn't mean it was some-thing he wanted to do.

"Good luck. The vet's coming out with the cat now. I'll take it home and let Hannah love on it for a few days. She always makes *me* feel better."

Smith didn't have it in him to bark at Griff for comments like that about his baby sister. Dread had consumed all other emotions. He ended the call and shut his laptop.

"Smith?" Mercy's tender tone pricked at the wound created in his chest by what someone had done to her. "What's wrong? Who was that?"

Swallowing down the singe of bile from his throat, he cradled her hand in his own again. "That was Griff."

"Oh God. Yoda." Tears threatened to escape from her eyes. No. No way. He didn't know what to do with girls when they cried.

"Yoda is good. He's going to be fine. Griff has him. My sister will take care of him."

"What happened to him?" The tremble of her chin and that crack in her voice that marked incoming sobs was the most devastating sound he'd ever heard. When he found the assholes that had done this, he'd shred them piece by bloody piece. "He was... uh... he was injured."

"How?" She squeezed her eyes shut. "He was in my apartment. How did he get hurt? I have to go home."

"Hey, it's okay." He wrapped his arms around her and drew her into his chest. If she cried, every tear would pierce him like a jagged blade, he knew, but he also wanted to be the one to hold her until she got it all out. She deserved someone in her life that held her when she cried, someone that at least tried to make it better. She'd lost her mother, and Julian told her she was lucky. Fuck-wad. "Shh, it's okay." He rubbed his hands up and down her back. She clung to him with more force than she'd had all day. He cradled her head in one of his massive hands trying to shield her from what he was going to have to say next. "Yoda was injured when your apartment was broken into."

She lifted her head. Her red eyes and running nose did nothing to diminish her beauty. "The FBI...?"

"No. Definitely not. The FBI does some things I don't agree with, but they would never have done this. Listen, there's more to this than the FBI wanting to arrest you."

"It was the people who stole the designs from Julian, wasn't it? I've been thinking about it all day, and I just kept thinking the FBI wouldn't have to steal designs. I mean, don't weapons manufacturers kind of work for the government anyway? And you told me that the FBI has hackers who are better than me, so they would have wanted their hackers to get the designs and erase them from the other server. That's why they're after me. They don't really know me, so maybe I'm the kind of hacker who wouldn't send the designs back to them. So... maybe the FBI did get them and erase them from the other server, and whoever stole them thought I'd done it somehow. That must be why they broke in. And if that's the case, the FBI maybe isn't still after me, so I could go home." Pleading desperation bled from every wounded word.

She'd managed to come up with every plausible scenario in the middle of a migraine while trying to outrun the FBI. How could she be so damned brilliant and still have everything so wrong?

Thankful for every moment of training he'd endured to become a Green Beret, he dismantled her explanation and picked out the parts he could validate. Someday, he'd have to tell her the truth, but he couldn't do it then, not when she was set to run. Motion was locked in every muscle of her body. "The break-in was related to the designs and the people who were after them, but I have no reason to believe that the FBI isn't still looking for you. Do you really think I'm going to let you go back home after someone broke in? You're still in danger, Mercy. Please let me keep you safe." With his thumb, he wiped away the tears escaping from her eyes. "It means a lot to me to know you're safe. It means... everything to me, actually."

Another tremble of her chin quaked through his soul. Her eyes closed, and a shuddered breath racked through her. He couldn't do it anymore. He couldn't sit there and keep lying to her. It was rending him in two. The alternative was equally as bad. If he told her the truth it would not only crush her, she'd set out to prove him wrong. He knew, because he'd do the very same thing, but he couldn't sit there and let her cry.

She should never cry. She should only ever be happy. And he was nothing if not the man who needed to save her. It was who he was. He saved the people he cared about. Hell, he saved people he didn't care about. That one day, one moment of his life when he couldn't save the people who meant more to him than anyone, still tore him to shreds. He couldn't save them, but he had to try to save her. He had to fix this.

Leaning in, absorbing her breath, taking on her tears himself, he brushed his lips over hers, and she responded like his kiss was the very thing that would keep her fighting. A quick gasp escaped into his mouth as she opened for his exploring tongue. Her hands went on an exploratory mission all their own, rubbing down his pecs and across his legs. The strawberry scent of the shampoo she'd used was intoxicating.

A jagged groan tore from his lungs as she neared his cock. It swelled out its hunger for her caress. She arched into him, so anxious for more, but there was a hesitance, almost an innocence, to her tentative touches. She seemed to be testing her tongue against his own. It all served to decimate him. The craving greed he only allowed in his fantasies, so rough and demanding, threatened to rise up from the depths, through his skin, out his mouth, from his cock. He lowered her chin so he could invade her mouth deeper, harder.

Some part of the man he'd always been resurrected at her almost self-conscious touches of his crotch. He had to stop before he took more than she would ever want to give him, but her fingertips traced along his denim-trapped cock, and a needy little moan made its way into his mouth from hers. Fuck him, he couldn't stop.

He molded his hand over her right breast. Her nipple strained between his fingers as he plied without finesse. He was driven only by raw need.

"Yes," she whimpered. Her hips moved against the couch needy for his friction, needy for his cock to take away the ache.

No. This was wrong. She trusted him. He was her protector. Other than the day of her mother's death, this had to be the worst day of her life. Here he was taking what he wanted without any consideration. There was no way she'd be willing to give up the things he wanted, the things he desperately needed.

It took every ounce of strength he possessed to pull himself away.

She panted for breath. The tears were gone from her eyes, but the devastation wasn't. "Why... did you stop?"

"Mercy, baby, I should never have done that. I'm sorry."

"But I wanted you to do that. Did I do something wrong?"

"Oh God, no. That was... it was fucking incredible. But you didn't want that. I did everything wrong. I wanted to make you stop crying, and I took advantage. You've had an awful day. You were sick. Your cat's hurt. Like I said, I'm really sorry."

"I don't want you to be sorry," she choked over that admission, doing nothing to keep him from lambasting himself. "I wanted you to keep going."

"You don't really want that. You don't want to be with a man like me, someone who's supposed to be keeping you safe and then did... that."

"I don't know a lot of things, Smith. I don't understand any part of today, really, but I do know what I want. I'd really appreciate it if you'd stop telling me what you think I want and what you think I don't." With that, she stalked to the bedroom and shut him out with the lock of the door.

17

Mercy managed to shut the door to her assigned bedroom before she dissolved into silent tears. She slid down the door until her rear end collided with the hardwood floor. She wouldn't give him the satisfaction of hearing her cry. She had plenty enough anger to burn the tears away before they could turn to breathless sobs, anyway.

She could easily count on one hand the number of men she'd kissed in her lifetime. Smith's kiss easily outranked them all. He'd kissed her like she was air, and he'd been drowning. That's precisely the way she'd felt. His kiss had been all-consuming. He'd taken up her whole world, eradicating the fear and the sadness and all of her confusion. There'd been no room for those feelings when they were together.

Now, she was left with nothing but those emotions battling for dominance in her chest and threatening to close her throat completely. But, more than that, the emotion that was winning out above all others was the harsh slap of rejection. Why was everyone in her life so certain they knew what was best for her? If Julian had just listened to her... their mother wouldn't be... no. She couldn't go there. The wreck wasn't Julian's fault. It was hers. He'd been trying to help her. She just wished someone in her world would listen when she spoke her mind.

A shiver coursed through her, vibrating the door against its frame. Managing to stand, she flung herself on the bed. If he knew she was crying, he'd just apologize again, and having a man like Smith Hagen be sorry for kissing you was somehow worse than every other thing she'd been forced to endure that day.

She had no idea how she'd managed the words she'd used to communicate her frustration with him, but at least she'd said them. She'd been right all along. Society really wasn't worth it. Everything was better back in her tiny apartment where no one could hurt her. Back there she could go on pretending to be the kiss of death to websites who took advantage of people. If anyone she'd ever hacked knew she was the world's oldest virgin, they'd just laugh right along with the rest of humanity. Right along with Smith, surely. She wanted her kitten. She wanted to understand everything again, and she wanted to go back to where she knew how things worked. She wanted her apartment.

Her apartment. A brutal, hiccupped sob tore free from her lungs at the thought of someone breaking in and hurting Yoda. She buried the noise in a pillow and prayed he hadn't heard her. She hated crying. It was a stupid, useless thing to do. Hadn't she learned that after her mother died? It changed nothing.

Sitting up, she pressed the heels of her hands in her eyes until they gave up tear production. Still shaking, but refusing any other emotion but anger, she opened her laptop. The FBI had no idea where she was now. She had to find Julian. She had to figure out what the hell was going on, so life could go back to normal. Smith made her feel things, and that wasn't allowed. Feeling things hurt, and she had no use for it.

But when she opened her email, there was nothing from Julian at all. Surely, he'd want to know if she was safe. He'd hired men to protect her. Or maybe because he'd hired them he assumed she was safe. If that was the case, where was he? Because she *wasn't* safe. The searing pain hollowing in her chest, robbing her of breath, couldn't possibly be the way her body was supposed to be working.

Reality slowly crept through her, making her bones brittle and muscles hollow. She had no way to figure out where Julian was or if he needed her help. She couldn't go back home. There were too many people out to do her harm. She was stuck here with a man she was insanely attracted to, who'd kissed her to make her stop crying, and she'd completely misread everything. Clearly, he didn't want her, or he wouldn't have stopped. No shock there. A mercy kiss for Mercy. Wasn't that appropriate? Wasn't that the way it always went? Still, it infuriated her that he'd brushed her feelings aside with a careless hand.

THE NEXT MORNING, sunlight streamed in through the open blinds, forcing her to open her eyes. They were almost swollen shut. Great. So much for keeping Smith from knowing she'd been crying. Rubbing her hands over them, she tried forcing them to open wider without much luck. She could barely even roll them, which was the next task on her list.

Maybe she wouldn't have to see Smith that day. Maybe she could just stay outside all day long, and he wouldn't come looking for her. Even if he did, she had no interest in being around a man who didn't think she knew her own mind. Mrs. Holder had said they could come up to any of the houses to eat, so Mercy would take her up on the offer.

Determined not to let anyone know that she'd ever felt anything at all, she forced her limbs to move. Her muscles ached from the demons she'd battled in her nightmares. The face chased her through her dreams again. That same slightly-obscured face of a man whom she swore she'd seen over and over again but could never quite recognize. The squeal of her mother's brakes. The tires that couldn't gain traction against wet leaves and ground. The metallic rip of the hood as they finally came to rest against an oak tree at the bottom of the gully. The voice she'd been so certain she heard, but that had then disappeared as the roar of the ambulance and the flashing lights had muted out everything else.

Refusing to let those memories gag her again, she pulled on a different T-shirt, her old jeans, and her shoes. Then she listened. The shower water was running. Figuring God owed her at least one small favor, she prayed Smith was in the shower. She could stomach Voodoo that morning but not Smith. If she could somehow manage to fix it so she never had to see him again, that would be ideal.

Moving quickly, she slipped out the bedroom door, shut it behind her, and rushed down the hallway. Neither of the men were in the kitchen. She had no idea where Voodoo was that morning, and she didn't care. Escape was the only worthy goal.

When she made it out the kitchen door, she took off at a sprint. She had no idea where anything was on this ranch. All that mattered was that she was moving away from Smith. When the stitch in her side burned worse than her feet, she slowed to a walk. Several minutes later, she caught her breath and stopped at a tree-lined fence. She couldn't go any farther in this direction, so she hoped it was far enough away.

Letting her hand graze the fence post, she appreciated the rough wood and even the metallic prick of the barbed wire. They were real, and so much of her world wasn't. Suddenly, the ground shook to the even pounding of hooves. Another round of fear gripped her. She couldn't tell which direction they were coming. Before she could climb up the fence post, she saw them. The horsemen were moving cattle in the field beyond the fence. She watched them ride, strong and certain, not a single ounce of doubt in their movements. The only time she ever felt so self-assured was when she was in front of a screen with her hands on a keyboard.

Squatting down, she ran her hands over the wisps of grass, still anxious to feel something real, something that made sense. A cluster of dandelions grew a few paces away. She was much too old for making wishes, so she ran her fingers over the downy petals sending them flying out on the wind. Cause and effect. The way the world was supposed to work.

She walked along the fence line and allowed her thoughts to tumble in her mind. At least the sun-warmed earth and wide-open fields eased her mood. The wind whipped against her face, but she refused to close her eyes. She wanted them so dry they burned, too dry to ever cry again. Sweat dewed on her upper lip. She followed the low bellow of cattle and what sounded like the rumble of a tractor motor for several minutes without ever seeing either. She gasped when a bald eagle took flight just ahead of her. She envied its freedom and majesty. Eventually, she arrived at a massive barn.

Batting away a few flies, she peeked inside, uncertain if she wanted to find one of the Holders or if she wanted to remain entirely alone.

Her eyes took in every detail, the grooves in a salt lick, the rusty buckets on the ground, the chaff that floated in the streams of sunlight. She smiled at a cat in the far corner stalking what had to have been a mouse. She wished she could distract the cat long enough to pet it, but it likely wouldn't want her to interrupt its quest.

The stalls didn't have any animals in them, and there was no one in the barn that she could see. All of the cowboys must've been on the horses. Slipping inside, she replaced some kind of rope back on the hook it appeared to have fallen off of. She let the rough worn fibers prick at her hand. Everything there served a purpose. Everything on Holder Ranch was so very real, and absolutely nothing about her entire life seemed to hold any permanence at all.

The cat gave up on its conquest and came to investigate Mercy instead. Squatting down, she rubbed her hand back and forth over its fur. "Hey there. Maybe you'll get him next time." The cat's contented purr made her smile. The clop of boots and voices reached her in the odd sanctuary. People were coming.

Scooping the cat up in her arms, she whisked back outside before anyone entered the barn. Continuing along the fence she studied the grooved earth where some kind of truck had probably driven thousands of times.

She was certain ranching was hard work, but she'd give most anything to wake up every morning and know what was expected, to know what her day would look like, and that the next day would be same. What she wouldn't give for somewhere to call home that didn't actually belong to someone else, that wasn't available to be broken into because it couldn't be reached.

The cat seemed perfectly happy to be carried on a walk, so Mercy kept pacing forward toward whatever lay ahead. Eventually, she came to a stream with a few cottonwood trees along its bank. Setting the cat down, she edged close enough to the water to touch it as well. Smiling, she splashed the cool water over her face and tried to let it wash away all of her unwanted emotions. She forced herself to feel the freezing cold droplets as they raced down her face.

Everything before that kiss the night before had been muted. She wanted to feel something, anything, as strongly as she'd felt him. The water made her shiver, and it was nothing at all like the heat produced from the friction of Smith's lips moving in time with hers. Bracing her back against one of the trees, she sat and stared at the water.

Her four-legged friend climbed readily in her lap and nuzzled against her chest.

18

Smith noted every single lowered blade of grass he could see from the kitchen door of their safe house headed due west. Rushing, he ordered himself to remain calm. She had to still be on the ranch. There was no way she could've made it to one of the entrances on foot. Not from where they were.

Her petite footprints picked up again in the dirt near the barn. He raced inside, but she wasn't there.

Two men he'd never seen before both turned to face him. One was significantly older than him and the other about his age.

"You're Maddox's guest, right?" the younger one of them asked.

"Yeah. Have you seen Mercy?" he demanded. "Short girl. Long brown hair. These big green eyes that look like they could see right inside of you. Fucking beautiful. She's... well, she so fucking beautiful I don't know how to describe it."

The older gentleman smiled and shook his head. "No, son, but anytime I've ever chased after a woman, which was only once and she's now my wife, it was because I told someone else how pretty she was instead of telling her. Might try that next time. Maybe she won't take off on ya."

"Yeah, maybe I'll do that." There was a shit ton more to it than the old cowboy knew, but he appreciated the man's words none the less. He'd fucked up big time, and there wasn't a clear path to correct his mistakes. He'd tried apologizing the night before, and that obviously wasn't the right answer. Why did women have to be so confusing?

Finding her was all that mattered. After that, he'd figure the rest out. The five hours distance between the ranch and the cartel compound in Ft. Worth wasn't enough. There would never be enough time or enough miles for her to be away from that malignant world to ever drain him of the worry he felt over her. He'd have to personally burn the compound to the ground before he'd ever have peace. Given the opportunity, he would do just that.

Heading back outside, he searched the ground until he saw more footprints and took off again. Voodoo was headed to the closest gate to make certain she didn't leave. Maddox and some of his cousins were covering all of the other entrances.

She'd followed the fence line. Was that because she wanted to use it to find her way back or had she just stormed out and started running? *Dammit, Mercy.* Where was she?

He took the feed truck line to the closest stream. Relief threatened to topple him over when he saw her there along the banks, sitting against a tree. Thankfulness welled inside of him, rushing breath to his lungs. He stopped and gave himself several long moments to just appreciate the sight of her. Then he texted the news to Voodoo. She was safe. She was right there. He just had to figure out what to say to make up for taking advantage of her the night before. He had to fix what he'd done.

There was a dark calico cat in her lap. He watched her fingers stroke its fur as its tail curled against her arm.

"Mercy?" he tried, but his call was without volume. Clearing his throat, he moved closer. "You could call that one Chewbacca," he offered, not sure what he'd hoped to gain for himself with a stupid joke.

She whipped around to face him. Hatred played cruelly in her swollen eyes. If someone had driven an ice pick into his chest, it couldn't possibly have hurt more than knowing he'd had a part in making her cry that hard. She cocked her jaw to the side. "Did you come to tell me what I'm thinking again, or are you here to try to make me feel better about you not finding me attractive? Save your breath. I'm fine. I don't care."

"What?!" He made it to the bank in three long strides. He couldn't possibly have heard her correctly. Her creative explanations for Julian's whereabouts and everything that had thrown them together in the last few weeks seared through his mind. She definitely had imagination enough to devise something that was so utterly unbelievable. How could she not see how gorgeous she was? Even worse, how had he made her doubt for one second that he found her insanely attractive?

Fix it. He had to fix it. Right then. That was the only thing that made any sense at all. When he sat down, she tried to stand, but he grabbed her hand and kept her in place. "I've been following you for weeks," he informed her.

"What?"

"Yeah, that was part of my job. I had to know your every movement, so if anything happened with the designs and the FBI made a move, I would know how to rescue you. That's why I was in the coffee shop."

Her mouth dropped open, closed again, then reopened. She shook her head. Her audible breath seemed to deflate her body. "I should've figured that out on my own. I'm so sick of not understanding any of this. I know there's something you're not telling me. There has to be."

"I'm trying to ...tell you ..." That sealed her lips shut. "From the moment I first saw you, I just kept thinking, my God, how could I be lucky enough to be assigned to follow someone so beautiful. I know you've only known me a day, and this is probably going to freak you out, but I've been attracted to you for weeks. That's why I apologized last night. I know you better than you know me. Yesterday would've been too much for most people. I'm in awe of your strength. I took advantage of where you were. It had nothing to do with not wanting to kiss you. For fuck's sake, kissing you is the only thing I've wanted to do. Well, that and a few other things. If you don't want me telling you what you're thinking, don't sit over there deciding you know my mind either, because you have no clue what you're talking about." There. He sat back and studied her to see what she made of that.

She stared up at him like he'd just sprouted two other heads out of his shoulders. "You... think I'm beautiful?"

He wanted to find whatever asshole had convinced her otherwise and pluck his eyes from his skull. Clearly, they didn't work anyway. "Why is that so hard to believe?"

"Because no one's ever told me I was beautiful. I don't do all of those things most pretty girls do. I'm just a computer nerd. I thought you'd just kissed me to make me feel better."

"You're the most beautiful hacker I've ever seen, and since I'm a white hat myself, that means something."

The sunlight filtering through the trees played in her hair and highlighted her furrowed brow. "You're a hacker? I thought you were in Special Forces."

"The army uses hackers. I was the comm sergeant for SF Team Seven. We were the best of the best, which means I know my way around a database and secured networks to say the least."

"Wow."

Smith was hesitant to take another guess at her thoughts so he asked, "Is that a good wow or a bad wow?"

"It's just a wow. So, you're saying you're actually ... I mean...you want me?"

"Very much so."

"And you stopped kissing me last night because you decided yesterday was too much for me?"

Again he couldn't tell if he was about to get his ass chewed for deciding that on her behalf, or if she was just trying to get this all straight. Resigning himself to the ass chewing, he lowered his head and nodded. "Yeah, and because I have no business being involved with someone in a current case. I'm also supposed to keep you safe, not take you to my bed which is where we were heading last night."

"Is the not being able to be involved with someone you're protecting like a hard and fast rule, or is that just your gentleman thing again? Because shouldn't I get a say in whether or not we get involved, since we're both attracted to each other?"

This was not at all going where he'd planned for it to go, and his stupid ego latched onto her compliment like a dumbass. Searching the recesses of his mind, he landed on the one thing he was certain would work. "I'm not always a gentleman, Mercy. I'm most certainly not a gentleman in bed. I just told you how attracted I am to you. If I got you under me, I'm honestly not sure what I'd do, but I promise you being gentle wouldn't even make the list. I told you that you didn't want a man like me. I wasn't lying to you. Keeping you safe and taking you to my bed don't work together."

Shock, intrigue, and lust paraded through her eyes. He drew measured breaths and told his cock to give him a break. It was in full-on protest mode. The need for him to throw out everything he knew was right and take her as hard and as dirty as he wanted swelled his balls until he was certain they were twice their normal weight.

Her bottom lip slipped through her teeth, and his eyes locked there. "Once again, you told me something that isn't true."

Shit. What else had she figured out? And what he'd just told her was the most truthful thing he'd said to her so far. Confusion swamped a little of the desire racing through him.

She continued on without him having to prompt her. "You not being a gentleman in bed is pretty much the hottest thing I've ever heard, and that's exactly what I want. I have no interest in gentle sex. What's it going to take to get you to stop deciding things for me? That's really starting to piss me off."

Of all the things he'd thought she might say, that wasn't one of them. He was trying to scare her, and that had blown up in his face quicker than a second-hand explosive. But she couldn't possibly mean that. She had no idea what was on his mind, either. It was time to up the ante. "I'm not sorry it's pissing you off. You have no clue what I could become with you, what I want to do to you."

Defiance lit in her eyes. "So, tell me. If I were naked in front of you right now, what would you do?"

"Mercy." The word fractured and choked from his throat.

"Smith," she came right back. Christ, if she had all of those gorgeous curves in front of him right then, he'd turn her into nothing more than a wet, desperate, needy little mess. And that would just be the beginning. His kisses would be bruising. He'd leave fingerprint markings on her hips from his grip. He'd fuck her so hard she wouldn't be able to walk.

His mouth watered, so anxious to know her flavors. Sweet. He knew her juices would be sweet for him while she melted on his tongue. Her innocence the night before didn't mesh with her online persona of being the kiss of death. He wondered which version of herself she became when she was with someone who knew how to cater to all the facets of a woman's personality.

His fingers curved into fists to keep from jerking her into his lap, so she could feel what she was doing to him, feel how hard he was, how deep he wanted to drive into her. Maybe that would prove his point.

She released the cat who scampered off toward a patch of sunlight on the shore. The next thing he knew, she was right beside him on her knees. Fuck him. "Tell me what you'd do if we'd just met, and I wasn't your assignment. If we were just two people who met at that coffee shop yesterday and both admitted we were really attracted to each other."

"No."

"Yes. You made me feel like the ugliest duckling in the lake last night, so I think you kind of owe me this."

Shit. That did it. Fixing the way he'd made her feel was suddenly his number one priority. Scaring her off became a distant second. He jerked her into his lap, splitting her thighs over his own. She rose up on her knees, her body trying to climb up the wall of muscle she was pressed against. Then she sank back down, grinding the crotch of her jeans against the fierce swell in his own. An onslaught of pure, driven need consumed him. He gripped her ass as she rode. "You feel that?

You feel how fucking hard I am for you? I can't fake that, Mercy. You're so damned gorgeous. Do you have any idea how badly I want to drive that into your tight little pussy? Until you're soaked, until you're sticky, until you're sobbing out my name, and then I still won't be done. Don't you get it, baby? I'm not always the nice guy my friends think I am."

19

Mercy had no idea how she'd managed to find herself in Smith Hagen's lap, but she certainly wasn't complaining. Every cell inside her body had joined some kind of "Hallelujah Chorus" of thanks. *Finally* was the only word that pulsed in her mind.

She'd never had any interest in sweet, gentle sex. She certainly wasn't an expert, since she'd never actually had it, but she definitely knew what she liked to read and what she wanted to watch. With every book, with every video, she gained a little more knowledge about herself.

To be wanted, to have some kind of proof that she wasn't completely undesirable was a heady sensation. It shattered over her, drowning out a few of her insecurities.

Smith's right hand latched into a fist in her hair as he brought her mouth to his own. True to his warning, he was not gentle. And true to herself, she knew she was right. His rough power did nothing but amplify the desperation for friction between her legs, or maybe it was pressure she needed there. She wasn't sure. All she knew was that she required something to take away the constant ache. She continued to grind against his tented fly. The anatomy between her thighs felt swollen and more than ready.

A pained sound that echoed precisely how she felt filled her mouth.

His drugging kisses were loaded with that same intensity they'd held the night before. It was the same determination he used in order to be a gentleman for everyone else. The knowledge that he was letting her see some real part of himself only made her fly higher. She of all people knew about existing as two halves of a whole. The virgin kiss of death would make no sense to anyone. She knew that, but Smith was wrong about himself. He was more than capable of keeping her safe and indulging his darker side with her. She wasn't made of glass. The only way she was going to break was if he didn't do something about the raw emptiness that threatened to split her in two.

She knew she should tell him she'd never done this before, but that would make him stop. He thought he knew her better than she knew him, and maybe he did. She still didn't know what to do with his confession about following her, but no man who worried about her the way he did was capable of not fussing over her virginity. The entire thing was ridiculous, anyway. Surely, he'd never really know that she'd been a virgin before him. It was some stupid concept made up by chauvinists in the third century or some such nonsense. It didn't even have a real definition. Something that insubstantial was not going to keep her from being with Smith.

She concentrated on keeping him going. His right hand moved from her backside, to under her T-shirt, and then skated up her belly. That worked for her, given the painful throb of her nipples, and it appeared that they would be his very next stop.

Without much finesse, he shoved one cup of her bra downward and folded his hand over her breast. A harsh tremble shook through her, drawing another pained grunt from him. Did all men sound this sexy when they were turned on? They couldn't possibly. All she wanted to do were things that inspired him to keep making sounds like that.

His voice was one of the many things she found so intoxicating about him. He spoke with gentle authority, with wisdom, deep and rugged. Yet somehow, those grunts of need and moans of hunger were even better.

When she couldn't hold her breath any longer, she let her head fall back, gasping for air, as he made a rough exploration of her breasts. And once again she was struck by how very real his touch was. That knowledge only drove her harder. He caught her nipple between his thumb and index finger and squeezed. There was nothing tender in his touch. His eyes were indeed dark, the only light in them a primal flare of warning. Heady in finally understanding something, a low moan wrenched from her own lungs. Some pulse point of electricity seemed to exist between her nipples and her pussy. Need rushed back and forth on the arc.

"You like that, baby? That's just the beginning."

"Yes," strangled from her. She molded her own hand over his as he continued to ply and taunt her breast. His rough touch was the only thing keeping her anchored to the world around them. She swore if he released her, she'd never recover.

Introduced to every act of intimacy via books, she tried to remember what knowledgeable heroines would do next, but his mouth covered hers again as he made a feast of her kisses. Her reality blurred into nothing but the two of them.

She gripped his shirt and wished the fabric of their jeans would somehow disintegrate with the force of her grind against him. Restraint pulsed behind his powerful touch. It existed in every broad plain of his giant form. Hills of muscle bunched and flexed under her touch. Her lips were going to be bruised, as was her right hip where one of his powerful hands was still latched on with punishing force. And until that moment, with thoughts of his possessive hunger marking her, she had never known just how turned on she could be.

"Smith, please," she whimpered when he allowed her another round of breath. "More."

His eyes flashed with uninhibited carnality. She trembled from its force. "Are you already begging for me, baby? That pussy already soaked for me?"

"God, yes. Please," she begged again.

Suddenly, he wrenched back and moved his hand from her breast to her face. He gave her nowhere to look but directly into his exacting gaze. "Promise me something, sweetheart. Promise me when it hurts to walk, hurts to even sit down because I held you down and fucked your tender little pussy so hard you're raw, that you'll tell me so I can make it better. I'll put you in my lap and rub your pussy until you're so needy for more you'll beg for the very thing that made you hurt. Then I'll kiss it all better, run my tongue as deep inside of you as I can get, until you're nothing more than a sobbing mess. That's what you're telling me you want when you decide I don't know what's best for you. Just remember that I tried to warn you."

Shock shattered over Mercy. Her pulse stuttered through her veins. She should probably have slapped him for saying things like that to her, but she was much too busy being thoroughly aroused. His detailed scenario somehow read like a script of her dirtiest fantasies, as though he had reached into her mind and extracted it. He knew her better than she knew him indeed, and she wanted to live every single step of his warning. She longed for him to hold her down and she craved the friction-induced pain, anything that would replace the aching emptiness between her legs. She craved his touch, craved his tongue. She was desperate for his fullness to fill every hollow she possessed, over and over again, to tear away every single thing she didn't understand. She'd waited so long to really feel all of those things.

"I don't need to be warned. I want that. Now," she urged again.

"Not until you promise me."

"I promise." Her breathing thinned to nothing more than wisps of yearning that failed to fill her lungs, and somehow, she didn't care.

"And you're not afraid?" Disbelief grated in his rough voice.

"Not at all." She tried to think of what else she could say to convince him. "I hurt, Smith. I hurt right now for everything you just said you'd do."

"Oh baby, I'm gonna make that hurt go away, make that little empty ache feel so much better."

"Please."

"Then get up," he growled.

"What? Why?" His length felt like it might be unending, and it was aligned perfectly with the pain he'd just promised to soothe. Moving seemed highly unnecessary.

Another cocky smirk lifted the left side of his painfully gorgeous face. "Damn, you are needy, aren't you, honey? Because I'm not going to fuck you on the ground in broad daylight in front of anyone who happens to wander by. I don't share. If we do this, you're mine. No one else gets to see your beautiful curves but me. When I ride you hard enough to make those gorgeous tits bounce, that's for my eyes only. Think I'll fuck those, too, while I'm at it."

With that promise, she climbed out of his lap and tried to recover both her breath and balance. He squeezed his eyes shut and pressed his palm to his crotch. She didn't understand. "Why are you doing that?"

"So I can walk out of here without showing the entire ranch just how hard you make me."

20

Those compelling green eyes continued to stare down at him, willing him to move. Smith lumbered to his feet, grabbed her hand, and tugged her back toward the house. She wanted him. Hell, she'd begged for him. Everything about this was wrong, and yet he had no hope of stopping himself. Instead, he leaned and lifted her up into his arms so he could get them to his bed faster. One of his strides equaled three of hers, and he just couldn't wait that long.

But with every puff of air laced with her ripened strawberry scent and every pound of his boots against the ground, a little more of his good sense permeated his haze of lust. "Shit," he spat when reality caught up with the fantasy.

"What?" she all but whimpered.

"I don't have a condom." There, that was a legitimate roadblock neither of them could overcome, but agitation locked tightly in his gut at the thought. Dammit. Surely either Voodoo or one of the endless numbers of Holder men had one somewhere on this big-ass ranch, but he knew he shouldn't hunt one down. This was reason trying to shake him from the stupidity of his decision.

"We don't need a condom." Frustration pricked her declaration.

His mind offered up a lengthy list of things he could do to ease her pain, because his sweet baby clearly needed to be tended, but he knew better. If he sank his fingers deep inside of her drenched pussy, he wouldn't stop there. He'd need so much more. He needed to know the flavors of her cream as he lapped it from her swollen pussy, and most certainly needed to open her all for himself. "We do need a condom. I seriously doubt you're quite ready to have a baby. We've known each other twenty-four hours."

She ground her teeth. "I'm not an idiot. I also can't get pregnant. They put me on the pill a while ago for my migraines, and I don't have anything." There was a quiver to her voice now, like she was either afraid he was going to confess that he wasn't clean or refuse to sleep with her even if he was.

He vowed to reassure her just as soon as blood flow reversed course from his cock back to his brain. All his cock was interested in was taking her bareback, pounding inside of her with nothing between them. "I'm clean," he ground out.

"Then we don't need a condom. Like I said."

Fuck him. He was going to do this. Nothing would keep him from her. God, he had replayed it in his head too many times to deny himself now. All restraint was long gone, evaporated with every throaty whimper he drew from her when they kissed. He picked up his pace, and had her back in the kitchen of their safe house in record time. He kicked the door shut, but that was as far as he could go without feeling her. He'd been patient long enough.

Like a man possessed, he stood her on her feet, popped the snap of her jeans, and dove back in for another kiss simultaneously. She opened her mouth for him. He'd take care of opening her other set of lips with his hands, then his tongue, then his cock, and then he'd start all over again.

Desperate to feel the swollen, fevered skin of her mound, he sought it with the urgency of his next breath. "Feel how wet those little panties are for me. You are hurting, aren't you?"

"God, yes."

He met that admission with a grunt of understanding. His cock thickened until he was certain he was being strangled. "Me too, baby. Me too."

He teased at her clit while his tongue tangled with her own. The kiss was wet and hungry. He'd kissed enough women in his life to know he was fucking it up. He'd lost all finesse, all restraint. His very existence threaded to nothing but pure, driven hunger.

Taking more was the only thing that made any sense at all. Her rapid pulse quickened against his touch. That slick, slippery heat continued to drip from her. His mouth watered. It was all for him. Dipping his hand lower, he teased at her slit, certain it was actually the entrance to heaven.

Closing his eyes, he reveled in the hungry clenches he could just make out as he rubbed his fingertips back and forth between her lips.

"Smith, please." It was a breathless plea for his offer, and it was all he'd been waiting to hear.

He pressed two fingers inside of her, and had just enough intelligence left to notice her slight wince. Cringing, he slowly eased one back out. "Sorry, sweetheart. You're so damned tight. Jesus, you're going to feel good. Like fucking a virgin with my big cock." His own realization kicked up a rumbled groan from low in his gut.

But her eyes flashed open with a look he couldn't quite read. He ground his teeth and forced himself to really study her. Frustration? Yes, that was there, too, but this was guilt. Maybe. He tried to think of what might've brought that on.

"Please keep going," she urged.

"I have every intention of that, but tell me why you look so damned guilty all of a sudden. I'm the only one who should feel guilty for what I'm about to do to you."

Her eyes shifted to the cabinets like they were the most fascinating thing in the room at that moment. She gnawed her lip.

"Mercy."

"What?"

"Whatever is going on in your head right now, say it. If you don't want to do this, tell me now, before I get you in my bedroom."

"I want to do it. Right now."

"Then you know what you have to do, and don't even think about lying to me." She cocked her jaw to the side and rolled her eyes. He forced himself to withdraw his hand, though that was the absolute last thing he wanted to do. "Talk." With a huff to assure him she was pissed, she tugged at the ends of her own hair again. He'd take care of her being pissed with him just as soon as she made her confession. "I'm waiting," he demanded.

"Fine. I probably feel virgin tight, or whatever you said, because... I am."

The screech of a thousand brakes sounded in his head. "What the hell is a virgin doing on the pill?"

"Migraines, remember?"

She had said that. Damn. Her confession ripped away his desire to take her hard and fast like the removal of a layer of skin. If that wasn't enough to make him stop, the sound of voices outside the door certainly was.

"Smith, please. Please don't... just... I want this. I want everything you said you'd give me. I want it exactly the way you said it. Don't let this stop you. I'm begging you."

Before he could respond, Voodoo and Maddox flew into the house. He managed to zip Mercy's jeans before Maddox noticed. Voodoo, on the other hand, was more astute and his delighted chuckle was all the evidence Smith needed to know they'd been caught.

Maddox made himself at home, which Smith supposed wasn't all that rude given that this was his ranch. That didn't stop him from wanting to forcefully eject both of them through the back door via his boot.

"Please," Mercy whispered.

Damn him to hell and back. Her plea was fervent, almost wounded. It bruised his ability to turn her down. Why couldn't he just tell her no? The answer was in her imploring eyes, still red-rimmed and swollen from the night before. Because he wasn't that strong. Sure, he'd carried grown men and their gear two at a time out of harm's way. He could leg press well over a ton. But turning her down about this, there was no way in hell he would ever be that strong. Her first. He'd be her first. He'd open her and fit her to him and no one else.

"Do you want me to find something for Mad-dog and me to go do?" Voodoo spoke between his teeth when Mercy excused herself to her bedroom. Everything about the way she moved said she was crushed.

Smith stared after her and shook his head. "No. But don't be here tonight."

"You got it. Hey, Mad-dog, I'm staying at your place tonight," Voodoo informed him as he flipped on the television and fell into one of the ancient recliners.

Maddox took the recliner beside Voodoo. "No problem. We're all watching the fight up there tonight, anyway. Wanna come, Smitty?" he offered as Smith stalked to Mercy's bedroom.

"No." He opened her door without knocking. A shocked gasp rang from her lungs. He swore a hundred different emotions paraded through her eyes. He closed the door and the distance between them in one step. "Listen to me. If you're certain you want this, and I mean damned certain, you come find me tonight. But this has to be your choice, so you think about it long and hard. God knows that's what I am for you, but I can deal if you decide I'm not who you want doing this."

Hope rushed to her gaze. He swore fireworks went off in her eyes. "Are you serious? You'll really do this?"

A mirthless chuckle was all he managed for a quick moment. "God help us both, but I can't seem to find reason enough to talk myself out of it." That wasn't entirely true, but it was why he was telling her this. Left to his own devices, if he could stay away from her long enough, he'd manage to remember what an asshole taking this from her was going to make him. He'd been battling his baser nature for so long it was almost an automatic response. But if she came to him that night, climbed in his bed, begged again, that would be all it would take to strip away anything but the desire to make her sweet little cherry belong to him alone.

"And you'll be just as rough as you wanted to be before I told you?" She was killing him.

"No, I won't. I may not always know what you're thinking or wanting, baby, but I can guarantee that you don't want that. Not this time. After tonight, if you're needing more, I'll take good care of you then, too."

She nodded. "You made me promise that if I hurt I'd ask you to fix it. Now, you promise me that you won't change your mind."

He would make no promises to that effect. If he could find some semblance of sanity anywhere on the hundreds of thousands of acres of ranch land surrounding them, he'd cling to it. "Come find me tonight." He breathed the words over her lips as he indulged himself in one more kiss. His tongue already missed the flavors of those lips of hers. He wasn't certain he'd survive without them until that night, but he wanted her to have time to think about what she was asking him to do. It would, no doubt, be the longest day of his entire life.

21

Smith lay bare chested in bed that night counting the slow turns of the fan above him. She'd said nothing more about their arrangement, not even when they'd played *RexArmis* for hours. Just having her beside him had been pure torture. Occasionally, he'd catch her staring up at him in anticipation, with curiosity penned in those eyes of hers, and those moments were responsible for the marks on his cock from the compression of his zipper against it.

The house was silent, save for the occasional screech of a hunting owl nearby. Still torn between two distinct camps, horny and guilty, he continued to search for some reason to turn her away, assuming she came to him at all.

Maybe she wouldn't come. Maybe she'd located her good sense since his was nowhere to be found. The sheets pricked at his back. His own awareness was rubbing him raw. The very air he breathed was laced with yearning.

He tried to devise a plan. It had been almost twenty years since he'd been with a virgin. Of course, he had learned a thing or two since then.

If she wanted this, he had to prove to her that he could be gentle with her, and that wasn't something he was certain he could do. He wanted her too damn badly. What if his control continued to slip? God, what if he hurt her? Self-hatred clawed under his skin at the thought. He had to be careful with her. She was so little, so innocent, so trusting of him.

That did nothing to soothe the frantic debate in his head. She trusted him enough to let him have this, and he was still lying to her about her brother and the cartel and everything else. God, he really was a bastard. She deserved better.

That thought didn't have time to take hold before the timid knock on his door had him scrambling from the bed. He jerked open the door and took her all in. He'd seen her at dinner an hour before, and had somehow forgotten just how beautiful she was.

"Voodoo left with Maddox and Cole," she explained hesitantly.

All he could manage was a nod. Her entire being was drawn taut, tensed, and timid. That was more than enough reason to call this off. "We don't have to do this, sweetheart. No one should ever pressure you into doing anything you're not sure you want to do." Unable to keep his hands from her, he stroked his fingertips over her cheek and then tucked a stray strand of hair behind her right ear. The shiver he elicited sped his breath. She gave him a sweet grin that got his heart in the game. By the time this was over, he was going to sound like he'd just run a marathon.

"I know you think you're some kind of bad guy because you want to hold me down or whatever, but you're wrong. Your friends are right. You are one of the nicest guys I've ever met."

A humorless laugh escaped the trap of his lips. "Guess we'll see if you're still saying that in the morning."

"I will be."

"Don't be so certain."

She rolled her eyes at him. "Can I come in?"

Dammit, he was already letting his manners slip. He had to get it together. "Sure." He stepped back and drank her in as she crossed over the threshold to his room—a timid fawn stepping into the lion's den. Regret slithered through him at his own comparison.

When she turned to face him, her eyes widened in shock. He probably should've put a shirt back on. Truthfully, he'd been trying to find something to do while he awaited her, and removing a layer that would stand between them seemed like a good idea at the time. He did have a fair amount of chest hair and several tattoos, but surely she'd seen a guy with that before. Or maybe not. Jesus, was she really that innocent?

"What happened to you?" she whispered. It wasn't until her fingertips gently traced down the scars marring his right shoulder and side that he understood what she was referencing. If the woman distracted him enough to make him forget the worst day of his life, maybe there was more to this than him being an asshole who wanted to own her innocence more than he wanted the next beat of his heart.

He followed the path of her hands with his eyes and tried to come up with something to explain the bullet wounds and scalpel markings. "Uh... bad day at the office."

She managed a slow nod. "Does it still hurt?" Her hand tended and caressed his pecs, scattering his thoughts.

Closing his eyes so he had some hope of concentrating, he forced a joke. "Does it make me sound like an old man if I admit that it hurts when the weather is bad? Voodoo says the scar tissue gets inflamed or something."

"It doesn't make you sound like an old man. It makes you sound like a hero. I'm sorry you got hurt."

He wasn't feeling particularly heroic, but if she thought that about him, he'd be damned if he was going to correct her. Being a hero for her was akin to the heavenly way it would feel when he eased her open and took her all for himself. "Nothing but a thing, right?"

When she withdrew her hand, he swore the absence of her touch physically hurt. "Is that what you say when you don't want to talk about something?"

Damned brilliant woman. "Pretty much."

Her bottom lip slipped through her teeth, and she perched that sexy ass on the edge of his bed. He followed after her like she was a magnet and he was nothing more than a metal ball bearing thoughtlessly seeking her.

She played with a loose thread on the quilt. "Am I allowed to ask you about other things?"

That depended. If she wanted to know things about him, he'd provide as many answers as he could all night long. If she wanted to know about Julian or the designs or the case, he was going to have to continue the lies. Never before had he ever hated his job, and yet, without it he never would've met her. How cruel the world could be that someone who fascinated him so thoroughly had existed just a few hours from his home, and he never would've known. "Baby, you can ask me anything you want, and we still don't have to do this." He gestured to the bed, certain she knew what he was referring to.

"It's just something you said to me earlier." Heat climbed in seductive curves from the lush swells of those tits under the T-shirt until it bloomed across her face.

He tried to turn his hungry grunt into a cough. "What did I say?"

"That you know me better than I know you. I guess I was wondering if we could change that a little bit."

Dangerous territory. "What do you want to know?"

"Well...," she considered, "there are so many things. Like, what do you do for fun when you're not rescuing geeky virgins who inadvertently tried to hack the Department of Defense? And do you like *Lord of the Rings* because they're my favorite books but not movies. I don't know why that matters, though. You told me your dad was a general, but are you close with him? I never knew my father, so I like it when other people get along with their dads. You know, the way it's supposed to be. You don't have to tell me what happened to you, but could you maybe tell me something you don't tell other people? I don't know why that's important. It just is." She sealed her lips shut with the might of her teeth, but one more confession sprang loose. "I'm sorry I'm rambling. I guess I am a little nervous." He started to tell her, yet again, that they didn't have to do anything at all, but she wagged her finger in his face. "But not so nervous that I don't want to do this. You promised."

Grasping her hand, still loving how completely it fit inside his own, he shook his head. "I never promised, and I'm glad you finally admitted that you're nervous."

She pursed her lips indignantly at that. "Are you going to answer my questions?"

He nodded. "Let's see here, when I'm not working I tend to fully embrace my own geekdom. Video games, learning new programming languages, reading. Griff, that's the guy who rescued Yoda, used to be my roommate before he married my sister. Since he moved out, I realized how much I like quiet. Whole damned world is so..."

"Loud. Yeah, I know. I think that's part of why I stay in my apartment all the time."

He got that. He really did. "The past few months are really the first time I've lived alone. Before that, we were almost always deployed, so we lived out of rucksacks and called a tent home sweet home."

"I can't imagine that." Fascination colored her features.

"Living alone?"

"No. I like to be alone, too. I can't imagine living outside on purpose."

Smith chuckled. "Does that mean if we keep this thing going for any length of time, I won't be able to convince you to go camping with me?" He hadn't camped since he'd been discharged, but teasing her was far too tempting.

She wrinkled that cute little nose. "I have a deep and abiding affection for electricity and Wi-Fi, but this going on longer than tonight sounds pretty amazing."

"I think I can live with that." He winked at her. "Uh, I have read *Lord of the Rings* like a dozen times each. You can quiz me, if that'd make you feel better. The movies are okay, but the books are better. That's always the way it goes. You asked about my dad. Yeah, we're close." Smith let his father's face form in his mind, complete with the grey hair and wrinkles he hadn't had ten years before. "He's not always easy to be close to, though. He's the kind of man you know loves you, but you're also not sure if you measure up. I spent most of my life never wanting to disappoint him. I don't have any memories of him telling me I'd screwed something up, but he wasn't around much when I was growing up. I guess I was never sure." He had no idea where that half confession had come from or where he was trying to go with it.

"Maybe try thinking about it differently. Has your father ever disappointed you?"

22

Mercy had no idea where her question had come from. She just knew she needed to rescue Smith from thinking he'd ever not been good enough. That wasn't even possible. She may not know his favorite ice cream flavor or what color underwear he wore, which she supposed she'd know soon enough, but she knew him. There was some kind of invisible tether between the two of them. Something she didn't fully understand, but she felt.

Smith ran his hand over his beard and glanced away. "Yeah. My dad has disappointed me a few times."

Giving the tether between them some slack, she scooted a little closer to him, feeling braver now. "Then why would you hold yourself to higher standards than you hold him?" He didn't seem to have an answer for that, and Mercy suspected the way he'd been raised was part of his guilt over his preferences when it came to sex. Well, she'd prove to him that he didn't have to be a perfect gentleman with her. In fact, she'd prefer he wasn't. That was an impossible standard she didn't want him to have to live up to. "It's like that with me and Julian, kind of. Sometimes he does crazy things, and he always wants all of this attention, and then I end up having to clean up his messes. Like with the designs, but that doesn't mean I'm disappointed in him, or that I don't love him. He's my brother. He means the world to me. He always will."

Something she'd said seemed to have drawn out a story he wanted to share with her. "I went to West Point because that's what my father wanted me to do."

Mercy sealed her lips shut. Whatever he was about to say, it must've been brewing just beneath the surface of his restraint.

"I didn't even really want to go. I knew it would be hell. In the army, they're not nicer to you because your dad is a general. They're harder on you. But that's what he wanted so that's what I did. I didn't hate it, but I resented it sometimes. Then I graduated from the Academy and went through the motions because that's what was expected. I was General Gerald T. Hagen's son. Every choice had already been made for me. I was up for promotion to captain, and I thought everything would go on just the way it always had. Making captain isn't assumed, but it's not that difficult, either. But it didn't work out that way. I did my job... I always did whatever I thought was expected of me, only I always tried to do it better and faster because that's what my lineage demanded. When the promotion board met, I ended up being passed over for the promotion because of bad ratings from this prick lieutenant colonel who hated my father. He was deter-mined to get me out just to stick it to my dad. I don't even know what happened between the two of them. I was just out."

She felt her own brow furrow. "You mean like you got fired just because you didn't get a promotion? I didn't even know they fired people from the army."

"It's not quite that dramatic, but yeah, if you get passed up for promotion, you're out of a job. I always thought my father could've done something about it. He could've stepped in. I don't know, maybe he couldn't, but I'd done everything he ever wanted me to do, and I was the one who got fucked. All he said was, 'Son, the army, just like life, isn't always fair. Either play the hand you've been dealt or reshuffle the deck.'"

Mercy tried to smile at Smith's impression of his father, but the anger in his gaze betrayed him. The lamplight spilled around him, sharpening some angles and distressing a few others of his impressive form. He looked like he'd been carved out of rough granite and then honed with a chiseled blade. Colossus indeed. "What did you do after that?"

"I pissed around for a few weeks, sulking mostly. Then I decided I was going to do what I'd always wanted to do in the first place. I enlisted and set my sights on Special Forces. It finally occurred to me that maybe my dad never realized how hard I always tried to please him. Maybe that's why he didn't step in. Maybe he couldn't. I don't know. Talking was never our strong suit. He told me he was proud of me when I graduated from the Academy, and I let that drive me for years. Realizing that I didn't have to let his expectations define my life might've even been worth it. I don't know why I'm telling you all of this, except that you asked me to tell you something I don't tell a lot of people."

Mercy had heard enough. Her heart pricked both because of his story and the scars that sharpened his already impressive physique. She had no idea how many hard memories he'd had to endure. His father might not have been there for him when he needed him to be. God knew hers hadn't been able to be, either. But she was right there, and the pain in his eyes was potent. If she could soothe any part of his life, that's precisely what she wanted to do.

Crawling to her knees, she leaned in and brushed her lips tenderly against his own. When his eyes closed and those hands, she knew had been asked to carry far too much, closed around her waist, she opened her lips, loving the craving grunt that filled her mouth.

He moved one hand to her cheek, caressing and cradling her face with so much tender care she melted against him. When he lifted his head to allow her breath, his eyes had that warning flare glowing in them again. A harsh swallow tensed in his throat. "Does that kiss mean you don't want to quiz me on *Lord of the Rings*?" He'd tried for a joke, but there was far too much ragged hunger in his tone.

"Maybe later." She dove back toward him, starved for him, but he held her back.

"You're sure about this? Because baby, I want you so fucking badly I don't know if I'll be able to stop once I get started."

"Good. I don't want you to stop. I want this. I want it from you. I just need you to let yourself have it."

23

Her encouragement disintegrated another layer of his worry over her. He lost all ability to deny himself any part of her. There were so many things in his life he'd told himself he shouldn't want, so many things he never sought because of the expectations that had been carved out on his behalf.

But he was going to take her all for himself. The lies, the case, her brother, the General—they could all take a fucking number and wait outside the door. This night was for the two of them to exist without intrusion.

Never before that moment had he ever ordered himself to be hesitant. Hesitance would get you killed in the field, but there in his bed with her it was necessary for his very survival. All of the things he wanted to do to her had to come after the things he wanted to give her. If he hurt her, he would never forgive himself. He lived with enough regrets. He couldn't stomach another.

She ran her hands down his chest and then caressed over the sword and cross tattoo on his shoulder. Like flint on steel, her inquisitive little touches set him on fire.

Skin. He needed to feel her silky skin. Needed her in his hands and against his body. The boulder of greed he'd tried to push back all damn day compressed against his chest. He couldn't fight it. He could only appease it.

Shoving that T-shirt aside, he splayed his hand over her soft belly, but that wasn't enough. He wondered if he'd ever be satisfied. He melded their lips together again to test his theory. Every kiss before had only amped the rampant craving. This one was no different.

She gave as good as she got, and kissed him like air wasn't necessary for survival. He pressed his tongue inside her mouth the way he intended to press it inside her pussy, tasting every square inch, absorbing her, devouring her. He trailed kisses to the hollow of her throat and down her neck. She might've forgotten to breathe, but he needed her to have breath.

"Smith," gasped from her, needy and cautious at the same time.

"What, baby?" He lifted her shirt over her head battling with his own desperation.

"I don't know how to do any of this. I don't know what to do next. I want you to like this, too."

That comment effectively throttled his need at least for the moment. "Look at me," he demanded. "Absolutely nothing that you do is going to keep me from loving every second of this. My God, a man should have to sell his soul to get to be your first. I'm a lucky bastard. I know that. Trust me, everything you're giving me, I'll never take it for granted. I'm going to take good care of you, honey. You don't have to know a damn thing. You just have to relax for me. Let yourself enjoy this."

With that, he popped the clasp of her bra, groaning out his pleasure as her breasts spilled forward, their heavy weight no longer restrained. He slipped the garment down her arms and tossed it away. "Lie back, baby. Let me see you. You're so damned beautiful."

Her immediate compliance, coupled with the sway of her tits as she reclined, shot another hot surge of lust to his cock. He throbbed out his pleasure. Cupping her breasts in his hands, he let them spill through his fingers. She'd loved it when he'd been rough with them that morning, but he didn't want to frighten her now. Later, he'd rake his teeth over those rosy-pink tips and suck until he left marks, but not tonight.

Instead, he spun his tongue over every raised bump surrounding the flushed crests, and then drew her right nipple into the heat of his mouth and sucked. Her short fingernails clawed against his scalp as she wound her hand into his hair and arched her back, needy for him to take more. Oh, fuck yeah. Losing another modicum of restraint, he gave in, sucking harder.

Her hips grew restless with her need. Soon. He'd take care of that needy little slip of heaven between her thighs all too soon. His lips descended the hills of her breasts. He kissed a trail of fire to her navel and spun his tongue there as well, drawing a quick gasp from her.

Intent on his goal, he popped the snap on her jeans.

ONCE HER JEANS WERE OFF, he was going to see all of the many things men probably didn't find very attractive. Not that Mercy had a great deal of knowledge about what men liked, but she knew she lacked a thigh gap. Most men didn't seem to care for her weight. In fact, her thighs were complete with dimples. She hadn't seen the inside of a gym since that one semester her freshman year of high school when she'd been forced to learn badminton. All she'd successfully managed was to get the birdie tangled in her hair and her racket tangled in the net.

At that moment, every nerve ending she possessed seemed to tangle themselves up just like that racket. He peeled her jeans and panties away at the same time. She braced for some kind of rejection. She couldn't even look at him. Dread coiled low in her belly.

She certainly hadn't expected another one of those greedy grunts to reach her ears. "Damn, it's as beautiful as the rest of you. I should've known." He grasped her knees and spread her legs as if to get a better look. Cold air taunted the sensitized skin between her thighs, so swollen and heavy she knew whatever he did, it would only make it feel better. "I should've fucking known. So damned gorgeous," he admonished himself as he leaned in and spun his tongue at the crest of her mound.

"Oh God, yes," tore from her lungs. Her eyes closed, and though she searched the recesses of her mind, she couldn't find any of the worry over her own body that had threatened to drown her a moment before.

"You smell like heaven, too, baby. So damn good." He took a deep inhale of her scent at the apex of her thighs. "You have no idea how long I've wanted to know how good you taste."

But she was too lost in the ministrations of his tongue to give his accolades much thought. With tender restraint she was certain he'd rather not have to use, he separated her swollen folds with his thumbs and lapped his tongue at her opening. She shuddered as every whisker of his beard taunted her pussy and inner thighs, certain nothing had ever felt that good. The way his mouth moved over her was pure, unadulterated decadence. Some devious part of her hoped her thighs were chafed, evidence of his possession.

"That swollen little clit is peeking out at me. Is it needing to be tended, baby?"

She hadn't been aware she was going to have to answer questions. A reedy moan was all she could come up with, but that must've sufficed because his tongue roved to the spot where her pulse throbbed, hot and fast. Blood rushed behind her ears. The world seemed to spin faster, perhaps too fast, as he drew her clit into his mouth and soothed its need.

She began to beg. "More. Please, please I need more." More of his tongue maybe. Something to fill the aching emptiness. Something to sate the swollen folds of skin that pulsed all for him. She didn't know more of what exactly, but she knew her very existence required more of him.

"No, baby. We're going to leave this virgin pussy innocent for me right now. I'll open you nice and wide in just a few minutes."

"But I'm going to..." For some reason she couldn't quite relate what was about to happen to her. She walked a jagged edge of arousal, and she was going to fall. That same pulse that pounded between her legs moved up her spine. Her entire body timed itself to the strokes of his tongue. A knot of pressure throbbed behind her mound.

"Come?" he chuckled. "That's what happens when I lick your sweet pussy, baby. Don't worry, I'm gonna give you something to come around when I think you're ready. Now, relax and let it go for me. Don't fight it. Let me feel your cream going down my throat."

With another stroke of his tongue and soft suckle of her clit, the levee that held back a flood of pleasure shattered, and a tidal wave of heat and relief ripped her apart. A harsh gasp choked from her as he devoured everything she gave up. Her jaw clenched tight, but frantic whimpers escaped through her locked teeth. She did indeed soak down his tongue and his beard. She should've been ashamed but couldn't quite manage it.

"You come so sweet for me. Jesus Christ, I'll never get enough," was his only warning as he drove his tongue deeper, consuming relentlessly and perfectly. The low grunts of pleasure and the distinctively male scent filled her senses. His heavy forearms held her thighs apart, forcing her open for him, and the soft swirls of his tongue set her entire world on fire. There was nothing but him. It was so fully consuming, she tried to memorize the heat and the feeling, but found herself without the brain capacity to contain it all.

24

A crackle of possession shot through Smith's musculature. She was his. She had to always be his. Her flavors danced on his tongue. He'd only just tasted her, and he knew he'd never get enough.

Letting his fingers replace his tongue, he dragged them gently between her folds spreading her own heat and his saliva over her.

"Smith, please." Her head shook back and forth on his pillow. Her dark hair splayed across the white sheets. Utter ecstasy at his hands contorted her beautiful features.

"Please what, sweetheart? You trying to tell me you need more?"

"Yes," she whimpered. Sweet baby. So certain she wanted something that was going to hurt her no matter how much tenderness he managed to cling to. Those restless hips bucked all for him. Good. He wanted her so drunk on desire and on him that the pressure she required would quell the pain he would inevitably bring.

With delicate precision, he eased one finger inside of her and brought his mouth back to hers. "Taste your juices in my mouth. So damn good together." The tug-of-war in his mind was relentless. He constantly tried to remember that she was a virgin, and yet, he wanted to pound inside of her, claim every inch of her all for himself, with no reprieve. Neither side seemed willing to drop the rope. When one side managed a few inches, the other yanked back with equal force. Her protector dueled her corrupter, both housed deep inside his soul.

Not certain what she'd make of his letting the dirty talk loose, he hesitated for a split second. She looped her arms over his back and tried to pull him down on top of her. Okay, then. Worried he'd crush her, he managed to brace on the hand not currently tracking toward her G-spot, and devoured her mouth. Her pussy cinched so tightly around his finger, he could barely stroke. Damn, she was going to feel good on his cock.

"Relax for me, Mercy. Relax and let me open you."

At his urging, she tried. She spread her legs open further and writhed. He watched all of her luscious curves dance to the rhythm of his touch. It was the most beautiful thing he'd ever seen. Another rush of wet heat coated his hand, allowing him to bring her friction. When the rhythmic pulses he'd sought began, he cradled her head in one hand. "I love how small you are. Love that I can touch all of you. Most beautiful thing I've ever seen, having you in my hands. I need you to take a little more for me, baby. Just a little more."

"Please," she urged frantically. He added another finger, crossed one over the other, and felt her stretch to accommodate. If it was possible to die of pleasure, being inside of her was going to completely destroy him. He was fine with that. If this was the last thing he ever did, she was more than worth it.

And those thoughts fueled the beast housed inside of him. The beast he'd tried for years to keep at bay. The very beast he was certain if he freed with her, would not only bring her harm, but also terror. But she summoned it, sang for it, taunted it. Every harsh cry, every stuttered whimper, every whispered moan of his name had the beast pulling at the chains until they were taut against their shackles in the caverns of his soul. One gave way, snapping from the force of her desires.

A rumbled growl quaked from inside of him. "I'm the reason this tight little pussy gets wet, baby. Only me. I'm the one who keeps it satisfied because it belongs to me. All mine. Tell me you understand that."

Though she didn't give him the response he wanted, she did something even better. She shattered at his filthy words, like a detonated bomb screaming for him. Her fingernails clawed at his back. His name sang from her lips. Nothing would ever be as fulfilling as making her come.

As she crested at the height of pleasure and tumbled back toward the ground, he centered his cock at her pussy. His thighs pressed hers further open. The beast was busy licking his chops at the way she'd come for him, so Smith leaned hard into the sanity he needed to gain ground. "Tell me what you want, baby. Say it by name." This had to be entirely her choice.

"You," she whispered. "I want you."

"By name, sweetheart. Tell me."

Her brow furrowed and a quick shiver shot through her. It shook his resolve. Leaning further over her, needing her to understand that he would always stand between her and the world, he reached and dragged his cock against the tender folds of her pussy.

"Yes," she gasped. "Please. I want to see you inside of me. I want to..."

"What, baby?"

"To see you... enjoy me.

Holy fuck. He had asked for specifics. That wasn't precisely what he'd thought she'd say, but once again, it was so much better. She never did quite what he expected, and that only amped the ecstasy that pulsed in the very air surrounding them.

Damming the beast back to its cage with his own immeasurable strength, he swiped the head of his cock against her clit once more and then tucked inside of her less than an inch. When he met with resistance, he forced himself to stop and give her time to adjust. A rough groan vaulted from his mouth, however.

"More. I need more." She wiggled under him trying to draw him deeper. Smith wasn't certain if he was in heaven or hell.

"Are you sure you can take more, sweetheart? You're so damn

tight." He closed his eyes, reveling in the silky grip of her body surrounding his.

"Please." This time her movement lured him deeper without his permission.

"Fuck," grunted from him as he allowed her a little more. "I'm big, baby. I'm a big man, and my cock is no different. I don't want to hurt you, but it's going to."

Her hands cradled his face, forcing his gaze to her own. "The only way you could ever hurt me is by not giving me more. I want it all. I don't care if it hurts. Nothing could hurt as much as you not being inside of me right now."

Her body didn't quite agree with her mind. She didn't make entering her easy. She was cinched so tightly he only managed another inch, maybe two. He shook from the tightening ecstasy surrounding him. "Try to relax for me," he soothed. He had no idea where this patience had come from, but he was thankful he'd located it.

When she eased ever so slightly, he made it deep enough to thrust, but denied himself that as well. He grinded against her, ordering himself to remain deep until her body gave way.

When her hips lifted fractionally against him, he pressed to his hilt and shook, not just from the pleasure but from the shock. How could anything possibly feel so perfect? "So good, baby. God, you feel so damn good." Smith was certain he was somehow too big for his own skin. The armor of expectations he forced himself to live within shattered. She simply wasn't big enough for him to keep it locked around him anymore, and he would only ever want to be whoever she needed him to be.

He'd spent years becoming whatever he needed to be to accomplish the job. He'd worn every assigned mask, never questioned the missions. Years of pretending he wasn't the man he was. Years of existing only in his father's shadow. Years of denying himself, desperate to become something acceptable to the world.

Never before that moment had he ever stepped into his own timeline. Never had the two sides of himself, the savior and the sinner, the hero and the villain, aligned as one. Never had his dark desires been washed by the light. Never before her.

He took more, pressed deeper, withdrew by fractions and then sank further still, only so he could claim more of the redemption she offered. His demons met their conquering angel. He wrapped his arms around her and vowed to himself that somehow, some way he would forge a path for the two of them to be one forever.

25

The rough invasion tore the air from her lungs. Mercy decided that was an acceptable sacrifice. The pain and the pleasure seemed to separate into two distinct, yet peaceful, camps. With his every gentle thrust, the pleasure expanded its territory, and the pain willingly gave way.

She swore the erotic rhythm of them moving together wrote itself on her soul. How would she ever exist without this? She couldn't. The frantic beating of her heart insisted he fill her to overflowing. She melted around him. Her softness was pliant under his strength, like the gentle snap of two pieces that fit together. There was so much more about him she needed to know, so much she needed to tell him, but there was far too much of him for the doubts to continue to exist. He took up her entire world and loomed so large over her she should have been intimidated, but it was another thing she required to go on.

When he leaned up, removing the firm press of his chest against hers, she started to protest, but then his roving fingers found her clit again. With tender care, he spread her further, allowing every thrust to stroke her there, as well. Her protest turned to whimpers of ecstasy.

"Can you come again for me, baby? Can you come on my cock this first time?"

This question was different. He didn't seem to know if she was capable. Until he began stroking tenderly against her, she wasn't certain she could. The pain was still there. She focused only on the bliss in his dark eyes, the rough shudders of his body, the restrained male groans that vibrated through her.

Her breath stuttered in her lungs.

"That's it, sweetheart. Give yourself to it. Just let it go. I'll be right behind you. Gonna fill you full of me. Soak down your walls," he grunted, "so you know who you belong to."

And with those words, that dirty reassurance that he didn't want this to end either, she crested the mountain once again and flung herself off, certain he would catch her, certain he would keep her safe.

Every muscle in his massive body tensed. He cursed. His eyes squeezed shut. He shook against her and did indeed fill her full.

He showered kisses over her cheek and kept her tucked tight against his form. His hands soothed and nurtured her constantly. "Let me give you a bath." He sounded almost desperate to do that very thing. Sleepy satisfaction perforated his already deep voice. She wondered if he said her name in that same tone if she couldn't orgasm from that alone.

She grinned. "Why?"

"It'll help."

"But then I have to move, and I don't think I ever want to get up."

She could hear the smile in his response. "I love hearing that. How about if I get in with you? Assuming the bathtub is big enough for me, which most aren't."

Exhaustion and satisfaction sated Mercy, but there was that annoying burning sensation between her legs. She felt a little like she might've been rubbed raw. But neither of those things were as pressing as the questions she had.

"If I let you give me a bath, will you promise to be honest with me?"

"About what, baby doll?"

"I just need to ask you some things."

"Okay," more kisses on her shoulder and neck, "ask me."

"Um... well, when you've... you know... done that before does it..."

"Does it what?" He leaned up on his elbow and studied her. Concern darkened his gaze.

"Always feel like that for you?"

"No. And I swear to you I'm not just telling you that. That was incredible. *You* are incredible."

Delight filled her, not quite as thoroughly as he had, but almost. "Really?"

He nodded. "I promise. When my sister married Griff, Voodoo told me that the universe knows when two people are made to wreck the world together. I didn't believe him. Not until now."

That did it. Despite the protest of movement from between her thighs, she turned and wrapped her arms as far around him as she could manage and squeezed. "Wow."

"Yeah, wow." He leaned back and sank his lips to hers in another one of those drugging kisses. She patted his shoulder when she required breath. "Sorry." His cringe made her giggle.

"Do you think my butt is too big?" She had no idea why she'd asked that. Surely, she didn't actually want to hear his answer, but in all of the things his force had stripped from her one of them had been her inhibitions. He'd promised to be honest, and she wanted an answer.

His brow creased. "What?" She couldn't say it again. What if he was just stalling, anyway? He rolled his eyes. "The only thing I think about your fucking gorgeous ass is that I can't wait to spank it, both when I'm deep inside of you and when you ask me things like that."

"So, when you tell me I'm beautiful, you actually mean that?"

"Yes, when I tell you that you're beautiful, I mean it." There was an odd change in his voice at that declaration. He didn't sound like he was lying, but something had shifted inside of him. He eased down on his back and drew her up onto his chest. Her head rose and fell with the waves of his breathing. It soothed her. She reveled in the slight tickle of his chest hair against her cheek and the rhythmic pound of his heartbeat. "You know when you asked me what happened to my arm?"

"Yes. Are you really going to tell me?'

"Yeah, just let me get through it. It goes along with what Voodoo said to you last night about knowing what it feels like to be the survivor when part of you will always wish you'd been the one to go instead." She brushed a kiss over one of the grooved scars on his shoulder, wishing that small act could really heal whatever he was about to share. She knew it wouldn't, but she had to try. "Anyway, the day I got those, our team was attacked by some men we'd been working with. I was climbing down out of the vehicle and took multiple rounds in my arm. They thought I was dead when I went down, and that ultimately saved my life. Over half of our team didn't make it."

"I'm so sorry." Her tone reflected the break in her heart at his story.

He gave a haggard nod. "Yeah. Me too. But I'm telling you this because I know what it means to know someone is going to be there no matter what. So, you asking me if I really think you're beautiful, it just doesn't make any sense to me. I'm falling for you fast, baby. I'm falling for all of you, not just your gorgeous body, or brilliant mind. Everything about you fascinates me and turns me on. I can try to stop it, but let's not pretend that this thing between us is going to follow normal cause and effect functions, like some program we write, because it doesn't. I know what it means to have the weight of your hand inside mine, and sweetheart, that is the only weight I ever want you to worry about. Your curves drive me wild. I'm pretty sure I just showed you that. The world is so fucking hard. Is it wrong that I love how soft you are? Even if it is, it doesn't change the fact that I do."

Mercy leaned up so she could stare down into his eyes. "It's not wrong at all. I love how safe I feel when I'm with you. I love how strong you are. I don't see how that's any different than you liking that I'm softer. Let's see if we can't wreck the world together."

The pain in his eyes altered but never left. He gave her a haggard nod like there was something he wished he could say but didn't allow himself. "Sounds like a plan."

26

His cell phone's frantic vibration against the bedside table sounded entirely too much like mortar fire in the distance for him to have ignored it, no matter how well he'd been sleeping.

Keeping Mercy cradled to him, he shut the damn thing down but not before he saw the caller's name. *Roman.* He squeezed his eyes shut, trying to wish the phone call away, but that wasn't going to work. How could he have said the things he'd said to her the night before? How could he have done the things he did? My God, when the truth finally unraveled about why they'd even met, she would hate him forever. He was nothing but a liar. Why would she ever believe his vows about how attracted he was to her, how he wanted to remain with her, to wreck the world together or whatever it was that had spewed out of his mouth? She'd stripped him of everything but the absolute truth, but how would he ever be able to prove that to her?

No matter what Roman wanted, Smith was certain it was only going to bring about the end of this relationship faster, and he just couldn't allow that. It was cruel. It would finish what the M-4 in Iraq hadn't been able to. That would be the brutal blow that he wouldn't be able to survive.

He brushed a kiss in her hair and stared down at her as she slept soundly tucked in his arms. So small, so sweet, so unaware of what was inevitably going to destroy everything he'd fought to build the night before.

But the phone calls wouldn't give him peace. The next buzz was somehow even more urgent. *T-Byrd* glowed on the screen. It was one thing to ignore Roman. He'd been Team Seven's CIA op back in the day, but he wasn't a part of the team that would always mean more to Smith than most anything else. *They don't mean as much as she does.* His mind didn't have to remind him. He already knew, but he still wasn't going to just ignore T.

Easing away from her, he answered the phone with a gruff, "I'll call you later."

"We have to talk now."

"In a minute." He ended the call and pulled on a T-shirt and a pair of jeans. Stepping into his boots, he leaned and brushed another kiss on her temple and made certain she was tucked in and warm, before he marched out of the room. He didn't stop until he'd exited the house and made it to the fence line. A volatile combination of dread and guilt slithered under his skin. Cursing the earth itself, he returned T's call. He was certain liars, sinners, and men who spoke the way he'd spoken to a virgin the night before didn't get their prayers answered, but he made a breathless plea anyway. Just give him a little more time to figure out how to explain himself and some way for her to understand he'd only ever wanted to protect her.

T's chuckle was the first thing he heard. "Called Voodoo first and found out he was no longer staying with you. I guess things are working out just the way you wanted."

Smith rolled his eyes. T hadn't gotten it yet. There was a death date already stamped on their brand-new relationship. "How's Maddie?" He wasn't discussing Mercy with anyone, not even one of the men he'd walked straight through hell with on numerous occasions.

"She can't see her feet. Her belly arrives in the room about five minutes before the rest of her. She swears the baby's sitting right on top of her bladder, but as far as I'm concerned, she's never been more perfect. How are you?"

"I've been in this game long enough to know that the answer to your question depends on what you're about to tell me."

An audible breath reached Smith's ears from six hours due north. "Roman made a deal, and you're not gonna like it, especially if what Voodoo says is right."

Whatever the deal was, Smith didn't want to know, so he asked the more palatable question. "What did Voodoo say?"

"That you'd already fallen for her before you ever took her to bed last night. That she's the one."

The concept that someone else saw it as well should've sutured some of the gaping wounds tearing through him, but all it did was douse the gashes in vinegar. "What makes him so sure of that?"

"I don't know how he does it, but he always knows. I figure the guy has seen enough death to know when life is going to come through for us."

Smith shook his head, trying to combat the words that staged mutiny on his tongue, but it didn't work. "Even if he's right, it's not going to matter. I've been lying to her the whole fucking time."

"You've lied to her to keep her safe. That has to count for something."

"It doesn't have to. It's not going to, so go on with this deal of Roman's. I'm listening."

"It counts, man, just trust me on that." He sighed. "You're going to have to bring her to Dallas to attend a dinner... with the Castellas cartel and several other key cartels in the Mexican drug trade."

Outrage shook the phone from his grasp. Gall ignited deep in his gut. He stared at the vile thing on the ground before bringing it back to his ear. "If you think I'm doing that, you're out of your fucking mind."

"I knew you were going to say that, but listen to me. It's a deal. There are two sides to this. If we agree, the FBI will stop pursuing

Mercy, and I'm saying *we* because you know all of Tier Seven will be there to keep her safe. The feds have been digging. A few of her hack jobs were slightly south of legal. If we don't do this, they'll never give her peace. They'll keep pushing until they have her in prison. Then they'll parade her in front of the media for the trial as long as it takes, until they lure the Castellas hitmen out of their lair. You and I both know her brother would rather her be dead then talking to the feds. We'll all be there. You know we would never let anyone hurt her."

Pure hatred seared from his gut to his throat and lodged there. He couldn't even speak. He was certain he was going to vomit. How was he supposed to put her in danger like this?

And how could he not? T was right. This was the only way out for her, and the way out meant placing a pistol to his own head. Once she figured out how deep his lies went, she'd refuse to be anywhere near him. He'd no longer be able to protect her. This was the only way he could make certain she was safe while he remained at a distance. Devastation would meet him at the end. Without her, he had no interest in going on anyway. "When?" The one word cost him his next breath. He couldn't say more. The throat-punch of a deal wouldn't allow it.

"Friday night. Roman will play the part of host. He's spreading it through the embedded agents that he has the designs, and that they'll be auctioned off to the highest bidder at the end of the dinner. She'll need to play the part of the hacker who got the designs. The FBI believes if she's there, the Castellas will report back to Julian that she's working for a different family. They're hoping to confuse him enough to draw him out. They also want information on Wakefield, and hope to gain that at the event. It's semi-formal. She'll need a dress, and you'll need a nice suit. This has to look as legit as we can make it. Feds will be able to arrest anyone who offers up either a job or money for the designs at the end of the night. By then, you'll have Mercy far away from the hell that will rain down. I promise you, nothing will happen to her. You have my word."

Smith couldn't quite make out T's vow over the roar of fury in his head. How could he? And how could he not? The questions battered and beat him constantly. "I... can't." There. That's what he'd been trying to say for the last five minutes.

"I don't think we get to decide that."

"You wouldn't..." he tried again.

"If Maddie had done even half of what Mercy has and it meant keeping my baby out of a federal prison, I think I would. Especially if I knew all of Tier Seven would be there to make sure not a single hair on her head was moved out of place. I don't think I'd have any other choice."

He could've stalled longer. He could've asked how he was supposed to go about this since she had no idea her brother was working for the mob. There wasn't any situation anywhere that T-Byrd couldn't plan his way out of. But Smith didn't need to ask the questions, because he already had the answers.

Special Forces training made the decisions for him. For every scenario, there was the known and the unknown. Use the known to nullify the unknown. He already knew how to motivate her. He had to provide her just enough information that she would craft her own story, just like she'd done with everything else. He needed her to arrive at the idea that Julian was in danger, and this might save him. Her brother was the carrot. Until Smith proved otherwise, Julian always would be. And when Smith showed her the truth, it would be him and not her brother that she'd hate.

He already knew what he had to do, and every muscle in his massive body hated it with everything he was or ever would be.

27

Smith stared at the door to the safe house, certain when he crossed the threshold his entire life would disintegrate. He couldn't do it. He couldn't walk in there and tell her that he was going to take her to Dallas and expose her to men who would all be out for her blood.

The puff of dirt from the boots of the approaching cowboy shook Smith from his reverie. He had no idea how long he'd been standing there staring at that door, willing the earth to swallow him whole.

"You look like somebody just up and sold your saddle out from underneath ya, son. You okay?" The man offered his hand. "I'm Wyn Holder, by the way. I think we met once before, but it's been a while. I'm Maddox's daddy."

Still clinging to the edge of his own sanity, Smith only managed a nod and a, "Sir."

"Have a seat," Wyn pointed to the fence. "I've raised enough kids and enough cattle to know when something's bad wrong."

Before Smith could mentally agree to having a conversation with anyone about this, the words started to spill from his lips, "This is why everyone says never mix business with pleasure." That in no way explained anything, but it made sense to him at that moment.

Mr. Holder shook his head. "Now, I've never believed that was good advice. I happen to take pleasure in riding my horse, so I went into the business of horse riding, so to speak. Seems to me we ought to always take pleasure in our business. Makes our time on earth a whole lot more pleasant. But that ain't what you wanted to hear."

Smith turned to study the gentleman. "Have you ever had to do something you were fairly certain was going to kill you?"

A low whistle slipped between Wyn's teeth. "You know, my boys only get real dramatic like that when there's a woman involved. I'm guessing the sweet girl you're keeping safe on my ranch has something to do with this. Anything I can do to help you survive whatever it is you're so certain is going to be the death of you?"

"I've been lying to her ever since I met her. And now..."

"You've gone and fallen in love with her."

Smith's head fell in a nod. "I think so."

"Maddox said you didn't actually meet her until you were rescuing her though?"

"Yes, sir. She threw up on me, and it sort of went from there."

Wyn laughed heartily over their first interaction, but the circumstances kept Smith from joining in.

"I'd say if that's how you met and you're this sick over her, then it's definitely love." Wyn paused for a moment. "All right, so you lied to her. Any chance you could come clean now? From my experience, the best thing to do when you're in a hole is to stop digging."

"I can't. I lied to her to keep her safe, and if I tell her the truth, she'll leave, and I can't have that until I know she'll be safe without me. The FBI isn't going to leave her alone unless I take her to this thing in Dallas. I don't have a choice." He forced the words from the ashes in his throat.

Wyn nodded. "My great-granddaddy used to say not to take a saw to the branch that's holding you up, unless you're about to hang from it. Given what Maddox has told me about your mission and the look on your face, I'd say it might be your girl who's going to swing and you're the only one with a saw. Far be it for me to correct you, but if you need to keep lying to keep her safe, that has to be worth something in her book. And if it ain't, maybe this isn't quite as meant to be as you seem to think it is."

Mercy had been so fervent about their budding relationship the night before that Wyn's words took root in Smith's mind. He just had to prove to her that he'd only lied to keep her safe. He had to vow that he'd never lie to her again. He had to prove himself over and over again. He could do that. He just needed to believe he'd get a chance. "Thank you, sir," he offered the man his hand. "I think you might be right."

Wyn gave him another kind grin. "I wish you luck, son. Love ain't ever easy, but it is worth it, and you're welcome. My own kids get sick of listening to me telling 'em what they should do. It's nice to be appreciated. If it helps, Liz says there's something to the two of you. Never tell her I said this, but the woman is never wrong."

Smith had done an immeasurable number of difficult things in his life. He'd find a way to make this work.

MERCY REFUSED to open her eyes as she stretched her arms out against the warm indentation of Smith's sheets. The whole bed smelled like him. Turning her head, she pressed her face to the dent in his pillow and inhaled. The only way this would've been more perfect is if he'd still been in bed with her. She wondered where he'd gone. When she turned on her side, she was pleased to discover that evidence of his possession from the night before still twinged between her legs. She hoped she would feel it and remember every delicious moment until it happened again. And she hoped that was soon.

The longer he stayed away the more reality crept in. Smith seemed to be the only person who could keep it away from her. Testing her legs, she stood and took inventory of her body. It did hurt to walk a little. When she recalled his request that he be able to fix it if she was in pain, she grinned. He needed to come back. Now.

After she winced her way out of the bathroom, she pulled on one of his T-shirts and went after her laptop. Still nothing from Julian. She couldn't quite decide if that was good or bad. She also had no idea how to proceed with Smith. Where did they go from this safe house? They couldn't stay there forever, no matter how much she wished they could.

Before more questions could batter her psyche, he entered the bedroom again. His form took up the entire doorway, and she grinned. Nothing could ever make it through the wall he created, and that delighted her. But when her eyes made it all the way up to his, her delight faded. "What's wrong?"

He shook his head. There was a grave sadness locked in his gaze. "I have to tell you something that I don't want to say."

Her heart sped, and her mouth went dry. She wasn't ready for whatever had made him look that way. She wasn't certain she would ever be ready to hear whatever he'd come to say. "What is it?" Her own voice was distanced and tunneled like she might not even be in the room currently.

He settled next to her on the bed and took her hand. "The FBI has offered you a deal."

Her head moved in a mechanical nod. "What does that mean... exactly?" If the FBI was no longer going to be after her, did that mean that she went back to Kansas City and he went back to wherever he lived? How did she not know where he lived? Panic seized her empty stomach and filled it with dread.

"Hey, it's okay." He lifted her up into his arms and cradled her in his lap. "I would never let anything happen to you."

She remembered him saying something about the way the DEA would get the FBI to stop following her. She'd have to do something for them. "Can you please just tell me what the deal is because I'm losing my mind. What do they want me to do?"

"They want you to attend a dinner down in Dallas on Friday night."

Of all the things she thought he might tell her they wanted her to do, going to a dinner wasn't one of them. "What?"

"They want you and me to attend a fancy dinner with the people who tried to steal the designs. Do you remember when you figured out that it wasn't just the FBI who was after them?"

"Okay, so who are these people, and why would the FBI want me to meet them?" When he didn't respond, she placed both of her hands on either side of his face and forced him to look her in the eye. "Who are they?"

"It's a drug cartel. Their compound is in Fort Worth. The supply line is out of Colombia. It comes up through Mexico. If you agree to the dinner, the FBI will stop pursuing you."

"What am I supposed to do at this dinner? I don't understand. If Julian got caught up with some Colombian drug cartel, then this has to have something to do with him. What if he's in danger? Oh my gosh. I thought maybe he was working for the DEA or something, but he isn't, is he? He wanted to sell the designs to the highest bidder, and now he's in trouble."

28

Like a lamb to the slaughter, he led her right where he'd needed her to be. Self-hatred drilled into him from all sides. He couldn't tell her until after the dinner. She had to rely on him to remain alive. Closing his eyes, he forced Wyn Holder's words to the forefront of his mind to keep from collapsing over her and begging her forgiveness.

He was doing this to keep her safe. That was worth something. It had to be. He had to keep going. "They're planning to let a few key capos from other cartels know that they have the designs. Having you there legitimizes it. They'll tell people you were successful in stealing them. The people attending won't know that most of the attendees are either FBI or DEA. All of the company I work for will be there, along with me, to keep you safe. It's entirely up to you, baby, but if you don't agree, they have no reason not to pursue federal charges against you."

"I have to do whatever it takes to rescue my brother. I've always looked out for him. The last thing my mom said to me was to take care of Julian, and I've clearly done a terrible job of that."

"Stop," Smith soothed. "You haven't done a terrible job of

anything. You're the one in trouble, not Julian, but we're going to get you out of it. I won't stop until I know you're safe. Ever."

The shimmer of sunlight from the windows danced in her eyes at his vow. But her bottom lip found its way back between her teeth. Remembering how to maintain your role even when the hounds of hell were at your heels was another part of his training. "Hey, biting that lip is my job. What's my girl so worried about?" Playing the part of the man who adored her wasn't even difficult. Because it wasn't some part or some role he'd been assigned. It wasn't a mask handed to him to fit under his helmet. It was who he was.

She stared up at him. "I'm not worried about the dinner. I'm really not. You'll be there, and I've spent most of my adult life pretending to be a lot more badass than I feel, at least online. I can do that if it's to help Julian. I'd do anything for him. I was just thinking about what happens to us once the FBI isn't looking for me."

He'd known that was coming. Leaning down, he planted a kiss on her head. "What do you want to happen with us, sweetheart?"

Her brow furrowed, and she shook her head. "If I answer that, you'll think I'm one of those girls that celebrates one-week anniversaries and goes through your phone every day or something else ridiculous."

He shook his head. A grin formed on his features at the heat blooming across hers. "That sounds a little like a high school version of a real relationship. If you want to go through my phone, say the word, but I'd like to think I'm the kind of guy you'd trust more than that. As for the weekly anniversaries, if I get to spend those weeks with you, I'm fine celebrating them. Sounds like heaven to me."

God, she just had the most beautiful smile, especially when her eyes got in on the game. They lit up with thrill, and her cheeks lifted right along with his weary heart. "Are you serious? You'd want us to date. I mean... you'd be okay with that? I don't think I've had a boyfriend since someone asked me to check a box on a note they stuck in my desk."

His chuckle came easier this time. "I'd probably write it in code with some kind of functionality where your computer shuts down if you say no, but if you want to check a box, I'll make that happen, too."

"That's a little devious." She laughed.

"Yeah, well, maybe I'm tired of not going after what I want."

"Maybe I am, too."

"Then let's do this, for as long as you don't hate me." Damn, where had that come from? The excitement over their agreement was too distracting. The mask had almost slipped.

"I would never hate you. Why would you say that?"

Because he knew how this story ended. He shook off the inevitability of their ending once again. The lies had to count for something. Calling himself a bastard, he refused to answer and sank his lips to hers to indulge in her flavors instead. When she parted for his questing tongue, a hungry grunt escaped his lungs. She tasted like everything good in the world, but more than that he wanted to absorb the future he was certain he wasn't going to have. Torturing himself seemed appropriate, and indulging in her, but knowing ultimately this would all blow up in his face, was like swallowing liquid fire. He reveled in the burn.

When she finally pulled away, he let himself memorize the hunger in her eyes and the way her breasts swayed with her shallow gasps of breath. "I don't even know where you live."

He considered that. "I guess we didn't exactly go about this in the normal order. I live in Lincoln, so only three hours from Kansas City."

She made an effort to conceal her disappointment but ultimately didn't succeed. "Three hours seems like a long way, but you have a job up there and family and everything, I guess."

"Yeah, I'm tied to Lincoln. You might like it up there. How do you feel about cornfields as far as you can see in any direction?"

Her chuckle was worth the lame joke. "I'm not opposed to cornfields." She crawled up on her knees and wrapped her arms around his shoulders. "Especially if you're in them."

He latched his hand on her full, feminine ass and squeezed. "Are you saying you might think about moving to Lincoln? I'm not sure you're going to want to go back to your apartment anyway."

She laid her head on his substantial shoulder and gave him a contented sigh he'd spend the rest of his life trying to earn. "I don't know if I can move. I've always lived in Missouri. But maybe. That seems like a huge step."

"I tend to take big steps, sweetheart. Comes with being a big man."

"Then I'll try to catch up."

"You don't have to. I'll wait for you if that's what you want, and I'll carry you when that's what you need."

29

"I feel a little like Julia Roberts in *Pretty Woman*," Mercy exclaimed as she and Smith made their way to the Macy's dressing rooms. It was so bizarre to be shopping at the expense of the FBI, especially so she could attend a dinner with the mob. The extent of her knowledge of organized crime came from watching the Corleone family in *The Godfather II* when she'd had the flu a few years before and had felt too awful to change the channel.

How had her brother even found these people? Smith's job was to keep her safe at this dinner, but her job had to be to figure out where her brother was and how to help him get away from the cartels. Maybe he needed to meet a woman. Surely, if he felt about some girl the way she felt about Smith, money wouldn't be so important to him.

Smith's chuckle ripped her back from her mental planning session. "I really do not want to play Richard Gere as a John in this scenario."

"I used to think of myself that way."

"In what way?" He looked and sounded utterly confused.

"You know..." she glanced around to make sure no one was near enough to overhear them.

"As a hooker?" he gasped. "You were a..." he cut off the word virgin unnecessarily.

"I know, I know. But I pretended to be the sexy kiss of death when I hacked, and in real life I... well, I didn't know what to do with men at all." She lowered her voice and gestured to his crotch. "In that movie, I always kind of thought that Julia Roberts's character didn't really know how to do what she was trying to do either. She needed the money, so she did what she had to do. I love that movie, by the way."

He shook his head at her from behind the stack of cocktail dresses he was carrying on her behalf. "Someday I'm going to prove to you that you don't have to be one or the other. You can just be you, baby."

That same zing of thrill danced in her belly. It had been her constant companion the past few days. "I'm trying, but I've enjoyed *not* being a virgin," she mouthed the word, "very much."

That earned her one of his sexy grunts. She loved it when he did that. For a girl who stayed home as often as she could, it was distinctly odd to be out at a mall, especially since she was still technically in trouble with the FBI. They'd reached an agreement with Tier Seven that she could go shopping as long as they kept an eye on her. There were two guys in suits sitting in the waiting area with Voodoo.

"I'm her bodyguard. I'm going in with her," Smith informed the sales clerk stationed at the dressing rooms. Mercy tried to determine how she felt about that. He'd seen her naked plenty of times in the past few days, but this wasn't how she'd envisioned a day of dress shopping. Seeing herself in dressing-room mirrors was bad enough. Now she had to do that with him. She cringed at the thought, but she knew better than to argue. That stubborn determination she found so intoxicating rolled off of him in waves.

"Uh, I suppose that's all right," the clerk didn't sound too certain, but Smith pushed past her.

"Thanks," he added to soften the blow, Mercy assumed.

Once he had her locked in the dressing room, it was far less strange. When it was just the two of them together, everything made sense. "I think you scared that lady," she whispered.

"Good." He winked at her. "I wasn't taking no for an answer, and confidence will get you everywhere."

"I wouldn't know." She whipped the T-shirt over her head, and fought not to dance at the obvious delight that set in his eyes. Delight was never something she'd experienced in a dressing room before.

"Along with keeping you safe and keeping you mine, another one of my personal missions is to show you how brilliant and beautiful you are. I have no clue why you're not more confident. You're irresistible."

She popped the snap on her jeans, and his left eyebrow lifted in intrigue, making her beam. "I don't mind those being your missions. I plan to keep you being mine, as well."

"Good. Having the same goal makes it easier for both of us. Now, keep going."

She scooted the jeans down far enough to reveal her bare bottom and pussy. This time his grunt was even better. "You forget something, baby doll?"

Embarrassment and exhilaration fought for dominance in her bloodstream. Life itself filled her lungs. Those feelings were some of the many things she'd lost the day her mother had died. She'd gone on for two years unable to reclaim them. She wondered if she'd ever be able to thank him enough for the restoration he'd done to her soul. She wasn't even terribly annoyed with Julian for his stupidity. If he hadn't done this with the designs, she never would've met Smith.

Certain her cheeks were going to catch fire if they heated any more, she laughed. "Well, see, you had your whole backpack packed when you came into the coffee shop the other day. I had no idea my entire life was about to change, and I don't just keep spare pairs of panties in my laptop bag. So, I haven't had any to wear in a while. I'm going to get some while we're here."

He licked his lips, looking every part of the big, bad wolf, and she wanted nothing more than to be devoured. "Do you have any idea what it does to me to know that you've been walking around on that ranch for days now bare under those jeans of yours? I thought you were just coming to bed that way."

Her pulse quivered and then flew. The thundered pounding centered at her core. She'd never had any idea how to flirt, but with Smith she said and did things she never would've done before. She gave him an exaggerated seductive glare as she slipped on the first dress, a deep purple number with a flared skirt. "If you're saying you like me without panties, I guess wearing them is negotiable."

"Is it, baby?" Suddenly, he was off the bench and towering over her. That rush of intimidation spiked in her pulse and pure unadulterated lust ignited inside of her. Her nipples throbbed out their needy obedience, and a flood of wet heat coated her lower lips. Bracing himself against the wall on his forearm, he caged her in and traced the angles of her face with his rough fingertips. Her breath stuttered as it tried to make it out of her lungs. "Look at me," he growled in her ear. *Gladly.* She lifted her head. "It is not negotiable." His hot breath cascaded from her ear to her bare shoulder. She shivered, giving an odd response to the heat, but not the need. "Who makes your pussy wet?"

"You do," she answered in a breathless plea. Her body swayed between him and the wall, two entirely immoveable forces.

"That's right. I do. And I fill it full. It belongs to me. Might make me a possessive asshole, but I want to be the one who yanks your panties down your legs or the one who pushes the crotch aside, so I can have what belongs only to me. Make a deal with me."

"Anything." He could have asked her to remain naked and at his disposal for the rest of her life and at that moment she would've agreed, just to see what he'd do next.

"You keep that sweet little pussy all for me, and I'll always keep it satisfied."

For the past two days, Mercy had been trying to practice being the kiss of death, some kind of femme fatale, instead of being her awkward, still somewhat innocent self. She assumed she'd need to have it perfected for the dinner. That thought fought its way through

the haze of lust swamping her mind, but she shoved it away by
staring into Smith's greedy gaze.

Having sex in a department store dressing room seemed like the
kind of thing her alter ego would do. She wanted to live out an experience that would cement the two halves of her life, even more than
Smith already had.

Summoning every wile of her femininity that had been awakened
at his touch, she licked her lips. His responding groan brought her
hunger to fever pitch. Every harsh breath brought his distinct male
scent to her lungs. "It's feeling a little unsatisfied right now." Her
whisper was so low she wasn't certain he'd heard her. She'd intended
to come off as flirtatious but assumed she'd missed the mark. How
did other women have this down so well? Frustration mounted
behind the fear that she would never be able to convince the mob
that she was some kind of hacker vamp who wasn't afraid of
anything.

But just like every time before, when the terror began to bubble in
her belly and extend its claws to enclose her throat, he was right there
to scare away the demons. His right hand slid deftly under the loosened skirt of the dress. "I know what you need, baby. Your sweet little
pussy needs to be reminded of who keeps it happy, doesn't it? Can
you be quiet for me?"

Though she wanted to scream the word 'yes' from the Macy's
rooftop, she settled for a silent nod.

Crinoline grazed against her thighs as his hand sought the heat
gathering between her legs. She sank her teeth into her bottom lip to
silence the moan building in her chest. Her legs spread insistently,
trying to draw him closer still. Thick fingers teased at her slit, just
enough to frustrate. He spread the liquid invitation her body
extended him up and back, over and over.

She let herself get lost in the rough touch, in his corded forearms
covered in hair, and the intensity in his eyes as he watched the effects
he had on her body.

Like he'd held her hands to a live wire, she shook with her own
need. He circled her clit once, twice. His voice was nothing more than

a guttural growl. "Your swollen virgin clit is still confused, isn't it, baby? It doesn't quite understand what it needs, but I know." His heavy breath ran her internal thermometer up to blazing inferno, alerting her to his own need. "I know when you need to be laid out under me, fucked slow and easy, until you're sobbing for your maker, who'll have to wait until I'm finished with you, to save you. And I know when my sweet, innocent baby needs to be my vixen, smart as a whip and twice as lethal. I know when you're parading around in front of other men without your panties that what you really need is for me to take good care of that pussy and remind you who it belongs to. And I know when you're begging to be finger-fucked in a dressing room that what you really want is to know that I'll never let you go unsatisfied. When you get hot and wet thinking about me, all you have to do is tell me, sweetheart. I'll always take good care of you." With that, he dipped two fingers deep inside her, hard and fast. Her body cinched around them and drew them deeper. She needed more. Needed him to drown out everything else in the world.

She was certain her next gasped breaths were entirely dependent on him never removing his fingers from her. *More. Almost. Please.* Her body tried to beg on behalf of her mouth, since he had his free hand covering her lips. Swiveling her hips in an effort to ride his hand only served to make him lean into her, so she couldn't move at all. The dominant possession he took of her body rode her hard enough to almost bring her to climax. It was right there, and he was keeping it from her. She was certain he knew what he was doing. That knowledge only made her wetter.

A wicked, greedy grin formed on his features when her eyes fluttered open to beg him for more. "It's not enough, is it, honey? Not enough friction, not enough force for my girl." She shook her head and a whimper escaped the tight lock on her lips. "I know you want more. But see, this is my apology. I'm going to take my time, be nice and gentle with you." He did indeed rotate his thumb around her overly-sensitive bundle of raw nerve endings with more tenderness than a man his size should be able to summon. His fingers eased in and out of her, never quite giving her the force she craved.

Every nerve in her body began to converge in her core. The constant pulses of need in her pussy were off rhythm with her heart. Woozy with a hunger she had no hopes of understanding, she decided she just didn't care. He understood every single desire hidden deep in the dark recesses of her soul, even those she was ashamed to own. He brought them into the light, shattered her shame, and gave them life. That was all she needed.

"That's a good girl. You're gonna let it come for me nice and slow even though you know you need more. Want to know why this is an apology, baby?"

She managed to nod, although her head also shook back and forth so she had no idea what he was actually seeing from one second to the next.

A low curse hummed in her ear. His voice grew choppy from his own need. "I'm trying to be gentle now, because of how hard I'm going to fuck you when I get you back to the ranch. I've tried to take it easy with you. God, I tried. I swear, but you're too damn much... just too damn beautiful. I can't do it anymore. I need it. I'm going to lean you over that bed, shove your head down against that mattress, prop your ass up in the air all for me, and make sure you feel my sac slap hard against it every time I pound into you. So be ready."

Her body began its telltale spasms at the tantalizing promises he'd provided.

30

The vibration Smith had come to anticipate strummed through her body. He recognized it because the rhythm matched his own, one he hadn't been aware existed before her. She was threaded through him. He was unable to separate her wants from his need to provide them. She was the light and the dark, the innocent and the corrupt, the grey line that ran imperceptibly between the white and the black. She was his. And he was inextricably woven to her. If he tried to separate the man he'd been from the man he was with her, he would have to tear himself into pieces.

Somehow, she didn't yet understand that the climax to his every wet dream was a good woman with a distinctly naughty side that wanted to be cultivated. He'd make her understand. When this dinner was over, when she was free of the FBI and the cartel, he'd find a way to prove to her that Julian wasn't worth her worry.

Smith of all people knew life wasn't fair. The way the universe determined what stays and what is torn away was never based on someone's worth or goodness. How had someone as good as Mercy ended up with a father like Armend Castellas or a brother like Julian? How had half of his team, all decent men and relentless soldiers, been killed while following orders on their assigned mission?

How was Smith supposed to usher Mercy inside the lion's den and not lose his mind? None of it would ever compute. His father's words echoed against his skull. *Life will never be fair. Either play the hand you're dealt or reshuffle the deck.*

But when he had her like this, the stronghold of panic gave way to something he understood. After the dinner, he'd find a way to make his present extend into the future. Determination rooted him, not to the cheap carpeting of the department store dressing room, but to her. This would not be over.

He watched her body sway and toss in the dressing room mirrors. The effect had his balls so high and tight he swore he was choking on them, and he was still fully clothed. The Mercy effect. He knew. His cock was an iron spike tearing at the zipper of his jeans, like a prisoner at the gates. He released her mouth, and cradled her to him. He needed to feel her shake against him. When her teeth raked along his shirt and her hands gripped the cloth, searching for an anchor, what little blood remained in his mind rushed to his cock as she found the anchor in him. He would never let her down. He just had to teach her that. "Come on, baby, let me have it. You're right there."

Just like always, she fell apart in ragged spasms and gasps of satisfaction. Her pent-up need saturated his fingers. Watching her come apart surged pre-cum to his tip in desperate anticipation of unloading deep inside of her. She needed to pick out a damned dress. If he didn't get her back in his bed soon, he was going to press her up against the wall, wrap her legs around his waist, and sink himself so deep inside of her she'd feel him coming for days.

Heat streaked under the low neckline of the dress he'd shoved upward to reveal her all for himself. She quivered in his arms. He eased his fingers from her and wrapped her up against him. Her constant ballast in the storm. "I've got you, baby. Does that feel better now?"

She seemed to float back down to reality by degrees. That was fine by him. Keeping her flying had become the driving force in his life. When her eyes finally opened, she grinned. Mercy, with swollen lips and a just-been-sexed flush, was one of the most beautiful things he'd ever seen. If he could just keep her satisfied, maybe everything would really work out. That was another lie he'd been telling himself the past few days. He'd said it so often he almost believed it.

"So, does all of that mean you like this dress?" she giggled.

"I like you in anything you're wearing. I'm particularly partial to one of my T-shirts." He winked at her.

"I don't think I can wear that to the dinner."

That prompted yet another reminder he hated about this entire deal. "Roman said you needed to wear something relatively revealing. It plays to your alter ego."

She wrinkled her nose. "Do you think that's all it will ever be? That it's just a role I got good at playing online, and I won't ever be able to be some kind of sexy vamp, even for you?" Disappointment weighted every word.

"Hey." He lifted her chin so she had nowhere to look but into his eyes. "You do not ever have to be anything for me, except whichever version of yourself you want to be. Part of my job when I was in SF was to occasionally tell our enemies that I was someone other than who I am. Every time I took on another role I had to find some part of myself inside the mask I was wearing. We all have an endless number of selves, baby, and I've fallen for every single one of yours. Nothing is going to change that. You be whoever you need to be. I'll learn how to indulge every side. You seem to think you have to be only one version of yourself, one thing or the other." He turned her so she was staring into the three-way mirror in the tiny room. "The only thing I have to figure out is how to make you understand that you are every single thing to me."

31

Heat poured through the windshield of the FBI sedan as Smith drove Mercy to the staging hotel. She knew it was bulletproof, but if she gave that much thought she was going to vomit again. Making Smith clean her up a second time was not happening.

Tension locked into the stagnant heat filling the car. It was approaching dusk, but the Dallas weather didn't seem ready to relent to cooler evening temperatures. She focused on not throwing up and not freaking out. Smith would maim anyone or anything who tried to do her harm. That wasn't what worried her. What if she accidentally screwed this up and somehow caused him to get hurt? From what little she knew about the mafia, they didn't seem particularly forgiving of mistakes. She assumed these people would be no different.

Once again she promised herself to shake her little brother, when he finally surfaced, for being involved in this whole thing. She still hadn't heard from him, though. Another spike of terror drove through her every day she went without an email. Where was he?

"Hey," Smith soothed, sensing her discomfort, "I'd never let anything happen to my girl. You know that, right?"

"I know." Being his girl had become the single most important thing in her world. She'd managed to push this dinner out of her mind in order to focus on their new relationship, but she had to figure out where Julian was and what he was doing. She couldn't let anything distract her from that anymore, not even Smith. She owed it to their mother's memory. "I'm just scared I'm going to screw this up. I'm bad with people. I don't really even like them except for you, and Voodoo, and all of the Holders. What if I say something wrong or do something I'm not supposed to and... something terrible happens to you?" The last few words choked from the dry heat in her throat.

"Baby, I've been doing this kind of thing in one capacity or another for years. Adapting is one of my specialties. Nothing but a thing. I just want to get it over with. I want you safe at home with me."

He'd said things like that several times in the last few days. She hadn't quite had the courage to ask him exactly where home was. She hadn't agreed to move to Lincoln, but she hadn't refused either. After they got out of this alive, then she'd figure out what came next. Nothing after this dinner would compute anyway. The word 'drug cartel' took up all available brain space that wasn't filled with panic.

Words bubbled up from the terror. "You know what I don't know that I really should?"

"What's that?" His brow furrowed.

"Why is a drug cartel interested in drone radar designs?"

"The DEA uses drones to fly over cartel compounds. The images the drones return are admissible as evidence. If the cartels can do something to either destroy the drones or destroy the camera feeds, it works in their favor."

Her life one week ago seemed to shimmer through broken glass. Vague recollections of the time when government acronyms and drug cartels had nothing to do with her were distorted through the shards. If she tried to access any part of it, she'd slice her hands open beyond repair. There were parts of her previous life she'd never want back: the loneliness, the fear, the work that never quite satisfied. Mostly, she wanted no part of a life that didn't include Smith and getting to hear his sleepy, graveled voice calling her baby every morning. She never wanted to sleep in a bed without the angle created by his massive body that kept her tucked against him or the wiry hair that covered his chest pressing against her cheek when she laid on him and listened to his heart beat. The way his arms so thoroughly wrapped her up in a sanctuary of safety and contentment. She wanted nothing to do with anything that would separate those things from her daily existence. That fed the determination she needed to get through this night.

Smith parked the car behind the hotel near the kitchen entrance. Before Mercy could take one more deep breath, the car was surrounded by men in suits. An odd squeak vaulted from her mouth as she cringed closer to Smith.

He wrapped her up in his arms. "They're all from Tier Seven, sweetheart. This is my old team. They're here to keep you safe. Getting you in this hotel without being seen is the first mission. I'm right here. I will be right beside you all night. Okay?" He kissed the top of her head.

Calling herself several unsavory names that all basically meant coward, she nodded against him. "Sorry," she whispered.

"Don't apologize. We'll get out whenever you're ready."

She didn't want his friends to know how frightened she was, so she forced herself to open the door. "Let's just get this over with."

"Miss Valon, I'm T-Byrd. It's nice to meet you." Mercy accepted his offered hand simultaneously praying he wouldn't notice how badly she was shaking. He had that same confidence she'd come to expect from Smith. Maybe they all had that. He grinned at her like this was no big deal at all. She would've given anything to feel that confident.

"Uh... you can call me Mercy," she stammered. T was one of Smith's closest friends. Why was he being so formal? She knew Smith had told them they'd started dating, if that's what you called never leaving each other's sides while staying at a safe house.

"Let's not for tonight," he explained. "And we'll make the rest of the introductions once we're in the suite."

Voodoo climbed out of another sedan, and they headed into the hotel in groups of two and three. She clung to Smith's offered arm, certain if she released him she'd collapse. In an effort to distract herself, she watched the men he worked with. They moved with precision, an almost deadly accuracy with an air of rugged domi-nance. If any of them were worried, it didn't show.

Smith escorted her onto a service elevator. T-Byrd, Voodoo, and a man she didn't yet know boarded with them. No one spoke. She wished they'd say something. Smith's voice was always so soothing, but she gnawed her lip to keep herself from asking him to tell her again that everything would be all right.

As they exited the elevator, glimpses of navy scrollwork in the crimson carpeting and an endless number of doors with brass numbers passed in her peripheral vision. She tried to put the puzzle together, but nothing about any of this made sense. By the time they were standing outside room 1215, she'd given up.

Smith guided her into the room that was filled with more men in suits, all equally impressive as the ones on the elevator, and one woman who grinned at her. Smith nodded to everyone. "All right, this is Griff." He gestured to the man who'd ridden up with them. "We are the original Team Seven." He pointed to himself and his three closest friends.

"Oh, it's nice to meet you finally. Thank you for what you did for Yoda," she offered Griff.

He gave her a half smirk. "Nothing but a thing. However," he turned to Smith, "Hannah's dragged me to the pound twice now. I'm thinking we're either even, or you actually owe me at this point."

Smith huffed, but Mercy was pleased to see the smile on his face. "Three words for you, man. Fucking. My. Sister."

Griff rolled his eyes and flipped him off, and Mercy began to loosen up. If they were joking around, surely there wasn't really anything to be worried about.

"Could we move on with the introductions, Hagen? We have a lot of ground to cover," Mercy looked to see the speaker. He wasn't the only man in the room who looked perfectly comfortable in an expensive suit, but he had a hardened edge to his gaze that she didn't see in the room's other occupants.

"Sure." Smith threw him an annoyed glare. "Mercy, baby, that's Roman Becker. He's with the CIA but working undercover with Tier Seven." Then Smith pointed to the woman. "This is Rylee Mitchell. She'll be doing things like going to the restroom with you should you need to go." He moved down the line of men naming everyone in turn. "Rio Travers, Reid Cantori, Derek Kingston, Dean Hudson, Ryder Mathis, and these two are Jase Hughes and Clint Hardey." A contagion of single nods accompanied every introduction. "I'll be by your side all night, but if you need anything or get into any situation and can't find a way out, any one of us will come to your aid. Everyone else in here is either FBI or DEA. They'll all be pretending to be working with the cartels. Only Team Seven and Rylee will be your security unless things go south. Then any of us will step in to help you."

"Thank you." She prayed there wasn't going to be a quiz on names at the end, but she tried to come up with a few clues to help her remember them. Smith had explained that everyone there tonight would fall into one of two categories, either the good guys or the bad. Mixing up the two could be deadly for everyone involved. A cold sweat dewed on the back of her neck.

Roman approached her carrying a wired device she didn't recognize. "I'm assuming you'd prefer for Hagen to tape your wire inside your dress?"

Voodoo chuckled. "He'd likely destroy anyone else that tried."

"Yes, please." Since Mercy did not want to be undressed in front of anyone but Smith, that suited her just fine. She was far more concerned with the fact that she was going to be wearing a wire. She'd seen too many television shows where people were searched and then murdered when a wire was found. Somehow, she'd gone from viewing life through a screen to becoming the performer on the other side.

Roman handed the device to Smith but kept his hardened gaze on her. "Buck up, sweetheart. You're supposed to be a take-no-prisoners hacker looking to make bank on those designs tonight. It is imperative that you play your part without missing a single line. All of our lives depend on it."

Smith narrowed his eyes. "Hey, back off. This was your shit deal. She's nervous enough."

Annoyance rimmed Roman's coal-grey eyes that perfectly matched his suit. "Would you have preferred she spend the next twenty years in a federal prison? We all have to live with our choices. Let's not forget that." There was a distinctive note of regret in Roman's reminder. Its spiked edges pricked at Mercy's heart. She wondered what choices he was having to live with.

Pondering that, it finally occurred to her that she wasn't living with her own choices. She was living with Julian's.

Before she could be escorted to the bathroom to be wired, the hotel room door burst open. Every single person in the room besides Mercy raised a pistol and took aim. The air in her lungs seized.

A man dressed in a cowboy hat and well-worn blue jeans, rubbed in all the right places, grinned at every raised gun pointing directly at him. He held up a hotel keycard. "Lower your weapons, gentlemen. Let's play nice." He chuckled. It seemed absolutely nothing about this situation concerned him at all. Mercy noted how attractive he was. Nothing at all like how gorgeous Smith was, but lean and lethal none the less.

"Landry, what the fuck are you doing here?" One of the FBI agents spat as he restored his pistol to his shoulder holster. Everyone else followed suit, holstering their weapons.

Smirking, Landry rolled his eyes. "The Federal stench that rolled into Dallas tonight was so thick I knew you all were up to something. When I figured out what it was, I have to tell you, I got my feelings hurt. My invite must've gotten lost in the mail or something."

Roman shot the man with a hate-fueled glare. "Who the hell are you?"

"I'm Deputy U.S. Marshal Heath Landry." He stepped to Roman. "And which combination of Federal letters is it that you work for?"

Roman was set to detonate. "CIA," he snarled.

Landry let a low whistle slide between his teeth. "Got the big boys in here playing. Too bad you have no fucking clue who you're dealing with tonight, Mr. CIA?"

"Get out," Roman snapped.

The marshal's eyes narrowed. Mercy stepped back towards Smith instinctively. "I don't think so. The Castellas cartel is mine. I've been following Marino for years. You don't get to come piss on my turf just because you got bored sitting in your corner office. You take on the Castellas, you'll be outmanned and outgunned. You either let me in on this shindig you've decided to throw to make yourself feel like a badass, or you get the hell out of Dallas. This isn't a game for suits. This is marshal business."

T-Byrd cleared his throat. "Roman, we aren't really in a position to turn down offered help. If the marshals want in on this, I think we should get them briefed."

"Smart man," Landry drawled. "Let me guess. You're not actually a fed, right?"

"Former Special Forces," T explained.

"You really ought to listen to your friend there, CIA. Gambling on your own ego is a dangerous game. You'll eventually run out of chips."

"I'm running this show," Roman informed both T and Landry. "No one goes in or out of that event tonight without my say-so. If I'd wanted the help of Marshal Services I would've let you know. Now, leave or I'll call your Chief, and see if we can't come to some agreement on where you should be tonight. A prison cell suits me just fine."

"Roman, come on," T huffed.

"No. Javier Marino is mine. You want the rest of the cartel, Marshal, they're all yours, but Marino belongs to me. Until I get him, you stay the hell away from them. You show up tonight, I'll pull every string I have to make sure your next assignment is somewhere just south of hell."

The marshal cocked his jaw to the side and shook his head. He stepped around Roman and stood directly in front of Mercy. "You're

Mercy, right?" She nodded. "You look a lot like your mother. God rest her soul. Listen to me, if you need protection, you should let me handle that. I can keep you safe from the Castellas and anyone else. Witness protection is one of the many things we do well."

"But I'm not a witness," Mercy insisted.

"Oh, but you will be." He removed a business card from his pocket, wrote his personal cell phone number on it, and handed it to her. "If you get yourself in any trouble and the suits don't want to get their hands dirty to get you out, you call me. I'll be right there."

32

"You can do this." Smith tried to reassure Mercy when he finally got her to the bathroom after the invasion by the U.S. Marshal. Thoughts embattled his mind. He prayed she wouldn't ask him about the marshal and her mother. On the other hand, he agreed with T. They weren't in any position to turn down aid. He was a little annoyed that Landry thought Smith couldn't keep Mercy safe, but he was far more annoyed with Roman. The next time he and Roman were alone, he'd let him know precisely what he thought of the way he was running this ridiculous deal. Fucker.

Forcing himself to remember that Roman had always been there for Team Seven, no matter where they'd been sent, he knew the man hadn't intended to do anything but impress the seriousness of this evening on everyone involved. But scaring Mercy didn't sit well with Smith.

Focusing, he eased the zipper down the back of the dress Mercy had selected. She looked like a mortal sin he wanted to commit over and over again. If she'd been dressing up for his eyes only, he would've thought the skin-tight number was perfect, but since other men would see her, he had to resist the urge to wrap her up in his jacket, throw her over his shoulder, and run. *Just get through the night,* became his mantra.

"How did that marshal know my mom?" finally leapt from her mouth.

"I... don't know, sweetheart."

Mercy cleared her throat for the third time in as many minutes. "Don't you think someone might notice that I'm wearing a wire? I saw this movie once..."

"Baby, if anyone gets close enough to you tonight to feel this through your dress, trust me, that will be the last thing they do before they..."

"Shed their mortal coil." She managed a frantic grin.

He chuckled. "Exactly that." She needed a distraction. How had he missed that? He had to get better at this boyfriend business. Not that she'd officially called him that. "That reminds me. I shed my own mortal coil again this morning in the arena raid."

And there was her sweet grin. "Did you summon the Adarna?"

"I didn't have time before the cryofreeze."

He finished attaching the wire up the center of her spine and re-zipped the dress. She spun and stared up at him like she'd follow him right into the bowels of hell and never question a thing. They had to get through this night so he could come clean with her about every-thing. He couldn't stand the lying anymore.

"You know what I think you need?" she whispered.

He wrapped his arms around her. "I've got every single thing I'll ever need right here."

Mercy pressed her face against his jacket and filled her lungs with his scent. Damn. Those lush tits, on vast display in the low-cut dress, taunted his own chest and his resolve. "I was talking about the game, but that's the sweetest thing you've ever said to me, and you say sweet things all the time." She wrapped her arms around him and squeezed with all of her limited might.

"I meant every word, but what do I need in the game?"

"You need a partner. Well, actually, *we* need to become a duo. I could've summoned the Adarna for you while you were getting your ass kicked."

Grinning much too broadly at that, he cradled her face in his right hand and eased her head back until she was staring up at him again. "Are you saying what I think you're saying?"

"I'm saying we should always play together. I'm pretty sure that other than real-life marriage, there is no stronger commitment than teaming up in *RexArmis*. It can't be undone unless you start over." If he could bottle those giggles of hers, he'd become a junkie just for hits of them.

"You're making me hard, woman," he goaded.

A quick knock on the bathroom door tore at the moment he'd been trying to provide. Voodoo's voice reached them. "That vein in Roman's head is starting to throb. Y'all 'bout done in there?"

All of the air she'd inflated her lungs with came out in a defeated breath. "I guess we better go."

"We have a different room in a different hotel about twenty miles from here. This is just the staging area. In a few hours, this will be over, and we'll be back in our room. The only thing I want you to worry about tonight is the state of my cock from seeing you in this dress."

That earned him a full-faced grin that reached all the way to those beautiful green eyes. "I know how to take care of that. I'm getting pretty good at it, actually."

"Oh honey, pretty good doesn't even come close to describing the things you do for me."

"Before we go," she lost a little of that grin and it killed him, "I just want to make sure I have all of this straight. So, I'm basically playing K155 and you're...?"

He'd coughed over Roman's explanation of his role that evening, hoping she wouldn't ask. He should've known better. Curiosity and intelligence pulsed under her skin constantly, two things he found highly addictive. He cringed. "I'll be... your handler."

That went off about as well as he'd expected it would. She scowled. "Are you serious?"

"It legitimizes you to the cartel. It's something they understand. They don't just traffic drugs. Their dealers handle women as well."

She looked almost as sick as he felt. "So, you're my hacker pimp. That's just... gross."

"I agree. But for tonight it lets anyone who wants to talk to you know that they'll have to go through me first. I'd hoped that might make this a little easier."

That seemed to annoy her more than soothe her, so Smith assumed he'd missed the mark again, but her irritation eventually morphed to something closer to relief. "I guess that's good. I was kind of looking forward to playing K155 in real life, but I'd probably screw it up."

"Stop." He laid his index finger over her lips, which she promptly kissed. "We still need you to be my little kickass hacker. Don't hold back. All I want is for you to realize that K155 is you, Mercy."

"So, the thing about you making it easier for me is the part you recognized behind the mask, right? Like you told me about all of your missions, where you had to find some part of yourself in every role. You don't really want to be my *handler,* but you do want to keep me safe."

"Smart as a whip and beautiful too. I have no idea how I got so lucky."

MERCY WALKED into the opulent ballroom of The Cascadia Gardens with a little more confidence once she reminded herself that these men were no better than the assholes who ran revenge porn sites or worse, abuse sites. It helped that she had Smith's towering form beside her and her arm looped through his. She supposed being surrounded by Rylee and the rest of Team Seven didn't hurt either. The rest of Tier Seven Security was stationed strategically throughout the room all pretending to be working for one of the competing cartels after the designs.

Overall, it was pretty intimidating. When she pretended she had a screen and keyboard between herself and the real bad guys, she felt like she could stand on her own two feet, even if the heels she'd gotten to go with the dress were already killing her.

She was somewhat surprised to see a few women in the room as well, but she supposed she shouldn't have been. Women could be evil as well. Smith had almost convinced her that society wasn't bad enough to completely give up on. It was going to be difficult to maintain that decision that night.

Two men approached, both in suits and wearing fancy alligator-skin boots. Mercy had no idea who they were, but they did look rather thug-like, in her very biased opinion. Griff and Voodoo both stepped closer to her.

"Both undercover FBI. Stay in character." Smith spoke through his teeth and narrowed his eyes at the men.

One of them extended his hand to Smith, who did not accept the gesture. She couldn't recall him ever doing anything rude the entire time she'd known him. She didn't care for this version of him, but he did play his part well.

"I've always said the most dangerous things come in the smallest packages," one of the men drawled at Mercy as he visibly sized her up.

Griff's mouth opened, but before he could speak, Mercy beat him to it. "Is that what you tell yourself?" She directed a quick glance to his crotch. Smith gave her a discreet grin and a wink that made her belly do a few backflips. This was kind of fun. Griff glanced from her to Smith and back again. He looked perturbed maybe. Mercy couldn't really tell.

The feds feigned offense. "Are you going to let her speak to him that way?" The taller of the two huffed to Smith.

"I didn't tell you that you could speak to her at all. Walk away before you make another unfortunate misstep." Two down and about three dozen to go before the night would be over.

Waiters moved throughout the crowd, serving glasses of chianti. Mercy assumed all mob parties had waiters carrying pistols under their aprons. Since Roman was the host, she also assumed the waiters were safe. Smith handed her a glass and took one for himself. She noted that he never brought the glass to his lips, so she followed suit. Wine might help her loosen up, but she wasn't certain that would be a good thing in this situation.

She noticed a man and a woman, both speaking in rapid Spanish, heading out the doors into the elaborate gardens. She lifted the glass to her lips for the purpose of being able to follow them with her eyes. She could've sworn she heard them say her brother's name. How did they know Julian? Were they the would-be buyers he'd talked to? Did they have any idea where he was now?

"Maybe we should go outside and get some fresh air," she urged Smith.

But he shook his head and guided her deeper into the ballroom. She didn't get to explain why she wanted to go outside before another man approached them. If she wasn't mistaken, Smith had heard her brother's name as well, so he should've understood. Did he think she'd blow her cover and ask about him? She wasn't stupid. Irritation crept up her spine.

"So, eh, she's the chick, right? You really got them designs, sweets? They on you? You could hand 'em over, and we can make this night work in your favor." The man's thick New York accent was almost too clichéd to have ever been real, and yet, he appeared to be. Recalling that there were numerous cartels all interested in bidding on designs she really didn't have, she narrowed her eyes.

Before Smith could order him away, she cut across him. "I'm a little busy. Could I ignore you later?" With a heavy eye roll, she stepped forward. Smith and her security detail followed, since she couldn't really move him on her own.

"I told you," Smith drawled.

"Told me what?"

"One-part hellcat, one-part sweetheart, all the same woman. You're killing me, you know that? Like you stepped right out of my wet dreams, baby," he informed her under his breath. "I'm not sure if I love you more for your comebacks or because you're quicker than Griff, which is driving him crazy."

Her earlier irritation melted at that. "You love me?" Shock rang through her whisper.

Team Seven gave them a little more room than they had thus far. "Yeah. I do, but I know it's been fast."

He probably hadn't heard those people say Julian's name. She wasn't even certain she'd heard it. They were speaking another language after all. Certain she'd been wrong, she tightened her grip on Smith's arm. "Well, I love you, too, and I don't mind fast. Slow Wi-Fi is terrible. Maybe slow love is, too."

She did love him. She loved that she could make him chuckle with her stupid computer jokes. She loved the way he intimidated her, only to prove himself good over and over again. She loved that he wasn't afraid to tell her things, and that he'd never lie to her. She loved him, and she had nothing to fear.

She surveyed the room again. There were still several men giving her quick glances and whispering with their counterparts, but from where she now stood, they didn't look quite so intimidating. Perspective really was everything.

33

ercy Jackson and James Dean. Mercy reminded herself of the clues she'd made up to remember the names of the men who were heading their way. *Rio and Dean.* That was it. Rick Riordan was one of her favorite authors, and the other member of Tier Seven had those classic, almost nostalgic, good looks. It reminded her of the old movies of Marilyn Monroe and James Dean. Neither of them held anything on Smith, but they were nice looking.

Only, just then, they didn't look so nice. They'd been more than polite back in the hotel room. Rio had even gotten her a Dr. Pepper from the vending machine when she'd made an offhand comment about being thirsty. Now, they were fully in character, pretending to be mafia members anxious to score the designs either with money or with force.

How could the first night Smith told her he loved her also be a night she hated so badly? Shaking off that confusion, she narrowed her eyes as they stopped right in front of Smith.

Dean's tone held a far surlier snark than she'd heard him use before. "You trying to fuck with us?" The threat seemed implicit, but Mercy wasn't certain why he'd said it.

Roman approached on cue, entrance upstage left. "Trust me, if anything happens to our hacker, it won't be us who's fucked."

Mercy knew one thing for certain—Roman Becker was deadly. The return of the volleyed threat was not an act. It was far more menacing. He maintained eye contact and revealed himself as a force you didn't want to take on, and if you did, you weren't likely to survive. His words were measured, almost kind. His stance relaxed. He was a deadly combination of poise and danger, and he was far more terrifying than anyone else in the room.

Rio went next. The thick southern accent she'd found so charming was all but gone. "You got everyone down here, but we have no proof you even have the designs. You're parading her around like she could really pull something like that. If we find out you're shitting us, you aren't walking out of here, you got that?"

Roman offered up an amused chuckle. Mercy glanced back to see him, hoping stupidly that they'd all go back to being friends, just messing around. Of course, this wasn't a play and nothing about it was fun. Dean and Rio were putting on a show for the real-deal cartel members, and every eye in the room was on the exchange.

Roman gestured to a waiter who brought him a sparkling water. Mercy wondered if that had also been previously planned. If it hadn't, it had worked to his favor. It added to the air of disregard he held with ease.

When the conversation turned to nothing but a course in mean mugging, Smith wrapped his arm over her shoulders. It took all of her strength to keep from burying her face against his broad chest and letting the sanctuary of his giant body enclose around her. But surely that wasn't how hackers behaved with their handlers. Or maybe it was. She didn't attend the underground parties or events hosted by the big players in the game just so they could show off their spoils.

"Come with me, baby," Smith soothed. "Try to look like you don't really want to but that I'm not giving you a choice." Her mind scrambled. *What?* Managing catty one-liners was one thing, but pretending that she was being forced to do something by a man she was in love with was something else entirely. Her heart leapt to her throat and pounded out a frantic cry for help. She stumbled when he jerked her to the side, but he steadied her without ever breaking pace. "Stay here," he ordered his friends who'd all started to follow after them.

Mercy had no idea why he was doing this until he guided her into some kind of supply closet near the kitchen. "This'll have to do," he grumbled. "It's the only spot in this place not crawling with feds or thieves." He turned to face her, dropped her hand, and took a few steps back until he collided with a metal shelf. He righted a swaying bucket with an audible grunt of annoyance. "All I wanted to do is hold you until you don't look so terrified, but at this point I'm thinking it's me you're afraid of."

That did it. She flew across the limited space and practically crawled into his jacket with him. "I would never be afraid of you."

A contented breath ruffled a few strands of her hair as he wrapped her up in his arms. "Are you sure?"

She nodded against his shirt and relished the moment where they could just be Mercy and Smith. "Of course. Why would you think that?"

She felt his shoulders lift in a shrug. "I don't ever want to scare you, but I'm a big guy, and tonight my job is to be scary. That has to be... odd."

Begrudgingly, she lifted her head so she could reassure him. "Tier Seven is doing their job, just like we all are. I hate it, but I'm not afraid of it. And I must not have done a very good job of showing you just how sexy I think you are." Heat climbed into her cheeks, but she had to tell him this. "When I first saw you in the coffee shop, I thought you were the sexiest guy I'd ever seen in my whole life. I couldn't believe you stopped to talk to me, but you're not just good-looking. You're a good man. I did sort of call you *the giant* in my head for a while," she admitted just to hear his chuckle, "but I've never been afraid of you, and I never will be. I feel so safe in your arms."

Before she could continue, he cradled her face in his hands and slanted his mouth over hers like he couldn't wait one moment more to kiss her. She was also utterly addicted to the gentle power he used with her. Just like the first time, every kiss took up her whole world.

When he had her like this, everything aligned and made sense. If this wasn't love, she didn't know what it could possibly be.

Their tongues tangled until she relented and gave him the upper hand. He devoured her mouth like he was memorizing every detail of them together. The rough scrape of his beard on her chin made her long to feel it between her thighs. His right hand dropped to her backside and massaged. With every squeeze, she rocked against his groin. The way his body responded to her was still fascinating. She felt him swell and stiffen against her. Lifting up on her toes, she pressed herself harder against him, hungry for the friction she missed when they weren't in bed.

He throbbed, and a hungry moan spilled from his mouth into hers. He jerked his head back and allowed her to breathe. His eyes closed and shook his head. "I didn't intend to bring you in here to do that, and since you're wearing a wire Roman and T likely just heard me."

"Look at me," she urged. His dark-whiskey eyes were still alight with lust, and when they met hers, she grinned. "I don't care who can hear us. Thank you for bringing me in here and for doing that. You know how when you're a kid and you skin your knee and then your mom kisses it because that's supposed to make it stop stinging, but it doesn't really work? Your kisses really do make everything feel better."

A pain she hadn't expected to see formed on his rugged features. "I'm sorry you don't still have your mom, baby. That kills me."

It was such an earnest and unexpected response to her silly memory that hot tears threatened her eyes. She blinked them away and shook her head, trying to banish them along with the hot boulder that clogged her throat. He wrapped her up in his arms again and planted a kiss on top of her head. "I didn't mean to make you cry, sweetheart."

"I'm fine." She wasn't, but she had to be. Eventually, they were going to have to leave their supply closet refuge.

"You don't have to be fine." Using only a fraction of his abundant power, he squeezed her just a little tighter. "When you lose people you love, it's okay to not be okay. It took me a long time to figure that out. I don't want you to suffer like that."

"Thank you for saying that. No one's ever really told me that before. I had to figure it out on my own. But, I really don't want to think about my mom right now. In a few minutes, we're going to have to go back out there." She threw a scowl to the door. "And I have some questions before that, and then I want another kiss."

He traced his fingertips over her cheeks again. "You are temptation incarnate, woman, but we have a job to do. What's your question?"

"What's the deal with Marshal Landry not liking the FBI and when you call them feds you sound like you don't like them either."

His soothing chuckle set her at ease. "Most of the time we think it has to be a part of their academy's graduation requirements to get a corncob shoved up their ass. They drive Tier Seven insane. They're choking on their own rules and regulations. I have no idea how they get anything done. All we want is for them to let us do our jobs and stay out of our way. I imagine the marshal feels the same way."

There were a few agents she'd encountered that night who were definitely handling the undercover work with ease. Maybe those kinds of agents were few and far between. "Okay, and I was wondering what everyone out there thinks we're doing in here? Since I should probably act accordingly, right?" He hesitated far too long. A different version of his pained expression creased his brow. "Just tell me," she urged again.

"I'm sure they think I'm scolding you about getting mouthy with the buyers."

Mercy assumed a handler being unhappy with your performance would likely include being physically punished. "I hate this night."

"Me too, baby. So fucking much." Smith paused and took a deep breath. "You need to act like you're mad at me when we leave here."

"When I find my brother, I'm going to kill him."

Smith fixed his gaze above her head. *I've had that thought a few times, too* passed through his mind, but he stopped it before it ever hit his lips.

34

Smith kept up his angry handler routine, though he loathed it more and more with every passing moment. They made it through the first dinner course, some kind of Caesar salad and had moved on to lasagna. He trusted Roman, but wondered if serving Italian to mob members wasn't a touch clichéd. They all seemed to be enjoying it, so he ate and kept an eye on his baby.

She never dropped her cover. No one would suspect that she would never have intentionally stolen designs from the Department of Defense, but he felt her quick shivers, and saw the frustration she used to summon the anger she showed. It killed him. The quicker they got through dinner, the quicker he could get her out of there, and the FBI could have their day. No one who really mattered was there anyway. The bosses had all sent low-level soldiers who could be easily replaced. None of the attendees would know enough to be worthy of witness protection, should they try that. The kingpins weren't stupid. They likely knew this was a setup, but they didn't want to be left out in case it wasn't. Gamblers never quit. They just change their game.

There were three men who'd all gone several steps too far. Smith split his attention between them. Two were weapons dealers out of Miami. They'd been busted a year before for supplying AKs to the Castellas cartel, but they'd come back even stronger than they'd been before. Smith knew from the malignant look on their faces that they were going to make a play on Mercy. If she wouldn't hand the designs over to them, she wouldn't live, or at least that's what they thought.

Smith wished they'd try it. No one would ever lay a hand on her as long as he was breathing.

Griff leaned closer and lifted his glass to his mouth. "You noticed the fuckers, I see."

"As soon as they got here."

"Got another one at your ten. If he doesn't get his shit together and stop leering at her, I'm gonna whip his ass on your behalf."

Smith appreciated the thought, but that wouldn't work in Tier Seven's favor, yet another thing he hated about that night. "I saw him, too."

"Does she know anything other than what we've told her?"

"I don't want to scare her more."

"Always a decent plan, but you might have to scare her enough to keep her safe."

While Mercy chatted with Rylee, Smith angled away to talk to Griff. "I'm going to tell her after this, though. Everything."

Griff offered him a bereaved expression. "Be careful fucking with things too soon. Reducing an obstacle without taking down whatever shares its foundation is next to impossible."

Since one of Griff's SF jobs was demo and destruction, he certainly knew what he was talking about. Of course, Smith was already aware of the things he'd be tearing away from her if he explained her family's lengthy history with the Castellas cartel. He just had to make certain he'd constructed a stronghold where they could endure the fallout.

Doubt crept in and began eroding his plans. Perhaps, that night wasn't the time. Maybe they weren't quite as strong as he'd like to believe they were. The thoughts pummeled his brain. He analyzed every possible angle, but found there were too many to predict every outcome. How would anyone know when another person was ready to have the rug ripped out from underneath them? How was anyone ever ready for that? She'd been unknowingly living lies her entire life. How could she trust the truth no matter how crystal clear he painted the picture? He was battling for her heart, and he had no intention of losing.

Later. He'd tell her when he was certain she relied more on him than on the idea of her brother. When she slid her chair back, panic lodged in his gut. Had she heard them? But her sweet grin said she hadn't. She wrinkled her nose and sank her teeth into her bottom lip like she didn't want to tell him something. Clearly, if she thought there was anything she couldn't say, they weren't ready for him to levy the full truth on their relationship. "What's wrong, baby?"

"I have to go to the bathroom. I shouldn't have had that chianti."

Rylee stood. "No worries. I'm on it. Besides, I need to go, too."

Smith stood to escort both of them to the restroom to make certain no one else was in there before they entered.

Still pretending to be angry at him for whatever people thought had happened in that closet, she walked a few paces ahead of him. He hated the distance between them. It gave the truth room to stretch its legs and breathe. He'd always prided himself on his own morality, had always held himself to higher standards than other men. It was the way he'd been raised, but it was also the way of Special Forces. When they were separated, by even the smallest distance, light illuminated just how much really stood between them—far more than he was able to admit when her sweet body was pressed to his.

He'd never been in love before, but he'd certainly never expected it to be so closely tied to hate. He hated the way they'd met, hated her brother, hated this fucking night, and hated every single thing trying to pull them apart. But all of that hate had nothing on the love he held for his adorable hacker princess. Half angel, half villain, all his.

DREAD STABBED through Mercy when Smith kicked open the door to the ladies' room, but the shock faded quickly now. A human being could only endure so many alarming things before that became the norm. Constant shrills of the unexpected eventually became expected, and she hated that as well.

It seemed to her that everything standing between her current existence and a real life with Smith was actually all her fault. Julian was the reason this had happened, but he was really the supporting cast. She was why all of these people were here. How had she gone from avoiding the limelight to the center ring of the circus? She couldn't figure that out, but it didn't matter anymore. She just had to determine how to shut down the show because she didn't want to wear this ringmaster's hat that her brother had forced on her head.

Just like that stupid anti-gravity ride he'd pushed her to do, it hadn't all been bad. She'd found Smith, but it was also time to get off the ride.

"Is there anyone in the stalls?" Smith demanded of the bewildered attendant.

"No, sir." She shook her head and took several steps back. Mercy wanted to tell her he wasn't scary, that he was the most amazing man in the world, but she was supposed to be afraid of him, too. Yep, definitely time to unbuckle the seatbelt and get the hell off of this ridiculous ride.

"I'll be right here." Smith pointed to the square of carpeting directly outside the bathroom door. She gave him a weary nod that required no playacting skill.

Mercy and Rylee both retreated to stalls. How sad was it that her favorite places in this stupid garden ballroom thing were the janitor's closet and the restroom? Her neck twinged ominously. *Great.* She should've known the stress of all of this would ultimately result in another migraine. But the sudden flare of pain disappeared as quickly as it had come on. Maybe if they could get out of there sometime soon and she could relax, she wouldn't get another one. She'd bet a few more of Smith's kisses and a few more orgasms would bring the tension down better than anything Voodoo had in his pack.

She exited the stall before Rylee left hers and offered the attendant a kind smile, since Smith had terrified her. When she turned on the water, the woman moved closer. Then closer still. The hair on Mercy's arms stood to make room for the goose bumps that raised under her flesh.

Her heart pounded out the cry for help she was afraid to make with her mouth. Before she could convince herself to scream, the woman whipped a pistol out from under her apron and fired at the door to Rylee's stall. The noise was muted by a silencer. Rylee's groan was louder than the shot.

Everything moved much too quickly and somehow not fast enough. Her world became a blur. She acted on instinct alone.

"No!" Mercy leapt for the gun, but she wasn't fast enough. The woman wrapped her left arm around Mercy's neck and held the pistol to her head.

"Your brother is very concerned about you, dear. I think we should go see him." Her accent. For some unfathomable reason, the hot prod of the just-fired pistol against her temple didn't register as quickly as the woman's accent.

Smith bound through the door. Griff and Voodoo stormed in behind him.

The woman turned, forcing Mercy to become her human shield. Griff sported a cocky grin. "It doesn't look like this went down quite the way you thought it would. Let's play the odds, shall we? Sniper versus fuckoff. Do you really think you're the first person holding a hostage in front of them that I've shot? I guess you wouldn't really know since none of the others are around to tell you about it."

Mercy gave Smith a pleading look. Griff was currently taunting the woman holding a gun to her head. That seemed like a really bad plan.

But Smith looked like he was going to be sick. "Let her go, and we'll let you live," choked from him.

"It's the only way out for you," Voodoo's voice was almost soothing. He seemed to be playing the yin to Griff's yang. "If you fire, one of us will kill you. If she walks, you walk. Make the better choice."

"Her brother wants to see her," the woman struggled with English. Her words were clipped.

"As far as we're concerned you and her brother can share a ride to hell. Take the carpool lane," Griff snapped.

35

S mith knew precisely what he was supposed to do. He knew Griff wouldn't miss, but he also knew it wasn't going to come to that. If her mission had been to murder Mercy, she would've already done it. Her brother wanted her kidnapped but alive.

Smith knew this would work. He knew his role, but nothing could ever have prepared him for having to give the instructions to the love of his life.

Clinging to all of those sound facts brought him no relief. Life had taken too many things away. He would never endure this. If Mercy didn't walk out of this unscathed, they could just shoot him as well. He forced the words around the boulder in his chest. "Mercy, when I give you the signal, I want you to pull hard to one side or the other. Your choice. Griff doesn't miss. Ever."

Her nod dragged the business end of that gun against her skull, and he was certain he was going to lose his mind. As if he could read her very thoughts, he knew she was replaying every conversation they'd had in preparation for this event trying to remember the signal. But there wasn't a signal because this never should've been a possibility. Every attendant, waiter, and chef had been screened and hired by the FBI, and most of them were agents themselves. How the hell had this bitch gotten through? His mind was moving much too slowly. Clearly, she hadn't passed the rigorous screening process, which brought their body count to one already. Whoever was actually hired to attend the ladies' room was likely face down in the Trinity River.

Bile singed a path to his throat, serving to prod the rest of the words from his mouth. "Do you remember the signal?"

His brilliant girl knew what was up. She gave him another nod, cringing from the scrape of metal on her sweat-dewed skin. Griff took two steps closer and narrowed his eyes. Smith swore his own heartbeats had to be audible to everyone in the room.

"Not another step," taunted the woman holding a pistol to his baby's head. But she seemed aware she'd just failed the test. Everyone save Mercy knew she would have already pulled the trigger if that was her intention.

Griff kept up his end of the bargain, though. He laughed. "I don't need another step. You ready, Mercy?"

Control the situation. That's what they'd been trained to do. Own every possible outcome. Too many weapons were still at play to take anything for granted, and Mercy didn't have Special Forces training.

Voodoo shifted his weight to his right foot and glanced at the bullet hole in the stall door. The door slammed open and Rylee leapt out, tackling the woman as Smith yanked Mercy out of her arms. Griff kicked the pistol out of the woman's hand, picked it up, and shoved it in his own holster, all the while maintaining aim with his own Glock at the woman's head. Voodoo pointed his pistol at her chest, but that was probably unnecessary since Rylee had already produced a zip tie and bound the woman's hands.

If Mercy shook in Smith's arms any harder, he was going to uproot trees with his bare hands. How dare anyone frighten her like this?

A few vibrated words made it out of her mouth. "I don't understand."

"I know, baby." He swayed her back and forth.

Voodoo shook his head. "Shit's about to rain down from the sky. You gotta get her out of here. Now."

Before Smith could execute an escape, Roman slipped into the bathroom. His calculated glance took everything in. "Give me her phone."

Rylee pulled the woman's cell phone from her pocket and handed it to Roman. He made quick work of easing one of the woman's thumbs away from the tight clasp of her hands and using it to unlock the screen. He checked all recent calls, text messages, and emails, and then studied his opponent. "Where's the driver?"

The woman said nothing. Refusing to answer a CIA operative's question was not a good plan. It seemed everyone in the room knew that except maybe the silent woman. "Tell me where the driver is, or I start shooting. See, I don't play by the same rules these good men do, dear. When I shoot, I don't aim to kill. Our goals are very different. I've found that when people stop screaming, they become more talkative. So, I'm going to ask you one more time, where is the driver?"

She stared wide-eyed at Roman, but didn't weigh her options for very long. "The loop at Valdina."

"You're going to call them. Tell them you have her, but were compromised and need to be picked up out front. If they're not here in the next five minutes, my interrogation techniques will begin to sound rather kind. Is that clear?"

Roman touched the top entry on the recent call list and held the phone to the woman's ear. In perfect Spanish, he ordered her to speak in her native tongue. For the first time since he'd walked in, the woman looked incensed, knowing she could neither lie in Spanish nor signal her collaborators by speaking in English. Clearly, she hadn't counted on tangling with Roman Becker.

Letting the adrenaline continue to drive him, Smith continued to sway Mercy back and forth. "Let's take your wire off before we go," he phrased carefully to keep from giving anyone any clue where Mercy was being taken.

"Okay," she whispered.

He escorted her into the largest stall and made quick work of removing the wire. "Can you give me three more seconds of being the bravest woman on this planet, baby? We're going out the window, and then I'm getting you out of here." After that, she could scream, cry, hate him, anything that came out of this. Just so long as he knew she was safe.

"I'm fine," she told perhaps the biggest lie between them yet. She wanted to be fine. She wasn't, but he went with it.

Smith lifted the window up as far as it would go. It slid upwards far too easily. The would-be kidnapper had already greased the track. He wondered how long this had been planned. When would the cartel realize their mission had failed? They were clearly seeking her out. How long could he delay the inevitable? They could run, hide, and he could sequester her away, but eventually, they were going to run out of plays to make. At some point the truth was going to be what kept her safe, but that required her to trust him more than she trusted her brother. Otherwise, it would be their relationship that ultimately burned on the pyre, and she would still likely not survive Julian's wrath.

36

Aware she was speaking much too quickly, Mercy couldn't stop. "I don't understand how Rylee wasn't hurt, and I don't know why that woman didn't ask me about the designs. She kept saying Julian wanted to see me, but that can't possibly be true because if that were true why doesn't he call or email? Oh God, do you think he can't? Do you think he's still alive?" She couldn't stop moving her hands. Why wouldn't they stop moving? She was officially freaking out. "No, wait, he has to still be alive, or why would that woman have wanted to take me? There would be no point. Where is my brother? I have to know that. Now. And what's going to happen now that we've left that Garden thing? All of those people had guns. And that woman is from Colombia. I know that because my landlord, Edgar, is from there. I could tell by her accent. She sounded just like him. Should I have told Roman that? I mean, he seemed to know, too, but it's this certain city in Colombia. Medellín, I think. Edgar and Sophia, that's Edgar's wife, left back in the eighties. She said it was dangerous for them to keep living there. She told me about it while I was fixing their daughters' computer one time. Oh my God. Oh my God, what if... Edgar... no."

Realization tried desperately to shatter through her babbling. She didn't want to give in to what had to be the truth, but it added up much too quickly. Her apartment had been destroyed, but Griff had told Smith that the lock must've been picked because there was no damage to the door. That all occurred while the FBI was watching the apartment. Edgar owned the building. Destroying your own property wasn't against the law. They wouldn't have stopped him, and he had a key. What if the lock hadn't been picked? What if it had just been unlocked?

That led to a dozen other questions she didn't want to answer. What did this drug cartel have to do with her? What did it have to do with her brother? How long had this been going on? Had Sophia found her in the market that day and talked to her about moving into their building because of some drug cartel? That part didn't make any sense at all. Yet, her questions were met with glaringly obvious answers. She was frequently approached by sketchy companies to come and hack for them. But Mercy knew of the dark edges surrounding her career. She thought she'd steered clear of anything truly terrifying. What if she hadn't? What if, somehow, she'd done something to make someone mad and that was how Julian had gotten involved in all of this?

"I liked it better when you were talking, baby," Smith eased. He kept her hand clasped in his own while he drove with the other. "I know that look. What did you just figure out?"

"Edgar broke into my apartment." Her own whispered realization echoed against her skull. "He's working for them or something. Did you already figure that out?"

His gaze was pleading as he nodded.

"Why didn't you tell me?" Her chin trembled, but she refused to cry.

"I kept telling myself it wasn't the time. I didn't want to have to tell you. I can't hurt you. I'd rather be shot again than to say something that causes you pain. I think that's how I figured out I'm in love with you. I just... couldn't do it. I'm sorry. I should've. It wouldn't have changed what happened, so I told myself it wasn't worth it. I guess that makes me a coward."

"Not wanting to hurt me does not make you a coward. I just need to understand everything. Can you answer all of my questions?"

"Okay." His nod came easier that time. "Rylee could see what was happening in the gap between the stall door and its frame. Every person who works for Tier Seven has a code. We enter our code on a group text before we do anything like this, but we don't hit send. If anyone sends their signal, we know who needs help. She sent her code and hit the floor before the woman ever even aimed the gun at the door. She stayed down until the right moment. You were also wearing a wire, so T and Roman knew as soon as she started talking that you were in trouble. We went with our planned response."

That information only brought on another series of rapid-fire questions. "Was Griff just bluffing or has he really killed people who were using a human shield? Was taunting her part of the plan, or does he just do that? How did he know she wasn't going to kill me? Was it like a good cop/bad cop thing, and Voodoo was the good cop?"

Smith glanced in the rearview mirror one too many times.

"And why do you keep doing that?" she added to her list.

"I'm making sure we're not being followed. Try to breathe for me, okay? Yes, Griff has killed people who were using innocent humans as their shields. He wasn't bluffing. I've never seen another gunman with his skill. He doesn't miss, but we would never have bet your life on that. His goal was to get her to turn the gun on him. He's wearing a vest under his suit. In any case, if he had to, he could've taken her out easily, but he knew she was needed alive. Voodoo's job was to talk her into laying down the weapon. Griff is quick with smart-ass quips, and Voodoo puts people at ease, so we always try to play to our strengths. We knew if her mission had been to kill you, she would already have done it, but when someone has a gun to your head, we don't take anything for granted. You mean the world to me. Tell me you know that."

"I do know that. I saw how scared you were, and that made it so much worse. I was afraid to talk to you because I didn't know what she would do. But I was worried about you. I knew you'd blame yourself. I couldn't stand that."

"Baby," he shook his head, "I wasn't the one..."

"I know, but I also know you pretty well now. It finally occurred to me that you haven't told me everything about the day your team was attacked. You never hesitate to answer my questions, but I got a shortened version of that story, didn't I?"

SMITH WOULD FEEL the sucker punch of that statement for a long time. He never hesitated to answer her questions, because she wasn't asking the right ones. Her mind worked so fast she out-thought herself. She'd just done it again. The first questions had led directly to the next, and he was able to pick and choose which parts he wanted to answer.

She could see the forest. She could see the trees, but she couldn't quite put them together. The lies kept a blindfold over her eyes that blocked her view of the truth. She didn't yet know what she was missing. When he finally removed the blindfold, he had to make certain the truth didn't glare so brightly it robbed her of sight yet again.

If there was something she wanted to know that was in his power to tell her, he had to try. No matter what it cost him. He had to earn her trust in every possible way. If she wanted to know more about what happened in Najaf, now was the time to tell her. "They had help," he choked.

"Who had help?" she asked in a devastated whisper.

"The faction of the Iraqi Army that attacked us. They had help from an American weapons dealer."

"I'm so sorry." She'd just lived through hell, and she was offering him sympathy he didn't deserve. Her well of strength seemed unending. If only his was.

He tripped and stumbled over the next few words. "We were

waiting on intelligence from Roman. A man named Marcus Finch kept him from getting it to us. He was playing both sides against the middle. I thought we had a few more weeks before they'd make their move. I was wrong. They attacked us at a routine fuel stop. They arranged for the weapons to be there, and they couldn't have had long to make those kinds of arrangements because we were watching them constantly." Regret knotted in his chest and lodged in his throat, but he owed her this. "It was my fault."

"What? How could that possibly have been your fault?"

"It was..." but that was all he could manage.

She shook her head and squeezed his hand. "None of it was your fault. It was whoever helped them, and the man who got them the weapons, and the people who actually did the shooting. Not you. Never you."

"You don't understand. I had the most experience. My father is a fucking general. I should've known what to do to keep them alive. There had to be some way. I don't know how I missed it." The guilt once again enlarged until he could no longer contain it. It snarled and clawed around inside of him, ripping the breath from his lungs and crushing his bones. Smith yanked his hand away from hers. He didn't deserve the comfort. In fact, he needed to feel the pain, so he slammed his hands against the steering wheel, unable to either fight it or to contain it. He reveled in the throb of his palms. "I should've figured something out. We were the best of the best. I let them down. My father would never have fucked up like that."

"Hey." She eased his right hand away from the wheel and laced their fingers together once more. "I do understand. I know this isn't the same, but I get it. My mom's car accident was my fault."

For a man who prided himself on being able to predict every possible outcome, she just kept shocking him. For some reason, he loved that, too. "Baby, that can't possibly be true. Why do you think that?"

"So, it's okay for you to think it's your fault your team was attacked, but it's not okay for me to know my mom's wreck was my fault? I love everything about you, but it bugs me when you tell me what I know is wrong," she reminded him.

Fine. He'd dismantle the story after he'd heard her out. "Then explain to me how I'm wrong, because every single thing about you is good, Mercy. I know that. For some reason you won't let yourself just be who you are. You think there are parts of you that are unlovable. But I love every part of you."

37

His words washed over Mercy like a healing tide, but she had to tell him the story because she couldn't allow him to believe his team's demise was his fault. She let his love center in her chest and spread its warmth outward to her limbs. It washed away the terrorizing things she'd endured that night as she contemplated where to begin.

"Julian always wanted me to compete in bigger arenas as a hacker. He was proud of me, I guess. I never really wanted to. I was happy doing small jobs at home in complete obscurity. I liked helping good people and hurting bad people. I know that isn't the way we're supposed to be. I've always been a house divided, so to speak." She prayed the slight lift of her shoulders would also shrug away the cracks in her voice.

This time Smith squeezed her hand instead of the other way around. "Putting an end to people who do bad things is what I did in the army. Do you think I'm a bad person for killing men who wanted to inflict evil on the world?"

"No." But that was different than her taking down porn sites. He was a hero. She was not. "Can you just listen, please?"

"Sure."

"Our whole lives, my brother has wanted to be a hero like our dad. It seems like he always tries to take on these impossible situations without figuring out how he's going to get out of them first. All of the most notorious bullies at school, Julian wanted to fight. Some girl's lunch money got stolen one day, and my brother went table to table making people empty their pockets to prove they hadn't stolen it. He wants to be Superman or something. He wanted to join the marine corps when he was seventeen. He kept saying things about being the tip of the spear." She squeezed her eyes shut.

Smith chuckled. "The USMC does generally recruit a type."

"Yeah, and Julian's it. My mom flat out refused to sign his paper work. She paid him to stay out of the service because we worried he wouldn't stop trying to be a hero until he got himself killed. My brother wants so badly to do some amazing, heroic thing. He just doesn't know how. He never considers that people are going to react to his actions, and maybe not always in a good way. I know that's probably what's happened now. He's in over his head again, and he needs me to get him out. But it's not just him that he wants to be recognized as a hero. It's me, too. He won't listen to me, and when he does he still doesn't believe what I say. That's how my mother got killed."

Realization illuminated in Smith's eyes from the passing car lights. "I'm sorry if I ever made you feel like you don't know your own mind. I just have this inborn thing inside of me that wants to protect you at all costs, even if it's from me. I should've listened to what you wanted every single time you tried to tell me."

"Thanks." With a deep breath, Mercy pushed on. "He insisted that I compete in the local Cyberlympics thing. I'm sure you know the winners on a local level can go on to compete at bigger events, for cash and recognition mostly. He was so insistent about it that I went along. I thought I had it all figured out. I planned to fail. That would get Julian off my back, and I could go back to hacking my own way. But I made a fatal mistake. I let Julian enter me."

Smith shook his head. "He used your Kiss of Death name."

No one who wasn't a kickass hacker himself would ever have

guessed that right off. She should never have let Julian fill out the
entry papers. She'd kept putting it off, so he'd done it behind her
back. "Yeah. I'd spent years building a business based on the Kiss of
Death name. IT companies, cyber security firms, programmers everywhere knew that name." Defeat and devastation sank her lower in
her seat. "But it gets worse, he not only entered me under that name,
he attached it to my real name. He didn't know what he was doing. I
thought my only choices were either to win or lose not only the
competition but my entire career along with it. But right after I got to
the arena, I came up with what I thought was a brilliant solution."

"What did you do, baby?"

"I called my mom for a ride. If Kiss of Death never showed, no
one would ever know if she could've won it or not. My career is built
on secrecy, so not showing did no harm. If I'd known what that
phone call was going to cost me, I would've just competed. Even if I'd
lost, it wouldn't have been as bad as what happened."

This time Smith was silent. He seemed to understand that the
grief couldn't be soothed with words. It had to exist both inside and
outside of its time and place. Grief wasn't a straight line. It ebbed and
flowed constantly. Mercy assumed it always would. "Anyway, so..."
her voice fractured, and she clung harder to his hand.

"Baby, you don't have to tell me."

"I want to. I need to," she insisted.

"Take your time then. You have to let the pain breathe when it
wants to. Sometimes you have to let it have you, and I will be right
here every single time to make sure you have a lifeline to bring you
back out of it."

And she knew he would. No one else could ever be strong enough
to bring her out of the endless well of grief that closed its fists around
her throat and refused her breath. Her lifeline would have to be a
giant big enough to terrify the things that frightened her, to decimate
the shackles of her past, and to free her of the chains of guilt. It had to
be him.

"Julian had insisted on driving me to the event. He knew I didn't
really want to compete. He probably figured if he didn't take me I

wouldn't go. He kept saying if I knew how good I was I wouldn't be so afraid to do things. But he had to work that day, so he left after he dropped me off. I called my mom, and she came and picked me up. On our way home, she stopped at a yellow light and the guy behind us got mad. He was cursing and honking. It scared both of us. Then he started tailing us. She kept changing lanes, but he stayed with us. I have no idea why. The guy was an asshole. Eventually, he backed off, but my mom was afraid to go home. We drove around long enough that he turned off and went away. We also got lost, and it had started to rain.

"The last thing I remember was bright lights shining in the rearview mirror and my mom looking like she'd seen a ghost. She took a turn too fast, and we careened off the road and down an embankment. We hit a tree, and..." She couldn't ever seem to finish that story. She'd tried to tell the police about the truck, but there was no evidence, and the concussion had muddled the story when she'd gotten to the hospital.

38

Julian knew. Smith's blood quaked with the kind of vengeance only satisfied by violence. He longed to rip the steering wheel from the car itself, but he doubted that would satisfy the desire to see her brother burn for what he'd done.

He'd known. Smith was certain. He knew she didn't want to compete, knew to enter her under her real name, knew if he offered to take her and then left, she'd call her mom for a ride home early, and had them followed.

Savage brutality had long been the way of the Castellas cartel. It had only gotten worse after Mercy's father's death. To earn yourself a seat of honor at the Castellas table, you had to murder someone from your past life, someone you'd loved. She'd said she couldn't see the driver. Julian himself could've been driving that truck, or he'd gotten someone else to do his dirty work for him.

Suddenly, the dominos began to fall in succession. Realization rocked through him. Running a car off the road was not an appropriate entry requirement for earning one's bones in the Castellas cartel. It didn't guarantee death and would've been seen as cowardly. Was Julian intending to kill both his sister and his mother? Every muscle in Smith's body contracted with hot fury. Was Julian being punished now for the way he'd gone about it and because he'd only managed one kill? Did he send the woman tonight to bring him Mercy so he could finish the job himself to save his father's surname, the one Julian himself didn't go by? Valon had been their mother's last name. It wasn't until that moment, that Smith realized he was madly in love with Mercy Castellas. The name served to freeze his blood. She didn't even know her own name.

Julian was probably furious that Mercy wasn't killed in the accident. That's why he'd told her she was lucky. Perhaps, if Mercy had managed to hack the DoD and get him the designs, that would've been enough to restore his honor once he'd murdered her, as well.

It all made entirely too much sense to be random shots in the dark. Smith vowed he would never rest until Mercy was no longer in danger from her brother.

Her choked words ripped him from his vows. "That's why I have to find Julian. I have to know what trouble he's gotten us into this time. Not knowing is killing me. Whatever he's done, whomever he's working with or for, I can get him out of it. I just have to know who they are."

"What?" His mission was cemented in his soul by the desperation in her voice. "No. You are not going to find Julian. I will not ever allow you to be in danger."

Frustration pursed her lips. "Why do you think he's in danger? Do you think that woman really knows Julian? I thought maybe she was just saying that because she thought I had the designs, and if I thought she knew where my brother was, that I would go with her."

"I don't know what she thought or who she's working for, but the idea of you searching for Julian makes me crazy. It makes me want to dismantle this car piece by piece with my bare hands."

She gave him a defeated half grin. "You could probably do that if you really wanted to, but I don't think you understand. Julian is all I have. He's my only family. I have to figure out where he is and that he's safe. I won't put myself in danger. I promise. I just have to come up with some way to find him."

"Baby, I need you to understand several things. Your mother's wreck was not your fault. It was the truck driver's fault. None of it had anything to do with you wanting to leave that competition."

"But the police said it was some kind of random act of violence. If we hadn't been on the road then..."

"No." He couldn't believe he was going to make this concession, but he would do anything to rescue her from the guilt of responsibility that came from having to own your part in the death of someone you loved. "How about this? I will stop blaming myself for what happened to my team, if you will stop blaming yourself for your mom."

"Really?" Of all the lies he'd told her, somehow that was the one she doubted.

"I'll try."

She gave him a quick nod. "I'll try, too, then."

Smith managed to steer the car into a spot in the parking garage of their hotel, but his phone rang before he could continue their conversation. It was probably best. He wasn't certain he could've kept from shouting out the rest, and she'd been through enough that night. "Everything okay?" he asked Voodoo. He barely recognized his own tone, strangled with frustration and fury.

"Yeah, we're good. One of the DEA agents was hit, but it was just a graze. I bandaged him up. It'll hurt for a while, but he'll be fine. FBI made fifty-seven arrests. They were pleased, so I guess Mercy's off the hook, with them anyway. Roman's still questioning the woman and the driver. So far, they're pretty tight-lipped, but we both know Roman will get his way eventually."

Smith only managed a grunt of agreement. His mind was a house divided. He was thankful the FBI intended to keep their end of the bargain. At least he should've been. For some reason, at that moment, he hated anything that allowed Mercy to not need him as much. He also hated himself for feeling that way.

"Are you okay, man?" Voodoo inquired.

"Not sure."

"I bet I know who could get you back to stable ground. Why don't you see if she'll oblige. She had a pistol held to her head, so I'm betting she could use some reassurances, too. I just wanted to tell you that we're going to camp out at the Desco Hotel near the Gardens. It's just a precaution. We don't want to lead anyone to either of you, not that anyone walked out of there who'd be coming after you. And, hey, Maddie called T. Sounded like she was pissed he was down here. She told him she thought she was having contractions. Wildcat's flying him back home now."

Another heavy blow of guilt scrambled the already confusing emotions Smith was trying to sort through. "We should be there."

"She may be having contractions, but she's not gonna have his kid tonight. I've delivered a lot of babies. Trust me. I know. She's still not okay with him being gone. After what happened to Chris when she was pregnant with Olivia, I can't really blame her. That, plus her pregnancy hormones probably pushed her over the edge. There are no flights to Lincoln tonight anyway. We'll all head back tomorrow. Have you talked Mercy into coming home with you yet?"

"No," Smith tried to order his thoughts. She still wasn't safe. The cartel was obviously still after her. She needed him to keep her safe. He couldn't tell her about Julian, not yet. Most certainly not if she really believed her brother was all she had in this life.

"Better get to it. She'd be safer up there. According to Griff, her apartment isn't fit to live in anymore anyway."

"Yeah," he studied the concerned gaze etched on her face, "I'll work on it."

"Call us if you need us, just don't need me because there are several women in the hotel bar looking mighty lonely this evening."

Smith tried to draw a cleansing breath, but it was laced with Mercy's delicate strawberry scent. The grip he needed to survive the rest of the night didn't seem to be coming. He needed her. Nothing else was going to suffice.

He ended the call and stared her down. "We're room seven nineteen. Let's go. We need to talk."

Terror flared in her eyes. "Did something bad happen after we left?" The tremor of her voice rocked him to the core.

"No. Everyone's fine. One of the DEA agents took a shot, but Voodoo says he'll be okay."

"Then what's wrong?" Her heartbroken whisper ripped some of the anger from him.

"We'll talk about it in the room, okay?" He tried to modulate his tone to something more soothing, but he wasn't certain he managed it.

"Okay." Caution plagued her features as she watched him climb out of the car and open her door. He hated it. She should never be wary of him. He had to get it together.

Five minutes later, they were standing in one of Dallas's nicer suites.

Mercy ran her hands over the down bedding and then peeked at the skyline before turning back to watch him pace. "Please tell me what's wrong."

He rubbed his hands over his beard measuring each word and tasting them before he gave them breath. "I'm angry. No, that's not it. I'm furious. Mostly with myself, because obviously I haven't shown you how much you mean to me."

Her head shook in confusion. "Yes, you have. Why would you think that?" She stepped in front of him and halted his pacing, showing no traces of fear.

"If you think for even one second that Julian is all you have, that he's who you should be worried over, I fucked something up. How could you think that? What can I do, Mercy? What do I need to do to show you that you are everything to me? I'll do anything. You name it, but hear me when I say this—Julian is not worth your worry, or your guilt, or whatever else you've got going on in that head of yours. He sure as hell isn't worth your life. So please, tell me how I can show you that I love you, that I want to be there for you. That you have *me* in this life. That my team, my parents, my sister will all be your family. They'll love you because I love you."

39

His words shattered through the fear and the confusion that constantly threatened to drag her to the ground and press the air from her lungs. She knew she had him, and she knew he was right about Julian not being worth her life as well, but that didn't mean she could ever walk away from her little brother. That wasn't how family worked.

It was probably fighting dirty, but they had to reach some level of understanding. "So, if your little sister was in trouble, probably with the law, and you couldn't find her, you'd just give up? You'd just leave her to figure it out on her own? You're still not over her being in love with your best friend, but you expect me to believe that you'd just walk away from her if she'd done whatever it is Julian's done to get himself in whatever situation he's in now?"

Her questions hit their intended target. Shock reverberated from his massive form. He squeezed his eyes shut as if that would dam back the emotion he was trying to keep bound. He fought the words, the truth, but it came out anyway. "I was angry. Griff and Hannah lied to me for years. They should've told me."

She stepped closer, leaned up on her tiptoes, and grazed his beard with her fingertips. "I know. Julian should've told me what he was doing a long time before he got himself involved with some drug cartel, but he didn't. And when people that you care about lie to you it makes you feel like you're not worth the truth. I know you're still upset about them lying to you even though you wish you weren't. I know you're trying to get over it, but you're struggling. I understand that. I need you to understand that I cannot walk away from my brother no matter what he's done."

His head fell in a defeated nod. "I know that. It just... it makes me crazy to think about him getting you in trouble, about him getting you hurt."

"I'm not going to get hurt." She wrapped her arms around him and laid her head on his chest. "See, despite all of this, I fell in love with this amazing guy, who even knows what a VPN is and never speaks in sports statistics." She lifted her head to stare into his softened gaze. "And I know he would never let anything happen to me. I've never felt so safe in my life, but I still have to figure out where Julian is and how I can get him out of whatever he's done."

His jaw tensed in irritation, but he nodded. Before she could explain away the tension, his lips were on hers, his tongue was prodding and urgent. She opened for him and reveled in the possessive growl that invaded her mouth. *Mine.* The single word was steeped in the kiss. She devoured that as well.

She longed to prove that she wasn't going anywhere without him. An idea rushed to the forefront of her mind while a hot wash of need soaked her panties. "You know a few minutes ago, when you asked me what you could do to show me that you love me?" she panted.

A hungry grunt was his only response as primal need flared in his eyes. Deftly, he unzipped her dress. Her body rolled against his as his hands pawed her bare back. Yes. This was what she needed. She couldn't stand any more thoughts about their night or what might happen when she figured out where her brother was. For now, all that mattered was the two of them. "Show me," she urged. "Stop holding back with me. Hold me down. Take me hard. Stop acting like I'm so fragile you might break me, or that I'm already broken. I'm not. I don't need roses, or chocolates, or gentleness, or whatever else other women might want. I need you. The real you. I don't want to be safe with you. I want you to lose control with *me*." Tortured yearning heated in his eyes as he stared her down and started to protest. She shook her head. "Don't you dare ask me if I'm sure, or tell me to mean what I say. Don't you dare. I know my own mind. If you want me to believe that you know that too, then prove it. You promised to fuck me so hard I ached. Do your worst, then do more. I need that, right here and right now. So, get to it."

His choked groan was the only warning she received before his hands attacked her dress, tearing it off leaving her in nothing but a wet thong and heels. That drew a bellowed growl from him that she was certain the rest of the hotel probably heard. Her blood thrummed hot and fast through her veins. Every erogenous zone in her body took on her heated pulse.

She ran her hands under his suit coat smoothing the fabric of his shirt, anxious to feel the brawny flexing muscles that comprised him. She longed to be manhandled, forced, commanded to do his bidding. She knew if he'd allow himself the pleasure, that's precisely what she would get.

SOMETHING PRIMAL AND INSTINCTIVE, that he'd tried his whole life to keep at bay, roared to life at her demands. The sanity that would've proven to him that this was wrong, gave up the will to fight on. She needed him to rectify every terrorizing thing she'd endured that day, and every demon from the depths of hell wasn't going to keep him from doing just that.

He was too far gone. There were too many things outside of his control, too many things unresolved between them. He burned with the things he didn't know and clung only to the things he did. She wanted him to prove himself. Fine. He'd make amends in the morning. That night she was going to get exactly what she'd begged for.

He threaded his fingers through her long hair and gripped it with force. Before he could make his first demand, her head fell back offering up the tempting column of her throat and a breathy moan escaped her lips. "Yes. Please."

Those two words shredded the last fragment of his sanity. He raked his teeth to the hollow of her throat. "Remember that you begged for this, because I'm not stopping until I'm satisfied and you're screaming out my name."

Her eyes opened at that. "Good."

He released her hair, tore off his jacket, and ripped off his shirt before he fell into a chair. "Get on your knees," he ordered. She started to step out of the heels, but he shook his head. "I didn't say anything about those fuck-me heels, baby. I told you to get on your knees. I've been waiting on this for so long. I'm out of patience." Another reedy moan spilled from her lungs as she fell to her knees between his legs. "That's it." He used both hands to gesture to his crotch. It currently felt like it was on fire and the only cure was deep in her throat. His cock tented the fly of his dress pants, eagerly rising to the occasion. "Now."

Her breasts rose and fell with rapid pants mesmerizing him as she worked the buckle of his belt. He lifted enough to let the pants drop lower down his legs. "I want to feel those tits on my thighs while you taste how bad I hurt for you, how bad I burn for you. Did you think that tight little pussy is the only thing that makes it better? It's not. Your mouth is going to take the first load of cum I've got for you, baby. Now, suck me."

Her little tongue teased her own lush lips drawing another strangled groan from him. Her hot breaths whispered over his cock when she finally freed him of his boxer briefs. Beads of cum glistened at his tip. She leaned forward and spun her tongue over his head, consuming it readily.

"Fuck," grunted from his mouth as his head lolled at the exquisite sensation. She took a hesitant, exploratory suck, but then she pulled back. She made a show of licking his need from her lips. Who the hell had taught her to do that? He gripped the arms of the chair and bared his teeth. "Tell me I'm your first," he demanded. "Tell me my cum is the first you've tasted."

That seemed to summon her inner sex kitten. She stared up at him submissively through thick black lashes, her lips a deep flushed pink. "You're my first," she assured. The breathy words were another lash of raw pleasure to his engorged tip, wet from her mouth.

"I better be your only," he growled. "And I didn't tell you to stop." She went back to work, and his head fell back in rampant satisfaction. "I used to watch you read when we were running surveillance on you," he admitted stupidly. "I used to fantasize about you doing this to me." To his shock, that drew a loud moan from her lips that vibrated down his shaft. He lifted his head, certain he was going to die from the pleasure coursing through him. "You like that, baby? You like that I used to watch you, get hard for you, wish I could make you take me down your throat just like you are now?"

"God, yes," she admitted as she pulled away with a hard pop.

This woman, this gift from the divine, made specifically for him, was perfection in a very petite frame, and he could never possibly love anything more.

40

When he had her like this, when he allowed her to access the potent femininity the world around her tried to squelch, she swore she felt unstoppable. Her heart hammered against her rib cage, like it couldn't contain her love for this man, still trying to summon control over his own desires.

She was awed by the sheer amount of rugged power that sat before her in an opened suit. His thighs were boulders on either side of her head. His thick arousal, so engorged it must've hurt, beckoned her to soothe its strain. Curiosity deterred her momentarily. She needed to touch him first. Slipping her thumb up the throbbing veins that ran along the back of his cock, she watched him enlarge again, something she hadn't thought possible.

The chair creaked in protest, as if in fear he would reduce it to a pile of splinters if he gripped it any harder. Heady accomplishment coursed through her. She made this massive mountain of a man so needy he couldn't contain his own force. Lust sheened in his darkened eyes.

Determined to prove to him that he didn't have to control anything but her, she leaned in and drew him deep into the hungry hollow of her mouth. She'd read about women doing this enough to have some clue how men wanted to be blown.

As if he could hear her thoughts, his hand gripped her hair once again, this time with less finesse, and the words, "To your throat," choked from him. Since that had been her plan, she readily complied, delving deeper with each hungry suck. His salty flavor, all male and all hers, danced on her tongue.

"I love the way you taste." She had no idea if that's something he would care to know, but she was compelled to say it. She wanted more so she returned to tend his blazing need.

A string of curse words flew from his lips, making her grin despite her mouth overflowing with his cock. She wrapped her hand around his base and moved it in rhythm with her mouth.

"Jesus," he spat, "I don't fucking believe I'm your first," he groaned. His huge hips flexed, bringing more of his unending length toward her throat. "Sorry." That word took on the same harsh scrape of his curses.

She released him and watched the colorful display of need throb in his head. "Don't be, and you are my very first." She spun her tongue over his head, taunting him.

"I better be the only man you give that greedy little mouth to." His grip on her hair tightened bringing the combination of pleasure and pain she craved to her scalp. He pressed her lips back to his head, forcing them to part over his tip. Liquid need dripped down her thighs now. The white thong was translucent with her own craving, but desperation to please him was all that mattered.

With her free hand, she explored the strength of his inner thighs. Rough, wiry hair met her touch, enlivening the nerve endings in her fingers. That masculine musk she loved permeated her lungs with every breath she managed. She was entirely absorbed in his flavors, and that was all she would ever require.

He rocked forward, lifting his hips clumsily now. His sheer size and magnitude of his hunger kept him from being easy with her. Accomplishment shimmered through her lack of conscious thoughts. She was driven only by the constant need to tear down every wall he had erected around himself. She'd shatter through them all to prove that this was what she wanted.

A sheen of sweat glimmered across his stomach. She moved her hand there and then let it slip back down his thighs until she hesitantly teased his sac.

He roared out his pleasure. She paused only long enough to make certain he wanted more. Every plane of his unyielding form was drawn taut. She sucked harder. He managed a few less than intelligible words. "So good, baby. So... mmm... damn...good." The man was all but purring. Her own mouth had fostered those words. She drew his thick tip deeper in the wet heat.

She caressed beneath his length again, reveling in the tightened state he was in. She'd done that. Deep feminine pride welled inside of her as the two sides of herself united in him.

As HIS CLIMAX tore through him, filthy words spewed from his mouth. "Drink it like my naughty girl." He was certain some part of himself would eventually regret those words, but she'd demolished every well-practiced rule he tried so damn hard to live by. She'd awakened the starved animal housed inside of him, set it free, and offered him the delectable feast of her body. She wanted to see what he was like when he lost control. She was about to find out. "I know you want it. Show me my cum on your tongue before you swallow it all."

Her greedy groan vibrated down his shaft as cum spurted from his head, hot and fast. When she lifted her head, he not only saw his release on her tongue, he saw her own need glistening there between those thighs that drove him wild. She shifted back and forth on her knees, needy for friction there where she was soaked. Another deep growl sounded from him. "I'm not finished with you, honey. Not by a long shot."

"Good," she fucking cooed all for him. Damn him to hell. He wasn't going to survive her.

Though dizzy from the intensity of the release she'd drawn from deep in his balls, he lumbered to his feet and kicked off the rest of his clothes. Then he lifted her off the ground and cradled her, resurrecting some semblance of the man he'd always been with her.

She stared up at him with dark greed blazing in her eyes. "I need so much more."

He was certain his own expression was much the same. She had no idea what she was asking for, but telling her no was beyond him.

"Are you going to remember you said that in the morning, honey? Or am I going to get to kiss that pussy better because I'm about to fuck it raw."

"Please, please," she whimpered as he positioned her on her hands and knees, letting those heels hang off the edge of the bed. She rubbed her thighs together again spreading her own wet heat. Her body begged for his friction and his force.

"Head down, baby. Keep your ass in the air for me."

She must have had a script of the endless fantasies he had about her. She shook her thick, lush ass back and forth and then shook her head at his order as she stared back at him. He was taunted by everything from the curious gaze locked in her eyes to the sway of her endless curves.

Stepping behind her, he gripped her ass with punishing force, making certain she felt every hard angle of his body. "Playing with fire, honey."

She turned back once more. "Then let it burn."

With that, he landed his hand against her ass with a quick smack. Her ass glowed pink and jiggled under his force. His previously flaccid cock filled with ragged, desperate need all over again. "You think you can wear these naughty little panties and then tell me no and get away with it? Or is this what you crave? You wanted to tease me, didn't you? Drive me fucking insane with want?" Another smack, this one harder. Her cheek was painted with his aggression. When she moaned out his name, she obliterated him. "You did. I know you did. And now I know what my baby needs when she doesn't obey, don't I?" Another smack and then he rubbed away the sting. "You need that pussy filled so full you can feel it in that greedy throat that just drank me dry. Don't you? Say it."

"God, yes," she sobbed out.

With his free hand, he pressed her face to the mattress. "Then you keep your head down, and you take it."

Tracing down the satin strip of her thong, he toyed with the puckered rosebud between her cheeks drawing another frantic moan from her. Then he speared two thick fingers between the swollen folds of her pussy, in and out, with no reprieve. He shuddered from the feeling of what his cock was about to get. "So wet, all for me." He panted. "Gonna soak down my cock, aren't you?"

"Now, please," she begged. Her fingers clawed at the comforter seeking an anchor he would only allow her to find in him.

"Not yet, baby. First I'm gonna teach you to behave." Her pussy flexed constantly against his fingers urging them deeper. "Feel that. Feel how badly you need me. Think about that the next time you decide not to do as you're told." He fucked her thoroughly with his fingers. His cock throbbed out its demand to be satisfied yet again. Wrapping his other hand tight around his heavy strain, he jacked himself once, twice. It only frustrated him more. His own fist held nothing on the tight silky heaven between her thighs. He needed her. Nothing else would ever do.

His head shook back and forth, and words continued to free flow from his mouth like a man possessed. "How could you not know what you do to me? How bad I ache to have your gorgeous little body under me? How bad I need you?"

"Smith, please," she moaned into the mattress.

"That's right, baby. Scream my name. If you're coming, it's because of me. Tell everyone who you belong to."

Losing all ability to draw this out any longer as she continued to groan out his name, he climbed on the bed behind her and exchanged his fingers for his cock. Gripping her hips, he slammed into her with deep, destructive force, tearing away anything that kept them apart.

Certain he would never become accustomed to the otherworldly perfection of her tight, wet heat around him, a strangled groan lodged in his chest. "So fucking perfect. So tight. Gonna ruin you, baby. You wanted me to take what I want. I want the spoils of my war."

"Oh God," she panted as she met him, thrust for thrust, moaning each time his sac slapped her fevered skin.

"I didn't tell you to call Him yet," Smith reminded her. "I'm not near finished with you."

41

inally. Mercy's body clamored for his force, for his satisfaction, for him. Until she'd met Smith, her life had asked her far too many questions that seemed to have no answer. Now, she understood. He was the answer. Together they made sense. It was the only thing that ever had.

Nothing else mattered. Another husky groan of her name aligned the frantic pulses of need from the tip of her scalp to the bottom of her toes. They all centered in her core, now so full of him that she knew she would always feel incomplete when he wasn't occupying her body.

Two rough fingers circled her clitoris. The soaked satin that covered it served to amplify the heavenly sensation. Her entire world timed itself to his tender touch, the perfect juxtaposition to his rough invasion.

Unadulterated pleasure erupted from where they were joined and sizzled outward to her limbs. Ecstasy tensed her muscles. The hungry spasms of her pussy tore another growl from him as they collapsed to the mattress. His heavy weight on top of her only added to the perfection of her climax. She was surrounded on all sides by Smith, and nothing could hurt her there.

The orgasm blinded her. It shattered everything she'd ever thought significant. It both altered her and aligned her. She didn't have to exist as both a fearful naive girl and the kiss of death. Because of him, because he really did love both of her sides, she'd discovered that the two halves could become a whole.

Her release seemed to summon his own. With a roar of lust, or maybe love, he filled her full. Harsh male tremors worked through him. He tensed against her and another heady dose of feminine pride brought a grin to her face. His satisfaction became the largest jewel in her crown.

"Shit, baby, I'm sorry." He eased off of her and then sank back down on the mattress as if the quick movement had been more than he could take. He did manage to cradle her to him, though. When he brushed kisses in her hair, she grinned.

"Why are you sorry? That was amazing."

He lifted his head and stared at her through a sleepy gaze. "I'm sorry for crushing you. I'd say I was sorry for being so rough with you, but you don't look like you minded as much as I thought you might."

"Good. Maybe you'll finally believe me. I loved that. I love you." She ran her hands over the hills of hair-covered muscle that comprised his chest.

He drew a stabilizing breath. "I love you, too, sweetheart. You're the most perfect woman in the entire world."

"For you," she insisted.

"Yeah, well, it was my world I was referring to. I know it's been fast and there's still a whole lot of stuff that isn't solved yet, but I want you to move in with me. I'll never let you down. I'll never let you fall. I swear. Just please think about it."

She'd already been thinking about it. She was certain this was not how normal relationships worked, but nothing about this was normal. Most girls didn't start dating because they'd been inadvertently hacking into a government stronghold, and they most definitely did not throw up on a guy when first meeting him only to move in with him the following week. Moving on from that thought, before she could get embarrassed all over again, she nodded against him. "I want to move in with you, too, even if it is fast, but..." She knew he didn't want to hear the rest of her statement, but she still had to make it.

"But?" There was an edge of the demanding timbre he used when they were locked in the throes of passion in the single word. She wondered if that tone would ever fail to turn her on.

Trying to focus, she closed her eyes and listened to his heartbeat. "But I have to find Julian first."

HE HADN'T HAD to ask. He'd already known that's what she was going to say. It was his response that he was trying to calculate. With a quick, silent prayer, he pressed the words from his lips. "Baby, I need for you to consider for just a moment that your brother is only out for his own glory, that he wanted those designs so he could sell them to the highest bidder, not because he had anything to do with formulating them. Maybe he thinks that will make him a hero. I don't know, but isn't it a possibility?"

She leaned up on her elbow. The absence of her heat stung his chest. "I have thought of that, but that doesn't mean I'm going to give up on him. It's like I told you earlier, you wouldn't just abandon Hannah because she'd done something bad."

He weighed every word carefully. "You're right. I wouldn't, but if he asked you to steal the designs, that doesn't make me think that he values your relationship as much as you seem to. If Hannah thought I was in trouble, she wouldn't stop until she found a way to help me. The same way I would be for her. But, it's a two-way street. Would Julian throw himself on a sword to save you? From what I know of him, I just... don't think he would." He leaned up on his own arm to match her stance and tried to soothe her as he stroked his thumb tenderly over her face. "The difference between wanting to be a hero and actually being one is the things you're willing to sacrifice. It's not taking on the biggest bully so you get all the glory." He shook his head. "Sometimes, it's not seeing the people you care about the most for months at a time. Sometimes it's burying your best friends because they really did sacrifice everything for their country. I want you to have every single good thing this world has to offer. I'm honored you think I'm one of those good things. But see, I'm willing to sacrifice anything to make sure you get the best. I haven't heard much about the things Julian would willingly give up for you."

He was certain he'd stated that much too harshly. She'd stripped him to his core. The tidal wave of emotion and the combined climaxes had robbed him of strength, of smarts, of the ability to sugarcoat anything at all. The raw truth, even if he wasn't going to show her his proof, had to come out into the light if this was ever going to work.

She stared up at him. He couldn't quite read her expression. Panic threatened to take hold of him, and he simply didn't have the strength to manage it. When she offered him a pained half smile, he ached. "People don't change," she whispered.

His brow furrowed. "I don't want you to change. You're perfect just the way you are."

That got him a real grin. "Thank you, but that's not what I meant." She traced a fingertip over his chest again. Her touches were always intoxicating. He had no idea how he'd existed without her for so long. "My brother will always leap before he looks. The very same way you will always be a hero. You'll always fight for what you believe is right, always stand up for the little guy, always protect the people you love. Even if you don't see yourself that way, that doesn't change the fact that you are those things. You won't ever change because that's who you are all the way down to your core. Julian can't alter the way he is, either, but neither can I. I'm his big sister. I taught him that I would always get him out of any situation he gets himself into, and I won't stop that now. I can't. That would be like asking you to leave your team behind in the middle of a firefight."

But his team was the good guys. He wanted to scream. Instead he whispered, "The Sevens. We call ourselves The Sevens. That's why the security company is Tier Seven."

She nodded. "Okay, then it would be like asking you to leave The Sevens behind. You wouldn't, and you couldn't. I can't do that to Julian. Will you help me? Please. If you can just help me find him and figure out how to help him, then I can move in with you and really start living life. If you can't, I'll understand. I just thought we might find him faster if we work together."

Squeezing his eyes shut, the love for her and the hatred for her brother went to war in his mind again. "I don't know if I can do that," he choked. God, he never wanted to tell her no. Everything about it was abhorrent.

She nuzzled her head against him. Desperation driving him, he gathered her in his arms and held her tight to his chest. "I know you can't. You just proved my point. You're the hero. You'll always be *my* hero. And Julian will likely always *want* to be a hero and never quite hit the mark. He might even become a villain, if I don't stop him. I have to walk in the middle between a real hero and a wannabe, I guess. I have to exist as the woman who's so in love with the hero that she'll never have her own heart back because he holds it entirely in his big, huge hands. And I have to be the big sister who always saves the wannabe. I don't get to choose a side."

42

Some incessant and annoying noise kept trying to awaken Mercy. Had she not been wrapped in the tight cocoon of Smith with the full weight of his arm slung over her, she might've gotten up to seek out the offender and throw whatever it was off of the balcony. No one should ever be awakened from sleep like this. The noise stopped, and she reveled in being safe and warm, where the dragons of worry over her brother couldn't reach her.

When the buzzing started again, she finally accepted defeat. It wasn't going away, and she would have to get up and deal with it because Smith was still snoring lightly in her ear. Grinning at that, she wriggled as gently as she was able and escaped the sanctuary of his arms. A shiver shot through her naked body, now robbed of his warmth.

The man was like her own personal oven, and she swore she'd been freezing for most of her life. Her feet protested movement, but the plush carpeting at least muffled her quick steps as she tried to locate the source of the noise.

As a testament to how well she'd been sleeping, it took her awhile to determine that the sound was her own cell phone inside her computer bag. No one had called her in more than a week. Who on earth was calling her at five in the morning?

Realization gripped her. Grabbing the bag, she raced into the bathroom and eased the door shut. She unzipped three zippers all at once and finally found the phone.

Her brother's name glowed on the screen. Her heart leapt from her chest to her throat and pounded with such voracity she was concerned it might spill out of her mouth. "Julian?" She coughed. "Where are you?"

"Miss Valon," responded a voice she swore she'd heard before, but it was definitely not her brother's.

"Who is this? Where is Julian? Why do you have his phone?" She gagged on the terrifying possibilities that tallied in her mind.

The voice gave an ominous chuckle. "Your brother is here. He's... indisposed at the moment due to his continued failings of the Castellas name." The pause after that was entirely too long. "If you'd like to see him alive, you're going to need to come here as well, dear. And you'll need to come alone."

"Who are you?"

"That doesn't matter. We thought we'd sent you a more pleasant invitation to the little party your new friends hosted, but since you never arrived, we'll do this my way."

The memory of the hot end of a pistol dancing against her temple shot adrenaline-soaked fear from her gut to her throat. It seared through her chest and sliced her in two. "I'm not coming anywhere until you let me talk to my brother."

Another sinister laugh filled her ear. "So much like your father." Her father? Mercy couldn't fathom why he'd said that. "If you want to talk to Julian, go get in the car Mr. Hagen drove you to the hotel in. Once we see that you're in the car, I'll text you the address. Remember, you are to come alone."

"Why?"

Smith Hagen would no more allow her to drive herself to whatever this was than he'd... abandon The Sevens. As if her words had summoned this, she knew what she was going to have to do. He would always be the hero.

"Do as you're told, dear. If you can't follow instructions, I will make certain that you never see Mr. Hagen nor your brother ever again. In fact, no one will ever see them again. Your security detail isn't there anymore. Hagen is alone, and I am not. You have five minutes to be in the car. One hour to arrive. Or your little brother will suffer your tardiness."

The call ended. She shook as the realization shattered her soul, and frigid hands of dread gripped her. Hot tears cascaded down her face, trying to melt through the dread, but she didn't have time for that. Wiping them away, she slipped out into the bedroom and silently dressed.

She knew she should leave and never look back, but she just couldn't do that to him. He was the hero, and heroes never gave up. He'd come looking for her. He wouldn't stop until he found her. She loved him far too much to let him die for her, and she knew he'd never stop until they'd killed him. That's what heroes did. Grabbing a hotel notepad, she returned to the bathroom and scribbled, *I love you so much, but I can't do this. Please don't look for me. Just be the hero. The world needs that. ~ Mercy*

With shaking hands, she placed it on her pillow. She let herself have one last look at his gorgeous form, forcing herself to remember the way it felt to be in his arms, the way he laughed, and how he would look at her like maybe she was magic. She prayed, as she slipped out the door, that if there was any good left anywhere in the world, that someday they'd find their way back to each other. The weight of terror and agony crushed her, but she pressed on. She had to save her brother.

SOMETHING WASN'T RIGHT. Smith had been in Special Forces long enough to know if that thought was the first you had when you awoke, things were bad. Sitting up, he tried to determine why the tug in his gut wouldn't let up. Something fluttered to the ground when he threw back the bed linens. Far more importantly, where was Mercy?

Forcing his still-exhausted limbs to move, he lifted the note from the floor, and his entire world shattered. He stared at every word, dissected each individual letter, and determined that none of it made any sense. What couldn't she do? When had she left? The abhorrent pain of her not being in his arms and in his bed robbed him of the ability to determine anything with any certainty.

She loved him, but she left. His heart and mind fractured. How could those two facts exist in the same plane? One automatically negated the other, didn't it?

His cell phone rang from the bedside table. The pain had already carved him out, emptied him. He existed only to heal. Being able to go on hinged on him finding her and repairing whatever had caused her to love him but also to leave him.

"Mercy?" he choked without ever looking to see who was calling. It had to be her because no one else existed to him at that moment.

"Shit," Roman's gruff voice clawed against Smith's eardrums. "That answers my question. She's not there, I take it."

"Where is she?" Smith's own tone was unrecognizable, a broken hollow of the man he'd been when she was in his arms. Nothing made sense. Not Roman, not the Sevens, not anything. "She left a note."

"That said?"

"Uh," he stared down at her uneven scrawl, not certain he could read it aloud without dissolving into the hellish abyss he'd existed in when half of his team had been killed. "Not to look for her. And... to be the hero."

Roman's tone softened slightly. "All right, Hagen, get it together. If you're the hero, who is our villain?"

The conversation they'd had the evening before filtered back through his mind. "Julian."

"Precisely. DEA has a phone call made from his cell phone to hers a half hour ago. That's why I called you. Before he stopped checking in, Wakefield managed to get a tracer placed on Julian's cell. Julian is in a home that sits on several acres on the outskirts of Dallas. They're fifty miles from the last place Wakefield reported them being. I imagine that's where the Castellas have set up shop since Wakefield was compromised. There's been no communication from Julian until he called Mercy, so we had no idea where to find him. But now we do. So, let's go get her. And if anyone asks, that note you have said that she was coerced into going to this location. She left the address, and she asked you to rescue her."

Smith wished it had said that. At least that would've made him certain that Julian's phone call had prompted her disappearance. Surely, Julian would've told her that he'd never sent Smith to keep her safe. He had no idea where they stood, but if she was in a Castellas compound, he wouldn't rest until he knew she was safe. If she never wanted to see him again after that, then…

He couldn't go there. There were just too many losses attached to his name. He wouldn't survive another. He focused only on Roman's instructions. "Because if law enforcement believes she was kidnapped…" The thought gripped his throat. It had claws. It wouldn't let go and refused him more words.

"Then the rules all turn in our favor, don't they? T-Byrd isn't here. We're doing this my way."

43

Mercy clung to the tenuous remains of her sanity. Nothing would ever be harder than leaving Smith, so regardless of whatever was coming for her she'd already done the most difficult part. That did nothing to soothe her, but it was a complete, conscious thought outside of the fear so she focused on that. The things behind her were worse than whatever lay ahead.

Her brother was likely dead. If he wasn't, why wouldn't they have let her talk to him to ensure that she did as they asked? If she was going to suffer the same fate because of these people, at least Smith was safe. That was all that mattered.

The blue Lincoln was still behind her. She'd seen it before at the hotel parking garage, and it had been following her every mile she'd progressed.

She didn't even have a weapon, not that she would've known what to do with one if she had. Still none of it mattered more than Smith's safety, so she drove on. There was only one thing she had to do before she arrived. It was a last-ditch effort, but she wasn't going down without a fight.

. . .

EVENTUALLY, the GPS on her phone announced that she'd arrived at the texted address. It was a dirt road covered with overgrown clumps of trees. She made the turn and the blue sedan followed.

Her breathing was shallow. Vile revulsion constantly ran the length of her esophagus. Those freezing cold hands of dread strengthened their chokehold. The car bounced over a tree root, and she gripped the steering wheel tighter.

Slamming on the brakes, she came face to face with a wrought iron gate. She could just make out a few brick buildings in the distance. What happened now?

She wasn't left to wonder long. Two men stepped out from the trees bearing rather large, automatic weapons. One of them tapped on the window with the butt of the rifle, and she lowered the window slightly as he rattled off something in Spanish. If he was giving her instructions, she had no idea what he was telling her. The other man turned to face her and she recognized him immediately. "Paul?" she gasped. He'd definitely aged in the two decades, but there was no question as to who he was. What was her mother's old boyfriend doing here? How long had these people had something to do with her life? She'd been eleven years old when he'd dated her mother. None of this made any sense. His only response was a cold glare.

The other man made a clipped remark, still in Spanish. She thought she caught the words alias and angel. "She looks enough like him," he said, switching to English mid-sentence, but his accent said it wasn't his first language. Looks like who? For the thousandth time since the phone call, she wished this was nothing more than some game she'd stupidly decided to play. Her screened reality was much better than whatever this was. "Go through to the main building. They're waiting on you."

"But..."

"Now," the man spat. "He's tired of fucking waiting."

Terror crawled over her skin. Who was he talking about? Was Julian waiting on her? Surely not. The creak of a rusted metal hinge shot through her, making her wince. Her choices were obviously to drive forward or to face a literal firing squad behind her. Neither.

Why wasn't neither choice an option? The car seemed to move forward on its own accord. She must've eased off the brake, but she had no conscious memory of doing so.

Self-preservation eventually caught her. She turned her head left and right calculating how far she might make it if she ran. Not fast enough to outrun a bullet. There were patches of dried grass in the barren Texas dirt, but nothing other than buildings to hide in or around. Surely, wherever she was, they had men with more guns in all of those buildings. If there was a chance Julian was still alive, she had to go in and find him.

The dull thud of metal came a split second before her body bowed forward and smacked the steering wheel. It wasn't hard enough of a collision to deploy the air bag, but she'd definitely been hit. The sensation was all too familiar. She was yanked back in time to her mother's wreck. Turning around she stared into the cruel eyes of the man driving the car behind hers, and knew suddenly where she'd seen him before. "Move it," he snarled. "We're all fucking tired of being here."

EVERY MEMBER of Tier Seven and the DEA and FBI agents all gave Smith a wide berth, but there was not enough room. He paced from one end of Roman's hotel room to the other. He wanted to tear the building apart brick by brick so he could get out of this hell.

"I'm not so sure he's up for this," Voodoo gestured to him.

"I'd love to see you try to stop me," he threatened.

Voodoo's hands went up in surrender. "Just trying to keep you alive. Okay? We're gonna get her out of there, but we're thirteen stories up, and you look like you're contemplating walking through that wall. There are only so many things I can stitch up."

Griff approached without caution. He knew he was the only person in that room that could ever get through to Smith, and nothing about that frightened him. It never had. "Hey, I'm right there with you. If some fuckwad had Hannah, I'd walk through a brick wall to get her back, too. And you'd be right there with me. So, if you wanna go through the fucking wall, I'm right behind you." Smith had no appropriate response, but for the first time in the last hour, his best friend's voice managed to settle him. "Best damn team in the business. I'm thinking we can probably come up with a better way to get to her. Hey, do you remember Harar?"

Smith nodded. "Yeah," he forced the single word from the regret filling his throat. It was the most he'd spoken in the last half hour. Speaking hurt. Breathing hurt. Every fucking thing hurt without her. Julian had lured her to some compound, and now.... He shook his head. Now what? They were waiting on satellite imagery and formulating an extraction plan. It was something he'd done a hundred times. Why didn't anything make sense? A thousand thoughts churned through quicksand, but none could gain ground. Fury pummeled his gut. It rose and fell making certain his chest burned constantly.

Griff offered him his signature smirk. "Hey, if we can get an ambassador out of the consulate of a walled city, we can get your girl out of some rinky-ass drug cartel compound in the middle of Bumfuck, Texas. Right?"

Another nod. He wanted desperately to believe Griff's words. He had to. It wasn't that he doubted The Sevens' abilities. He knew they were the best of the best. It was just that, for him, the stakes had never been this high.

With that realization, several other thoughts forced their way through the scrambled mire in his head. His lies had caused this. He hadn't told her what Julian really was. He never said why the cartel was interested in her, outside of the radar designs. She didn't know what she was driving into when she'd taken his rental car. Even if she hadn't believed Smith, if any harm came to her, it was entirely his fault. If they got her out alive, he'd swear to her that he would never lie to her again. After that, she'd never want to see him again anyway. If he was going to go on, he had to know she was safe. That became his singular mission. Get her out alive. He deserved the pain when she left him. God, he deserved so much worse, but he could not allow her to suffer because of his mistakes.

Two more suits walked into the suite. Roman lifted his head from his laptop. "DEA Special Agents Carter and Mallory. They've been following the Castellas cartel for several years. They likely know Marino's pissing schedule. Direct any questions about the cartel to them. However, I would like to get this woman out of there soon, so if we could speed this up...?"

The agents both gave Roman a single nod. Carter cleared his throat. "As soon as we set the extraction teams, we should be ready."

Mallory spread a few documents out on the bed. "We have a few details to iron out, but we have coordinates and imagery of the compound now. It's definitely not one of Marino's nicer hideouts. They're out on the old Culten property. It's in one of the last parts of unincorporated Dallas County. Culten bought the property and built the main house and outbuildings during the oil boom. He pretty much hated everyone."

"What's this?" asked Roman, pointing to a straight line on the photo, obviously a man-made object.

"That's a large brick wall Culten had built, mainly for privacy. He wanted to keep everyone out. The Cultens were one of Texas's wealthiest families. I should've known Marino would take them out there. Whenever the cartel screws something up, he takes them to some shithole to remind them where they came from and how much they owe him. We don't know how long they've been there, so we're uncertain what it is that they screwed up. The place hasn't even had running water in fifty years."

Griff nodded. "Right, so Bumfuck."

Carter chuckled. "It's just a little east of there, actually."

"Ah, so the thriving shithole of East Bumfuck. Well, that changes... absolutely nothing. Let's get this done."

Smith deeply appreciated Griff's urgency.

Mallory eyed Griff speculatively. "Ranger?"

"Special Forces. Why?"

"You've got that army-bred look. We need to move quickly, but we can't just go in with guns blazing. Marino didn't take power after Castellas's death by being an idiot."

Roman cut into the conversation. "Let's get down to brass tacks. How many armed men are we going to find once we get behind that gate?"

"They always have four men at the gates. Only two show if someone tries to get in. The other two hang back as reinforcements. There will be four or five others stationed around the exterior of the complex, and three crews inside around Marino. Any exterior buildings outside of the main house will also have three to four armed guards. The last time Wakefield checked in they were still in Ft. Worth. There's likely a reason Marino has chosen to stay in the shithole he has them in. If I were a betting man, I'd say he's looking to get rid of the Castellas kids and then get out of town. He doesn't like competition or leaving anything undone. You said Julian made contact with them, right? That would've pissed him off, especially if the kid made him a promise on radar designs he failed to deliver on."

The shrill blare of a siren echoing against Smith's skull hadn't allowed him to hear anything beyond the phrase 'he's looking to get rid of the Castellas kids'. They had to get her out now. It made no sense that everyone was still staring at those plans and working their jaws. Why weren't they moving? He couldn't fully process the room, the people preparing for battle, or anything other than what he'd already lost and what he still stood to lose.

The DEA point man finally turned to the members of Tier Seven. "As for civilian security firms, the rule normally goes—if anyone points a gun at you, then you are free to engage."

44

Another all-too-familiar sensation continued to jolt Mercy's nervous system. She was entirely alone in the dusty relics of the old mansion that she'd been ordered inside of, and yet, she was beyond certain she was being watched.

The man who'd killed her mother was here. The panic had cleared her mind enough to finally recognize his face in the car behind her. Why were these people attacking her family? And where had the men gone? She'd followed their orders to come in the house, and then they'd driven away.

The squeak of her shoe on the chipped marble floor ricocheted through her. Every sound was amplified by the open space. Wherever this was, no one could possibly still be living here.

She came to the first room behind the curved staircase. She peeked inside, unsure if she'd rather find a human or a ghost, realizing the latter was probably safer. No one. Her pulse continued to pound out a cry for help, but even if it could've screamed on behalf of her mouth, no one would've heard her. Whoever owned this house had made certain of that. Closed off completely from any nearby town or neighbors, she wondered if they'd done that out of a fear similar to what she felt in being there.

She understood shutting yourself off because you were afraid. She'd just never seen what that looked like from the future to the past. Perspective. She recalled Wildcat's plane dipping below the clouds and the weight of Smith's hand holding her own. She lambasted herself for not appreciating it more then. Perspective was everything.

She tried to not think of Smith at all. She would never allow him to be hurt trying to save her. No matter the odds stacked against both of them, he would still have come for her. Hero through and through.

"Julian?" she whispered into the ether. Dust particles danced in the jagged light of the rising sun through a shattered windowpane. She wondered if it had been broken recently or a hundred years before her arrival. She gasped when she slipped over something on the floor. She lifted her foot and immediately wished she hadn't. The bullet casing suggested the window hadn't been broken for very long, and that she was likely to meet the same fate.

Her heart slithered to her empty stomach. Acid and fear fought for placement in both her gut and her throat. When her neck started to throb, she knew she had a crippling migraine coming on. Smith had been able to arrest the warning signs so thoroughly the night before, but as soon as she'd left the hotel room, they'd returned with a vengeance. If there was any way she was going to be able to see Julian and tell him how much she loved him, she was going to have to find him fast.

"Julian," she spoke with more volume this time. "Are you here?" The next words rushed from her mouth in a haunted whisper. "Please be here."

An ominous click reached her ears. Whirling around and kicking a storm of dust into the already filthy air, she tried to locate the sound she'd heard. A mere echo of footsteps had her ducking into the next room. Cloth-draped furniture was her only companion, but at least that gave her somewhere to hide.

Before she could duck down behind an old chair, the footsteps were upon her. A frantic yelp wrenched from her lungs when two men in expensive suits sized her up. "Where is my brother?" she demanded. At least the tight clench of her teeth made her sound braver than she felt.

His voice wove through her ears and gripped her throat. She recognized the accent she'd heard from both her landlord and the bathroom attendant. "He's indisposed at the moment. Restorations, you know. Come with me. The boss would like to see you."

"No," she huffed. "I'm not going anywhere with you. What restorations are you talking about? Are you people turning this into some kind of halfway house for murderers?" There. That felt better. She knew she was going down, so she had nothing left to lose. "You take me to my brother right now."

The men eyed each other cautiously. One of them shrugged as he turned back to her. "Fine. Come with me, but we did warn you."

~

GET HER OUT ALIVE. That was all that mattered. Smith slipped silently tree to tree, keeping his boot steps quiet on the hard dirt. Sweat dewed under his vest. Nothing he hadn't dealt with before. He'd done all of this before, and yet none of those times were ever as important as this one.

The DEA agents on his flanks likely had no idea what he was going through. No failure or accomplishment in this life would matter if she wasn't alive and safe.

Griff, Rio, Voodoo, and Reid all moved ahead of him, their footsteps just as silent as his own, like ghosts through a forgotten land and time. They were navigating the relics of a man who'd surrounded himself with monuments to his own money and efforts to keep out the rest of the world. Crumbling brick work, chipped wood, and peeling paint. Nothing worth owning. Everything that mattered was inside one of those buildings, and Smith would stop at nothing to find her because their ending had found them. He always knew it would. No matter how hard he'd tried to outrun it. No matter how many lies he'd told to keep it at bay. It had bested him. It bested everyone. He just had to make certain this wasn't her end. It could be his. He'd already cheated it once. He doubted it would let him win again.

Griff halted at the base of a large elm, the only kind of tree that would ever grow in these conditions. He began his ascent to what had been identified as the perfect sniper's perch. Reid took another tree nearby.

Smith, Rio, and Voodoo pressed on. FBI and DEA agents surrounded the compound, but everyone awaited Roman's command through the high-end radio systems mounted in their helmets.

Griff's voice sounded in Smith's ear. "Got eyes on four hostiles at the gate. All armed. Two more heading to your southeast. Have a clear shot from my position, but I can't take them all."

"Standby, Haywood," Roman instructed. "We're not in position yet. You're not doing this on your own."

Dean and Rylee were along the back wall placing explosives. Derek, Trent, and Jase were performing the same task along the western barrier. Everything had been planned down to the moment Smith would be able to cross the threshold and find Mercy. His only prayer was that she would survive this.

Special Agent Carter's voice sounded next. "Any chance you could get me a pic of the ones at the gate?"

Voodoo turned back to face Smith. They wore matching expressions of confusion.

"Say again your last. You want me to take a picture?" Griff sounded thoroughly nonplussed.

Reid came over the comm unit. "He's old. Can't handle his phone and a big-boy gun. I got it."

"Cantori, off is the general direction in which I'd like you to fuck," Griff sniped. Smith ground his teeth. They didn't have time for bullshit.

A text came through to all of their phones. Smith studied the image Carter had requested.

Carter's voice filled the helmets next. "That's Angel Del Santos and Paul Garcia at the gate. They call Angel 'the Reaper.' He's the lead in Marino's security team. I've no clue what he's doing on guard detail, but if we can take him out before we enter, that's all the better. Paul was a good friend of Castellas, but he pledged his honor to Marino as soon as he took power. He was always the guy in charge of keeping up with Castellas's wife and kids before Armend's death. He used to pretend to be the mom's boyfriend if I recall correctly."

Frustration mounted in Smith's chest until it finally flew from his mouth. "What's your position, Roman? Let's get this done."

Instead of Roman responding, Rylee did. "Feds took out two on the back. We're ready when you are."

Derek Kingston finally said the words Smith had longed to hear. "Claymore mine is ready, Roman. Just tell me when."

"You are free to engage," Roman answered.

The remotely detonated mine erupted to the west, and just as it had been planned, every Castellas guard spun in that direction turning the barrel of their own automatic weapons past Griff, Reid, and every other sniper surrounding the northern front.

"Haywood? I think they're pointing their guns at you," Reid taunted.

Four shots sounded and four guards hit the dirt. "Not anymore," Griff responded. Three others raised their guns and fired randomly in Griff's general direction. None of them hit their intended mark before they landed in pools of their own blood.

Smith and Voodoo led the charge through the gates.

45

Mercy began to understand, as she was led to the top of the stairs, that the reason she hadn't encountered anyone for so long was because she'd explored the wrong end of the mansion. Her sense of self-preservation must've been stronger than she'd originally given it credit.

They passed pairs of armed guards stationed throughout the long upstairs hallway. She wondered what they were guarding but knew better than to ask. Besides, there were other, far more pressing questions. "Where are you taking me?"

"To see the boss. Like I said," the man with the deep, jagged scar carved into his cheek responded. He muttered something in Spanish, and she was certain it was a derogatory name. The other man with them was younger, and suddenly she remembered him. "You were at the coffee shop when I met Smith. You offered to get me a refill." The man only stared at her like she wasn't terribly bright. "Why were you following me?" Still no response. She turned her attention back to the other guy. "How did you get that scar?" spilled from her mouth. *Shut up, Mercy.* Clearly, the migraine was already starting to affect her good judgment.

"You ask a lot of questions," he huffed. "Maybe I ought to tell the boss you didn't make it in this time either, and take care of this problem myself."

Mercy immediately understood that she was the problem that needed to be taken care of. Cold sweat turned her skin clammy while her heart continued to shoot hot blood into her veins in erratic bursts. Certain she was either going to be sick or pass out, she wondered if being unconscious wouldn't be better. It seemed a far more appealing idea than being shot while she was fully aware.

This end of the home seemed to have held up better than the other. It was still filthy and on the verge of collapsing, but there was uncovered furniture and signs of life. They reached a closed door at the end of the hallway. She closed her eyes and prayed that whatever was about to happen to her, Smith would never blame himself.

The man with the scar knocked on the door and then opened it without prompting. The air ripped from Mercy's lungs as she screamed.

A man had his fist raised over Julian's face. Blood was already seeping from his lips and a deep gash on his cheek.

"Mercy?" Julian coughed. "What are you doing here?"

No longer caring what they did to her, she rushed into the room. "Are you okay?" She wasn't certain how to comfort him. He looked like he hadn't bathed in days. Ripped clothes hung from his body, and he was hunched over oddly. Blood was caked in his dark brown hair. He didn't appear able to move. It took her far too long to notice the man seated at a leather inlaid desk, watching her brother be beaten. Glaring at the man hatefully, she snarled, "What is wrong with you? What is wrong with all of you? Look, I'll figure out some way to get you those stupid designs, but let him go."

"You have always reminded me so much of your mother," the man stated dryly as if that weren't a compliment.

"Well, I guess you would know since you all had something to do with her death," Mercy came right back. "Talk," she demanded as she landed her hand on a bloody knife laid open on the desk. "Now."

Julian's assailant lifted his fist again, and she spun his direction, spurred into action. "If you hit him again, it might be the last thing I ever do, but I will kill you myself." Her voice shook, and she wondered if she could really drive a knife into someone, but she was nothing if not resourceful.

He faced the man at the desk who seemed oddly amused. "That's enough for now, Marco. He won't make another mistake. Will you, Julian?"

Before Mercy could demand to know what mistake her brother had made, the ground rumbled ominously. The computer mouse on the man's desk moved of its own accord. Did Texas have earthquakes? She wasn't certain, but the rapid fire of weapons answered her question. Smith had come for her. Of course he had. He was her hero. Thankfulness and terror mixed in an odd cocktail in her belly. Dear God, please let him be okay.

Determination cemented her to the chipped flooring. If Smith was willing to stare down death yet again, she was going to be alive when he got to her.

The members of the cartel all began speaking rapidly in Spanish. A low boom echoed throughout the house as the front and back doors were blown off of their hinges. Two additional men entered the room with guns drawn. Since both of them were pointed at her, she assumed these were not associates of Smith's.

Her jaw throbbed, and her vision began to swim. No. She had to be alive when he found her. Gripping the desk, she ordered herself to remain upright despite the sensation that someone had already fired a bullet through her skull. The laptop on the desk caught her attention. If the man studying the computer was the boss, there would be enough incriminating evidence on the hard drive to land the entire cartel in prison.

Another acrid cough preceded Julian's words, "You need to get out of here."

"I'm not leaving you." She also wasn't leaving the computer.

"Neither of you are leaving." One of the gunmen inched closer to Mercy's face. She stepped deftly to the side. The man behind the desk calmly pulled a pistol out and took aim at the computer, but Mercy made one final step in front of him. "You've both proven to be nothing but disappointments," he huffed. "I'd hoped for more, but I can't say I'm surprised. We should never have left you with your mother to raise you."

The race of boot steps, the most welcomed sound she'd ever heard, made its way to her as her rescuers crested the stairs.

Mercy forced herself to fight on. Just a few more minutes, and there'd be people to help. "Put down the gun. Surely you can see you're not going to escape."

"Mercy!" Smith's low bellow sounded every bit as frantic as she felt. The vise around her head tightened. She couldn't answer him. If she lost focus for one second, the man would pull the trigger, killing her and erasing all evidence that would put them in prison.

She wondered why he didn't do it. Perhaps he wasn't as sinister as his men seemed to believe he was.

JAVIER MARINO FIRED TWICE as Roman and Rio dove toward him at the top of the stairs. Rio clutched his knee and fell forward as several colorful curse words flew from his mouth. Roman dove right and brought Marino to the ground. Smith kept running, but as he turned to race down another long corridor, Roman's voice gave him a half-second pause. Holding his pistol to Marino's head, Roman looked him in the eyes with unequalled hatred. "Federal prison or burn in hell—you decide. Tell me where Finch is."

Asshole to the end, Marino spit in his face, and Roman pulled the trigger.

The door flew open under the force of Smith's boot. The doorknob lodged in the wall behind it. Voodoo and two DEA agents were hot on his heels.

"You kill her, we kill you," Voodoo stated succinctly, but this time the odds were stacked against them. There'd been too many unknowns. Every agent they'd brought with them was currently involved trying to either arrest or kill someone from the Castellas cartel. They were indeed outmanned and outgunned... by one. At least the members of the cartel were now aiming at Smith instead of Mercy.

"Drop your weapons, and we'll start cutting deals," one of the DEA agents demanded.

Mercy's pleading eyes found Smith's. She was trembling. But, yet again, she proved to be one of the bravest people he'd ever met. Now that the man behind the desk was distracted by taking aim at Voodoo, she fished a thumb drive out of the pocket of her jeans and inserted it silently in the laptop. With a few quiet keystrokes, Smith knew she was downloading every bit of data onto the drive.

"What the hell do you think you're doing?" the man at the desk demanded. Despite the distraction, none of the cartel members turned to see what had upset their boss. They kept their aim steady. Smith had stared down the barrel of pistols more times than he cared to recall. He had no idea how they were going to get out of this, and no idea how he would get Mercy out alive.

"When I shoot, you all fire," the kingpin ordered. Smith's heart refused him another beat as the boss turned his pistol on Mercy. "Doesn't seem your boyfriend brought quite enough friends."

Mercy's frantic gaze met Smith's once more, but then shock flared in her eyes as she stared past him. She pulled the thumb drive from the computer and took two steps back. The boss followed her. A shot rang out from behind Smith, made it through the space between him and Voodoo, and the boss hit the ground. The odds all turned in favor of the good guys, for once. Like removing the head of a snake, the body continued to twitch. When all of the boss's security team turned to determine what had happened, Smith, Voodoo, and both DEA agents leapt. When guns fired, cartel members all scrambled. Smith landed his boot in one's back keeping him from moving while he brought another to the ground.

Mercy screamed but was unharmed.

"Glad you all didn't need any help from the marshals," Heath Landry stepped into the room and adjusted his cowboy hat.

"Thank you," Smith vowed earnestly. "How did you know we were here?"

"Your girl there gave me a call just before she arrived here. There's a few ambulances pulled up outside for the ones who're bleeding but no longer conscious. For what it's worth, I doubt he would've shot her."

"Why do you think that?" Mercy asked before Smith could. He stepped over bodies to get to her and drew her into his arms. She was safe. That was all that mattered.

"Well," Landry cringed, "I just don't think he would've shot his own daughter."

"WHAT?" A bolt of shock jerked Mercy away from Smith so she could study the marshal.

"That was Armend Castellas, your father," Marshal Landry eased cautiously.

"But..." she shook her head. For so long she'd wanted to understand, and now the answers lay dead at her feet. Her mind tallied and rebelled as the fragments of her life that had never added up all met their sum. "So..." her haggard voice struggled through the conclusions. "My mother lied to me, my whole life?"

Julian struggled to his feet. "She wanted us to have a hero."

Mercy shook her head. "So, she just made one up?" Hot tears threatened her eyes as she stared at her little brother. "Are you okay?"

"I'll be fine. I wanted some answers. I knew the police were lying about that random act of violence shit when Mom was run off the road. I just didn't know how deep we were in. I should never have come here, but at least I got that DEA agent out. That's why I was being punished." When he turned and spat on their father's body, the reality of what had happened solidified in her mind.

Her vision swam with tears as she turned to stare down Smith.

He squeezed his own eyes shut and shook his head. "I lied to you so many times. Julian didn't send me to get you. That's where it started. Then I kept letting you believe things that weren't true to keep you safe. If I'd told you who your father really was, or that your brother had come looking to join the cartel, you never would've come here."

"What?" Julian grunted and cringed. "I never wanted to join. That's bullshit. But I did make that Wakefield guy promise to find someone to keep Mercy safe, so if you're that guy then what you told her wasn't a lie. Once I figured it all out, I knew they'd want Mercy for her skills. I couldn't let them get to my sister, so I came down here and pretended to want to join, until I figured out that Wakefield was embedded here. He's down in Mexico. Talk to him. He'll tell you everything. I was scared they'd come looking for her while I was here, and I needed someone to keep her safe. He said he knew the perfect guy. I assume you're him."

Mercy located her own voice. "Why didn't Mom just tell us?"

Marshal Landry stepped in. "You have to admit that's probably not a conversation a lot of parents want to have with their kids. Your father faked his own death a decade ago. He knew the marshals were coming for him, and I guess he thought that would slow us down. I'd suspected that's what he'd done, but your CIA friend didn't want to listen to me. Marino was a proud man. If he'd really taken over, why would they still wear the Castellas mark and call themselves by the name? But maybe your mom thought he really was dead. I have no communication between them in the last ten years. Maybe she thought you were safe from him."

"What's the Castellas mark?" Voodoo asked.

"The scar on the cheek. They get it when they earn their bones." Landry gestured to the bloody knife Mercy had laid on the desk when she'd retrieved the thumb drive.

Smith wrapped her up in his arms. "I'm so sorry."

She burrowed into his chest, and he enclosed his body around hers. "Why?" She pressed her face further into him. "You took care of me. That's what you were supposed to do. Can we just please get out of here? I don't want to look at him anymore, and the light hurts."

"Migraine?" Smith soothed.

She managed a nod against his chest.

"Voodoo," he demanded.

"No," Mercy protested, "take care of Julian first. He's much worse."

Voodoo was already cleaning the gash on Julian's face. "You're probably going to have to do some big talking to get the feds to believe that you weren't looking to join and that you didn't have anything to do with your mother's wreck."

"Actually," Roman entered the room, wearing Marino's blood on his shirt. "If you can tell me where Wakefield is, and if he is still alive, I'll see to it that you remain out of prison."

"Who are you?" Julian grunted as Voodoo drew something up into a syringe.

"The man currently in charge of your destiny."

Mercy lifted her head. "Julian, tell him what he wants to know. I didn't do all of this so you could spend the rest of your life in jail."

"I helped Wakefield get to a motel on the other side of the border. I took his phone, but he has his pistol."

"Why hasn't he made contact?" Roman demanded.

"Probably," he spat the words, "because our father figured out he was an embedded agent. Wakefield told me the men he got to keep Mercy safe would ultimately end the cartel, but that he needed to lie low or risk his life as an undercover agent. I assumed he knew what he was talking about. I can show you the hotel."

Shock and nausea continued to pound against Mercy's skull. Her father was never a hero, but her brother was. Her entire world had been flipped on its axis, and yet everything about it finally made sense.

46

Mercy sat in a large conference room in the Dallas FBI field office. Smith sat beside her, holding her hand. Voodoo had given her another shot of pain killers. The adrenaline had waned and she was exhausted, though she tried to remain awake. She longed to collapse in Smith's arms and sleep.

"I'm still sorry," he continued to tell her.

"Would you stop it?" She sighed. "Most of the things you thought were lies, weren't lies after all. Just promise to tell me everything from now on. If you'd started out telling me everything, I never would've believed you. It wasn't like you had other options. I would've insisted that my brother occasionally made bad choices but wasn't going to join a drug cartel."

"You would've been right," Smith reminded her. That was true. Wakefield had been rescued by CIA ops in Mexico, and he had corroborated Julian's story.

"Okay, but I don't have the energy to argue with you anymore. I want someone to explain everything my sperm donor did, and then I want to go see Julian in the hospital. After that, I want to sleep." She would never refer to the man who'd ordered a hit on her mother as her dad.

The FBI agents sat down at the table. They'd been very kind. One of them cleared his throat. "Here's what we've put together so far with the help of Deputy Landry. We interviewed several of the men from the compound, and they were happy to trade information for lesser sentences. The emails you thought were coming from your brother regarding the drone radar designs were being sent from Julian's laptop, but not from him, just like they used his phone to lure you to their hideout today. Your mother knew who your father was and whom he worked for since before your birth. She told him that she would keep you safe and that she would prepare you for life in the cartel if he would leave you and Julian in her care and keep her alive. We found a few photocopied letters on Castellas's body that were from your mother. We'll be happy to get them to you after we've processed them. From what we can determine in reading the letters, that's why she decided to name you Mercy. She did a decent job of keeping him away from you, but when your brother entered you in the Cyberlympics competition he entered you under your given name, Mercy Valon. Your father had to lay low after he faked his death, but when he realized what skill you must have, he planned to have a man by the name of Alonzo Ventura grab you at the end of the competition. He believed your mother must've kept her word and prepared you for work in the cartel, and that by entering you with her last name she was giving him you as a gift as it were."

"But I left." The events that had been set in motion because of that competition tightened every screw currently drilling into her skull.

"Correct. You left, but your father had a contingency plan. If you didn't compete or if you didn't win, he wanted you dead. Ventura was tasked with killing you, your mother, and your brother. According to a few of the capos we have, Marino was looking to take over the cartel. Your father suspected that, but Marino was his biggest earner. So, Armend either needed you dead or working for him to make certain your mother never turned state's evidence with the things she knew. If he'd landed in jail, Marino was set to step in."

Landry nodded and took over the story. "I had a lengthy paper trail on Ventura. He escaped custody in Santa Fe, and knew I was coming for him. I was an hour outside of Kansas City at the time of your mother's death. He didn't have time to hide three bodies before I got to Missouri, so he tried to do it with a quick hit and run. I'm guessing I arrived before he could show up at Julian's apartment to stage a suicide, so he went into hiding without completing the job. He was only welcomed back into the cartel recently. I'd hate to guess what he did to earn his way back, but I'm betting it's somewhere on that computer you all still won't let me see."

One of the agents standing by the door grimaced. "We're happy to let you see what we find, Deputy Landry, when we're finished with it."

Landry rolled his eyes. "At federal speed I assume that means I won't be getting a look at it anytime this year."

"Here," Mercy fished the thumb drive from her pocket. The FBI had the actual laptop. Landry was the one who'd saved them all. If he wanted evidence, he should have it. "Take it. It's yours."

He gave her a broad grin. "I knew I liked you. And hey, I have the actual letters from your mom to Armend. I arrived at one of their safe houses about five minutes after they'd left. I might've slipped in and taken a few things. I'll get them to you. There's nothing in them that's gonna put anybody in prison. They're love letters. As much of an asshole as your daddy was, you should have them."

"Thank you." Mercy wasn't certain she'd ever read the letters. It was all too confusing. She'd loved her mother so much and now hated her father with equal force. But it would mean something to her to have anything her mother had written.

One of the FBI agents said, "We'll be wanting that thumb drive as well."

"What thumb drive?" Landry slipped it in his own pocket with a smirk.

"We may need it," the agent argued, "there's a portion of the hard drive that's encrypted. If she got it copied, we need to see it."

Mercy stood. "No, you don't. I can break through the encryption for you."

"Mercy, baby, you've lived through hell today, and now you have a migraine," Smith argued.

If it wouldn't have hurt like hell, she would've rolled her eyes at him. "Right, and I did not endure all of this so those awful people could walk free, but my boyfriend is a fairly decent hacker himself so if he'd like to help, we could get it done quicker. I'm pretty sure he was a big help with a certain site I may or may not have taken down recently."

"You need to rest," he insisted.

Despite the pain, she did roll her eyes this time. "Are you saying I don't know my own mind?"

He shook his head. "Never again. If you feel up to it, let's get it done."

SMITH SETTLED with his laptop at the desk beside Mercy. He joined the FBI network, and watched her fingers fly over the keyboard. With two password attempts, she was in. Spreadsheets of purchases and sales of what had to have been millions of pounds of cocaine and heroin were on the screen before them. The next one she accessed was a lengthy list of suppliers.

"You clearly didn't need my help," Smith rubbed his hands up and down her thigh. "How did you know the password?"

"He didn't shoot me, and he could've," she admitted in a fragmented whisper. "That had to mean something."

"Hey." Unable to help himself, he turned her chair and scooped her up into his lap. "You're safe. I will never let anything happen to you again, and I will never lie to you about anything ever again, either." She started to protest but he placed his index finger over her lips. "I know you don't think I lied, but I did. I knew more than I told you. That won't happen again."

"Thank you. The password had to have either been my birthday or my mother's. I look a lot like her. I think that's why he couldn't shoot me. Plus, I saw a picture of her on that desk. When Deputy

Landry explained that the cartel hadn't been there long, I knew that meant he traveled with it. I guess he loved her at some point. I don't know. He also had her killed. Obviously, he loved his money more than anything else. It's confusing. But that's how I knew the password. It should all be here. I just disabled the deconstruction program. It's wide open now."

"Do you realize that you're amazing?"

"And just how am I amazing?" Mock disbelief colored her tone.

"You found out your father was a living drug lord instead of a dead Special Forces soldier. You've had a gun pointed at you twice in two days. You helped take down an entire cartel, not to mention the low-level thugs of several others. You saved your brother. I keep waiting on you to fall apart. God knows anyone else would've by now. But you just keep fighting."

"After my mom died, I never had anyone who I thought would help me put myself back together if I fell apart, so I never let myself, I guess. I couldn't."

Smith swore that statement cracked his chest wide open. "Baby, if you need to fall apart, I will be right there for it. I'll hold you. I'll let you cry. I'll let you talk. I'll do anything you need me to do. I'm a big guy. Not a lot of things can take me down, but the thought of you not having anyone to hold you when you need to be held or to let you ruin his shirt with your tears, that kills me. I will always be there to help you do anything in the world. Not because I believe for one minute that you couldn't do it all on your own, but because I don't want you to have to." He cradled one of her hands in his own. "I know what it means to hold this, remember? I'll never forget."

She lifted her head and smiled. "I know what it means, too. Thank you for falling in love with me. I can't quite wrap my head around the drug kingpin's daughter falling in love with the general's son, but I don't ever want to do life without you. I've tried it, and it doesn't work."

"I know. By the way, I was eventually going to tell you that it was me who helped you take down that revenge porn site. I'd forgotten I hadn't confessed to that yet."

"Probably best not to do that in front of the FBI. I told you we make a pretty good team. *RexArmis* will never be the same."

Smith rubbed his right hand over his beard in consideration. "Are you still willing to move to Lincoln?"

"Yeah, but I do have to go see what's left of my apartment. I still don't know what part Edgar played in all of this." The momentary strength she'd summoned to hack into the computer drained from her. "I still feel like there are parts I don't know, and all of the parts I do know I hate."

"What was Edgar's last name, sweetheart?"

"Nuñez."

"Hey, Landry," Smith tried to call quietly, both because of the agents all hard at work and because Mercy was worsening by the moment.

With his hat leading the way, Landry appeared beside them. "She get in?" He gestured to the computer.

"Of course she did, but what can you tell us about Edgar Nuñez?"

His shook his head. "I'd have to go back through my files. The name does sound familiar."

"He's from Medellín, Colombia," Mercy's explanation was spoken into Smith's chest.

Landry studied her curled-up form in Smith's lap. "Has the day finally gotten to her, or is it something else?"

"Migraine, and likely the day," Smith allowed.

"Poor kid. All I can tell you is that your father was also from Medellín. Can I take a look? I might be able to answer your question now."

"Sure." Smith scooted them away from the computer, and let Landry take over. "I'm not really certain how to thank you for saving us. I'm pretty sure there's no etiquette rule for appreciating the guy who saved the love of your life from her father before he tried to murder her and her brother."

Mercy tightened her grip on his shoulders.

"We all have a job to do. I just happen to be really good at mine," he vowed. He hit several keys but then shook his head. "I don't see anything in here about anyone by that name. Let me get back to my office. I'll get you some answers."

Voodoo and Griff both spilled out of the office next.

"We gotta go," Griff urged.

Smith was certain if he didn't get Mercy into a bed somewhere, she was going to fall asleep in his lap in the middle of a federal office building. "Go where?"

Voodoo grinned. "Maddie's in labor."

"I thought you said she wasn't going to have it anytime soon."

"What do I know? I'm not the one who knocked her up."

"You're the medic though," Smith reminded him.

"Right, and when I said that, someone had just held a gun to your girlfriend's head. I knew if you felt guilty for one more thing, you were going to collapse under it all. So, as the medic, I told you what you needed to hear. My gamble worked for twenty-four hours so, all in all, not bad."

"So, you lied," Smith summed.

Mercy lifted her head. "Sometimes people who care about you lie to you because telling you what you need to hear is more important than the truth at that moment. He's being honest with you now. But who's Maddie?"

47

"I hate that we didn't fly back yesterday, and that you weren't there when T's baby was born," Mercy lamented again on their flight home the next day. She'd slept on his chest for most of the afternoon and evening the day before. He'd plied her with some food after that, and then they'd played *RexArmis* until late in the night after she was feeling better. Then he did a few other things that made her forget she'd ever been in pain at all. She grinned at that memory.

Smith chuckled. "I doubt there was much Maddie needed my help with, and my own baby needed me to take care of her. The Sevens will always be part of my family, but they're not as important to me as you are."

"It'll be nice to be around them when they're not all having to protect me. I hope they like the nicer version of me. I was kind of awful at that dinner."

"You were not awful, and I'm not sure who convinced you that there are sides of you that shouldn't be loved, but they were wrong. You're allowed to be anything you need to be, anytime, with me and with The Sevens. That's part of being a family. God knows they've put up with me when I was being a grouch."

She grinned at him. "I'm guessing grouchy Smith looks a lot like regular Smith only you talk even less."

"You know me so well." He brushed a tender kiss in her hair. "I also watch a lot of that *Forged in Fire* show because it gets on Griff's nerves."

"Have you ever counted the number of times someone says *dude* on that show? I kept a tally once. Forty-nine times in one episode."

"You watch *Forged in Fire*?"

"Of course I watch it. They build swords and cut through car doors. It's kind of cool."

"Most perfect woman in the world," he vowed.

"For you," she reminded him.

"It was my world I was referring to." He winked at her.

SMITH GUIDED Mercy into Maddie's hospital room and they joined the line of Sevens all smiling at T.

"Poor kid looks just like you," Griff teased.

"There's no overcoming that," Voodoo piled on.

After checking to make certain Olivia was preoccupied with her coloring book, T flipped both of them off. Maddie shook her head and smiled at Smith. "Are you going to make introductions?"

Smith grinned. "This is Mercy. Mercy, this is Maddie and that is Olivia." He pointed to Olivia who must've still been irritated that she'd gotten a baby brother instead of a sister because she was thoroughly ignoring everyone.

Mercy offered a tentative smile. "It's nice to meet you. Your kids are adorable. Are you sure you're okay with me being in here?"

"Family," Smith insisted as he pointed to the circle around the bed.

Maddie laughed and then grimaced. "Oh, that still hurts," she sighed. "But of course I want you in here. It's been me and Hannah for too long. We need more women on our side to combat the giant haze of testosterone."

Mercy grinned at that. This time the smile reached all the way to those gorgeous green eyes, exact duplicates of her mother's, Smith had learned. "I'll try to help, but trying to keep him from doing something he's determined to do doesn't work. I think it goes with the hero territory."

Smith had no desire to discuss his hero status amongst his team so he gestured to Olivia. "She still upset?"

"She's coming around," T explained.

Maddie rolled her eyes. "She started coming around much faster when T took her to the toy store and bought her pretty much everything she wanted."

"She's my girl." T scooped Olivia up into his arms. "And you love baby Drew, don't you?"

Olivia stared down at the little bundle wrapped in blue blankets in Maddie's arms. "Yes, but maybe you and Mommy could have another baby, and it will be a girl and I can put lots of bows in its hair."

Maddie's expression said there would be absolutely no more babies coming out of her. Smith wrapped his arm around Mercy and waited to see how T fielded this one.

"We'll ask Mommy about more babies in a few months," he explained.

Maddie shook her head at him. "I somehow forgot how badly that hurt last time, but I won't be forgetting again." She grinned at her little girl. "I think you and Drew are all the babies we need."

Olivia gently patted Drew's blankets. "But maybe."

"Just maybe, Mama." T chuckled and then planted a kiss on his wife's head.

Maddie stared down at the tiny bundle in her lap. "Fine. Maybe."

"Hey T, can I talk to you a minute?" Smith directed him to the hallway outside the door to Maddie's room.

"Sure."

Mercy's brow furrowed, but she didn't argue when Smith closed the door.

"You know how you hired two entire teams of people a few months ago, and then how Griff hired on Cantori and Hudson all on the spur of the moment?"

T grinned. "I seem to recall something like that. Let me guess, you'd like to expand Tier Seven's cybercrime unit by one?"

"She's better than I am," he explained.

"Come on, now," T balked.

"All right, fine, she's every bit as good as I am. I don't want her scrounging for jobs anymore. Stress brings on her headaches. She's never really had any stability in her life. I want to give her that."

"It's fine by me, but she's your responsibility. I'm a little worried about trying to get the daughter of a major drug kingpin any kind of security clearance." Smith squinted his eyes and tilted his head, and quickly, T gave in. "But ...we'll see."

Truthfully, Smith hadn't gotten quite that far in his considerations. "My dad still has a few friends on the Joint Chiefs. He owes me a big favor."

"Then call up the General, because that is definitely above my pay grade. But congrats to both of you. I wasn't sure I'd ever see the day some woman got you all twisted up in knots. I was a little worried you're so damn smart you'd always find a way to think yourself out of it."

"I tried." He grinned. "I'm sure she tried, too. That's the thing I finally figured out when I wasn't sure I'd ever see her again. If you fall in love with someone who overthinks everything, you can be sure they've come up with every possible reason not to love you. If we both made it through every barrier either of us has, there has to be something to that, you know?"

T slapped him on the shoulder. "I know, man. I definitely know."

"Hey, did you know that the Castellas cartel had something to do with Finch, or did Roman keep that from you as well?"

"Rio told me what he said to Marino right before he murdered him. I plan to have a long talk with Roman when I see him. He hasn't shown at the hospital yet."

"That marshal down in Dallas that we met. He's a good guy. He took out Mercy's father before I could. When he was rattling off all of the places the cartel had been recently, I couldn't help but notice that they all lined up with the places Finch had been back when you and Maddie were figuring things out."

Shock colored T's weary features. "I definitely need to talk to Roman."

"When you do, I want to know what he says. Finch is still out there. If there's a tie between the Castellas and him, I need to know about it."

"You'll be the first person I talk to," T assured him. "But for right now, I have a very tired and very sore wife who probably needs me to get everyone out of the room so she can feed my kid. And you have a cute little thing in there that looks up at you the very same way Maddie looks at me. Go enjoy that. We'll deal with Finch when the time comes."

EPILOGUE

Mercy grinned at her very large boyfriend who cradled her very tiny kitten on his chest while he dozed on the sofa. The house didn't have stairs, but it did have a fireplace, just like in her dreams of what her life might look like someday if she got everything she ever wished for. Best of all, it had Smith. She knew anywhere he was would be home.

"He's in my spot." She giggled as Smith kept his eyes closed but turned on his side so he could cradle her as well, but she remained on her feet. "We have to go soon."

He forced his eyes open. "What time is it?"

"Almost five."

"How many episodes did I sleep through?"

"One and a half, but it was the same one we watched before. You know the one with the guy who did the Viking sword."

A deep yawn woke up Yoda who stretched out his paws and then jumped to the floor. Mercy was pretty sure he loved Smith almost as much as she did. "That's a good one. I wouldn't mind watching it again."

"I know, but aren't we supposed to meet The Sevens at that diner you keep telling me about? This seems like a big deal, and I want to make a good impression before I start working with them next week. I don't want to be late."

"You don't have to impress anyone, baby. They already love you."

"Okay, fine, I'm starving, and I want some onion rings. And also Marshal Landry is supposed to meet us with the letters from my mom. I kind of want to see them."

"That's a better reason." He lumbered to his feet and ran his hands over his hair and beard. "Do you think I should shave?" he asked her suddenly.

"No!" she vowed. "Don't ever do that. I love your beard."

That seemed to surprise him. "You do? Hannah said you might not."

"Hannah doesn't know what she's talking about. Clearly, Griff needs to grow one and show her how amazing it feels."

He laughed at her outright. "Where does it feel amazing, baby?" He waggled his eyebrows.

Mercy felt the heat climb into her cheeks and was certain she now looked severely sunburned. "It feels good...everywhere."

"Uh huh, I think you like it one place specifically. Feel free to tell The Sevens that I specialize in fuzzy-lingus."

That did it, she burst out laughing. It felt so good to laugh and to feel no paralyzing jolts of sadness anymore. Julian had called earlier to tell her that he'd taken a job with the DEA. They'd apparently been impressed with his tenacity to catch their father. It suited him. He wanted to be the hero their father wasn't. She hated that he might be in danger, but she had to let him find the peace she'd found in Smith. She couldn't protect him from life anymore. He wanted to be a hero, and the DEA could show him how. "Can we please just get ready to go?"

"Does that mean you don't want to squeeze in a quick session before we go? I could go down on you in the shower. Take care of two things at once. That'll save time because apparently you need onion rings."

Mercy headed toward the master bathroom. "I don't need onion rings as badly as I need fuzzy-lingus."

"That's my girl."

SMITH WAS STILL SPENDING some time convincing himself that he wasn't too rough with her when he had her under him, when he was so deep inside of her neither of them could tell where he stopped and she began. His baby had proven herself time and time again, and she knew her own mind thoroughly. They'd both thought of every possible reason not to be right where they were. If there had been one single reason not to go buy her a ring, surely one of them would've come up with it. He planned to make the purchase the following week.

T was a little late to the diner, and he came in wearing baby Drew in a pack strapped to his chest. Griff chuckled. "I guess he is cuter than the Camelbak you used to wear there."

"Maddie's taking Olivia to a movie. She's been missing her mama, so little man and I are going to do manly things," T explained.

"By manly things, I'm assuming you mean napping and sucking on tits," Voodoo chided.

"Jesus, for one night, could you be a little less...you?" Smith gestured to Mercy. "Please."

But Mercy laughed. "I don't ever want Voodoo to be anything other than himself."

A cowboy hat in The Hi-Way Diner in Lincoln, Nebraska was not unusual, but Smith recognized the owner of that particular hat immediately and waved Heath Landry over to the table.

The marshal placed his order and joined them. "Thanks for the invite. I think my sister was getting sick of looking at me."

"I didn't know you had family in town." T threw a few fries in his mouth and located a pacifier from the diaper bag all at the same time. He was getting pretty good at multitasking.

"Yeah, my sister moved over here with her husband a few years ago. I'm...just passin' through." He lifted the hat from his head like it weighed more than he could bear, and tossed it on the table.

Smith studied him. He'd lost a little of his cocky edge. "It's a long way from Dallas up here. Where are you heading?"

"Cheyenne," Heath spoke the word like a curse.

"Are you chasing another fugitive?" Voodoo asked.

"No." He sighed. "I was transferred."

Concern tensed Mercy's brow. "Why were you transferred?"

"I have no idea. Chief just called me in his office and told me I was going back home. I grew up out there." Heath didn't seem like he relished any part of returning to his old stomping grounds.

He pulled a packet of envelopes out of his jacket pocket. "Here are the letters from your mom." He handed them over to Mercy. "And I did find out a few things about Edgar Nuñez before I left Dallas."

Devastation cast Mercy's eyes. "Is he going to jail? I hate that he was obviously a bad person, but I also hate for his daughters to live without him."

"I'm not so sure he was a bad person. He and your dad grew up in Medellín together. The families were close. When the drug trade went global from Colombia in the eighties, your father wanted in on the action. Nuñez tried to keep him out of it. It came to blows, but neither man ever changed his stance. Your father kept tabs on him for years and knew when he'd moved to the States. After your mother was killed, your dad had a change of heart about you. I think he hoped he would eventually be able to use your hacking skills in his organization. He had you followed until..."

"I moved into that building. My dad paid Edgar to keep an eye on me, right? That's why I stopped feeling like I was being followed when I moved in there, and why he came by so often. My father must've gotten Sophia to find me and talk me into moving into the building. And Edgar didn't destroy my apartment or hurt Yoda. It was the man who was at the coffee shop that day, wasn't it? Edgar just let them in because my father told him to."

This time Mercy's completion of the story was spot on. Smith squeezed her hand. The man who'd first been assigned to follow her after her mother's funeral would live out the rest of his life in federal prison along with the rest of the cartel. That was the only way Smith was able to sleep at night. She was no longer in any danger. Her father's cartel had met its end with her hands on that keyboard.

Smith's own father had come through with a security clearance sufficient for her to work for Tier Seven. It seemed General Hagen's hands had been tied all of those years before, but he'd more than come through for his son now. Smith knew he should never have doubted him.

They ate and chatted with Heath about Cheyenne. Smith couldn't help but wonder if Roman had something to do with the transfer. Was he really pissed Heath had shown up at the takedown? Surely, that couldn't be it, but he needed to speak to Roman at work the next day.

Heath ran a napkin over his mouth and offered Mercy a hesitant smile. "I really am sorry for how you found out about your father."

She shook her head. "Don't be. I've been confused for most of my life about him. I wish he'd been a different person, but he wasn't. It just makes me more determined to fight for good."

Heath nodded. "Yeah, believe me, I get that. I need to get on the road, I guess."

Mercy reached and lifted his hat from the table. When her brow furrowed, Smith glanced inside the cowboy hat to see what had fascinated her. There was a snapshot of a rather attractive redhead wedged in the pinch inside the hat.

"Who's this?" Mercy asked but then cringed. "Sorry. I'm just being nosy. She's very pretty."

Heath retrieved the hat from her grasp and placed it back on his head. "Yeah, I think so, too." With that, he offered everyone a wave and made a quick exit.

Just before everyone was getting ready to leave, all of the blood drained from Voodoo's face and shock formed on his features. Smith turned to see a rather pregnant woman approaching the table. "I take it you know her."

Voodoo managed a nod. "That's...Amber." The two-syllable name robbed him of breath.

Understanding lit in Griff's eyes. "Is that the Amber from Austin? Your at-home girl that you get with when you go see your parents?"

Another nod was all they got before she arrived at the table.

She offered the table a hesitant smile. "I went by your house, and then I remembered your third Thursday night thing here. And I was starving so I came over. Sorry. I tried to call, but you weren't answering. I needed to get out of Austin kind of quick. Could we talk, Voodoo?"

"Uh... sure." Voodoo climbed out of the booth with a little steadying from Griff, and Smith painted a kiss on Mercy's cheek.

"Approximately how freaked out is Voodoo going to be by this?" she whispered as Voodoo followed Amber out the door.

"On a scale of 'oh my dear god' to 'holy fuck levels of nuclear explosion,' I'd say we're probably going to feel the aftershocks from here."

"I had a feeling. But we can help them. That's what family does, right?"

Smith grinned at that. "That's right, baby. Whatever is heading our way, we'll all be ready when it gets here."

ABOUT THE AUTHOR

Bestselling author Jillian Neal likes her coffee strong and sweet with a shot of sinful spice, the same way she likes her cowboys. In fact, her caffeine addiction is quite possibly considered illicit in several states as are a few of the things her characters do. When she's not writing or reading, you'll find her in the kitchen trying out new recipes or coming up with ~~excuses~~ reasons to purchase yet another handbag or make an additional trip to Sephora. Though she'll always be a Bama girl at heart, Jillian hangs up her hat and kicks up her boots outside of Atlanta with her hunk-of-a-husband and her teenage sons.

For more information...
jillianneal.com
jillian@jillianneal.com

ALSO BY JILLIAN NEAL

Broken H.A.L.O

Camden Ranch

Gypsy Beach to Camden Ranch

Gypsy Beach